The Devil Has Tattoos

Angela Corbett writing as
Destiny Ford

The Devil Has Tattoos

Angela Corbett writing as
Destiny Ford

Copyright © 2020 by Angela Corbett

Cover design by Kat Tallon at Ink and Circuit Designs

All rights reserved. No part of this publication may be reproduced,
distributed, or transmitted in any form or by any means, including
photocopying, recording, or other electronic or mechanical methods, without
the prior written permission of the publisher, except in the case of brief
quotations embodied in critical reviews and certain other noncommercial
uses permitted by copyright law.

This is a work of fiction. Names, characters, places, and incidents either are
the product of the author's imagination or are used fictitiously, and any
resemblance to actual persons, living or dead, business establishments,
events, or locales is entirely coincidental.

ISBN 978-0-9892836-8-7

Published in the United States of America by Midnight Sands Publishing,
Utah

Dedication

For my dad, who, despite numerous threats from my mom, still told me the shrimp story.

Chapter One

"So, let me get this straight," I said, trying hard not to narrow my eyes. It was an exercise in futility. I'd arrived at the scene ten minutes ago and had so many questions.

Officer Bob, my favorite Branson Falls police officer and former high school classmate, crossed his arms over his stout chest, shifted on his heels and prepared for my onslaught of queries. Most times I thought Bobby liked me just fine, but sometimes his squinty eyes and pinched expression when he looked at me gave me the impression that I might not be his favorite journalist, or *Branson Tribune* newspaper editor.

"There was a burglary at the Popes' house," I said.

Bobby nodded.

"Your one and only witness is six-year-old, Cory Lawrence, who saw the alleged burglar."

Bobby nodded again.

"Cory identified the perpetrator as a man who looked like a spider climbing up the wall of the house."

Yet another shift of Bobby's head.

I took a deep breath and pressed a hand to my forehead to

try and quell the headache I was sure I was going to have momentarily. "That sounds like someone with ninja warrior capabilities, and if they have those kinds of skills, they probably aren't hurting for cash enough to resort to common burglary."

I checked myself as soon as the words came out of my mouth because I had intimate knowledge of someone who could easily put "warrior ninja, war hero, mercenary—probably, millionaire," and a slew of other titles on his resume. His name was Ryker Hawkins, Hawke for short, and he had less body fat than Superman and was a hell of a lot stronger. I knew Hawke well enough to know that he hadn't had anything to do with scaling a house and robbing someone...at least, I thought I did. And he certainly wouldn't have been dumb enough to do it in the middle of the day with witnesses.

"What was Cory doing outside?"

Bobby shrugged. "Playin' with other neighbor kids."

"But none of the other kids saw the man crawling up the Popes' trellis?"

Bobby scrunched up his nose. "Nah. Cory said the guy was super speedy."

I couldn't decide if "super speedy" was Cory's description, or Bobby's, but decided not to ask.

I wasn't sure what Cory Lawrence had seen, but I had a feeling it was just a spry criminal who was adept at climbing walls. Normally, I'd ask a witness questions, but even if I got permission from his parents, Cory was only six and I didn't think he'd be the best informant. I also didn't feel like I'd get any more information than the police had already given me. I could include Cory's account from the police report in my article however, and that would be enough.

"Have you finished your sweep with the Popes to figure out what was stolen?"

"We're still workin' on it, but so far we know they didn't steal cash."

My eyes widened at that. Most robberies were financially based. "How do you know that?"

Bobby pointed his thumb over his shoulder indicating the Pope residence behind him. "Because when Brandy and Scott Pope were walkin' through the house fifteen minutes ago, they noticed the hundred bucks in cash they'd left on the counter was still sittin' there."

I raised my brows. "Why did they have that much money in cash sitting out?"

"Their teenage son was supposed to take it to pay for his clarinet lessons for the month."

I'd taken band in high school. In the wrong hands, the clarinet was one of those instruments that sounded like a cat screaming violently. I'd pay copious amounts of money for my kid to practice it somewhere else too. "That's odd the money wasn't taken when it was sitting in plain sight. When do you think you'll know what was stolen?"

Bobby lifted a shoulder. "Hopefully soon. The Popes are going to do a more thorough walk-through once they're not in shock. I'll call you when I know more." Apparently, Bobby had decided to like me again for the moment, which made my job much easier.

"Thanks," I said. "You know you're my favorite police officer in Branson."

He pushed his brows together. "There's about six of us, so I'm not sure that's a compliment."

"Of course it is," I answered, giving him a wink.

I walked over to where the Popes were talking to some neighbors in front of their grey and white farmhouse themed two-story home that looked like it had been expertly styled by the crew of *Fixer Upper*. Scott was a dermatologist, and Brandy owned an aromatherapy company. They were recent transplants to Branson Falls, which automatically put them at a disadvantage in the social hierarchy of town. Small Utah towns are like royal families and names, family heritage, and Mormon Church attendance records matter. "Hi Brandy and Scott," I said. They both nodded toward me. "I'm sorry about the robbery."

Brandy wrapped her arms around herself. "The thought of someone coming into our home like this and taking things...I just feel so violated."

Scott put his arm around Brandy. The protective gesture was sweet. "Hopefully they'll be able to find out who did it," Scott said.

"Did anything weird happen leading up to the robbery?" I asked. "Like, did you notice any strange people around your house?"

Scott and Brandy both thought about it for a few seconds and then shook their heads. "Nothing odd that I can think of," Scott said.

That wasn't surprising. Most people weren't on the lookout twenty-four-seven for strange things that might cause trouble because most people weren't related to my mom. "You haven't lived in Branson Falls long. Do you think this could have been done by someone who knew you from your old city?"

They both thought about it for a minute before dismissing

the idea. "No one comes to mind," Scott said. "Can you think of anyone, honey?" he asked Brandy. She shook her head.

"Okay, well if you think of anything else, feel free to give me a call." I handed them my card and got back in my dark blue Jeep Grand Cherokee. The day was young and I had more stories to cover.

Branson Falls is a tiny farming community in Utah, surrounded by the towering Rocky Mountains. It has clean, crisp air, four seasons, and a slew of small town traditions that people outside of Branson—or a Hallmark movie set—might find odd. The town was built on agriculture, but it was growing, and that meant new businesses and more jobs. Some people still owned farms, but almost everyone else worked at one of the businesses that make up the Branson Falls Industrial Park. Everyone knows everyone in Branson, and attendance at The Church of Jesus Christ of Latter Day Saints, also known as the Mormon Church, is viewed as a barometer of a person's character. I'd left the church years ago, so my character had been in question ever since. I was fine with that, especially since most of the people doing the judging weren't supposed to judge at all—according to their beliefs—so that made them hypocrites in my book.

I stopped to grab some lunch and then went back to the *Tribune* office to eat and catch up on some messages. My inbox gave me anxiety and I tried to keep it at manageable levels, though with daily emails containing everything from story tips to suggestions that the *Tribune* publish a weekly list of "sinners" caught frequenting the new local coffee house, I had a feeling that I'd never be a zero-inboxer again.

"Heard about the robbery," Ella announced as I walked into the office, my foot snagging on the worn low pile black and sage green speckled carpet. I dropped my food on my desk, chipped from years of use, and sank into my chair.

Ella was a spry young seventy-something with bluish-white hair, bright amber eyes, and was roughly the height of a hobbit. She'd started volunteering at the *Tribune* as a way to get out of the house after her husband had passed away a few years ago. She pushed boundaries, kept me updated on the mostly untrue gossip about my love life, and drove her Lexus convertible like a bat out of hell. She retained her license only because she bribed the police force with pies.

I raised a brow at her robbery knowledge. "Facebook?"

She sliced her head down once matter-of-factly. "The Ladies are all abuzz."

I rolled my eyes and started eating my sandwich. "The Ladies are always abuzz about something." The Ladies are Branson's version of *The Real Housewives*, but with a lot less money, influence, and no hair and makeup team. I'd never met more gossipy, unkind women in my life. Considering I despised gossip, and was frequently the subject of The Ladies wrath because they didn't agree with my life choices—like drinking coffee, having pre-marital sex, and not being married with two kids by age twenty-five—I didn't get along with most of them and avoided them whenever possible. Ella was the only exception and I hadn't known she was a member of The Ladies until after we'd already become friends.

"What was stolen?" Ella asked. "No one seems to know."

I gave her a look. "I feel like if I tell you anything, you're going to immediately post about it in The Ladies secret Facebook group."

Ella discreetly put the phone she'd been holding, and poised to type on, down on the desk. "I'll keep it between us."

I didn't believe that for a second. But the news would get out fast enough. "The Popes couldn't find anything missing when they initially walked through. They're going to go through the house again and see if they missed something and if so, Bobby will call me."

Ella pinched her brows together. "Nothin'? Seems like a lotta trouble for someone to go through if they weren't even gonna take anythin'." Since I'd grown up in Branson, I usually didn't notice the Utah accent of dropped Gs, Ts, and words that all ran together like a stream of consciousness, but sometimes it was more apparent than others—and Ella was fluent in it.

I nodded in agreement and finished up my food. "I have to get to the tattoo shop grand opening. I'll be back in a while."

Ella gave a long whistle that sounded like a sigh. "Good luck. It's gonna be hairy."

I narrowed my eyes. "Why do you say that?" Ella often had helpful insider information that she didn't share until after the point when it would have actually been useful. I was slowly trying to get her to start imparting information before I walked into a FUBAR situation.

"People ain't happy about that shop and I don't think anythin' good is gonna come of it."

I sighed. "Everyone said that about the coffee shop too, but Satan hasn't risen from the underworld and life as we know it did not end."

Ella tapped a finger on her lips. "He doesn't live in the

underworld, and I'd say opinion on his current whereabouts depends on who you ask."

I rolled my eyes and had a feeling that it might have been suggested by some Ladies that my current whereabouts and Satan's were the same. "I'll watch myself at the tattoo shop."

"I would," Ella said, nodding in agreement.

Chapter Two

Inked AF, was having their grand opening today and I felt like it was absolutely cause for celebration. The fact that a tattoo and piercing shop had been allowed to open in Branson Falls was shocking in and of itself. Like the coffee shop that had opened in Branson a couple of months ago, people thought tattoos were a gateway to other morally reprehensible and even illegal things. There had been a fight during the business approval process, and additional fights ever since. I'd covered more protests in the last month than I'd covered in my entire journalism career.

Personally, I was in total support of the tattoo shop. I've always believed it's important to expose people to a variety of different ideas and cultures, especially the ones they vehemently disapprove of even though they've had no experience with them. The fact that the tattoo shop was named Inked AF made me chuckle every time I heard it; the shop owners had chosen a very clever name. The younger generation would get it, but the older generation and religious minded people of Branson Falls definitely would not.

The shop was on Main Street, next to the antique shop that had been there since before I was born. It was about two miles from the *Branson Tribune* office. I drove by Inked AF multiple times a day and had watched the progress as they got the shop ready to open. I was excited to see what it looked like, but as I drove up and tried to find a parking spot, I realized I couldn't even see the front of the shop. The place was jam packed with people, and based on the angry expressions and homemade poster board signs with opinions written in craft paint—or maybe strawberry jam, I really couldn't tell— most of these people were not supporters.

I got out of the car and realized that instead of covering the opening of the first tattoo shop ever in Branson Falls, Utah, there was a good chance I was going to be covering a riot over needles and ink.

Bobby hadn't been kidding about the size of the Branson Falls Police department. It consisted of six officers, and they were all trying to prevent complete civil disobedience. Some people were yelling that the tattoo shop never should have been allowed in Branson Falls. Others were defending the shop and saying it was about time Branson joined the current century. I sided with the current century activists, but as editor of the *Tribune*, I was being objective and would get both sides of the story regardless of my personal opinion.

I passed by the protesters first. I saw several people from the Branson Falls community, but by far, the biggest angry contingent consisted of The Ladies. They were out in force, wearing fall fashion acceptable jeans, sweaters, scarves, over-sized accessories, and holding pumpkin spice hot chocolate in one hand—which they'd bought at the coffee shop they'd also protested recently—with signs about the evils of ink on skin in the other hand. That seemed a little hypocritical, considering how many of them were sporting permanent cosmetics.

I walked up to Jackie Wall, the ringleader of The Ladies. She'd recently cut her blonde hair in a style where it was short on one side and long on the other. I had a feeling that particular cut hadn't been done on purpose and she was trying to pull it off as a new trend. She'd undoubtedly get other Ladies to follow her example and then they'd all look like their heads had been caught in a close encounter with a weed wacker.

Jackie and I had a history. She was older than me, which I liked to remind her of whenever possible, and she and her manipulative little friends had spent high school ridiculing me in every possible way. The nice thing about becoming an adult is that you realize you no longer have to care or give any energy to people who treat you poorly. So I avoided Jackie and her cohorts in my personal life. However, when they decided to make themselves part of a news story, I still had to engage them. "Hi, Jackie."

"Kate," Jackie said, her eyes going over my comfortable jeans, form fitting navy blue sweater, and my messy bun like she was getting paid to critique me. She tilted her sign so it blocked as much of my face as possible. Manners weren't part of Jackie's wheelhouse.

"Do you want to tell me why you're here with The Ladies protesting the opening of Inked AF?"

Jackie moved the sign and seemed like she was trying to melt me with her stare—a feat since she was wearing dark, oversized round sunglasses that made her strongly resemble a drugged up bee. "You gotta be kiddin'!" she said like I was the dumbest person on the planet. "You know tattoos are against church rules. This is horrible! And unacceptable! It's gonna teach our kids that this kinda thing is normal when it's not! And the nerve! Namin' the shop Inked And Fantastic to lure kids in!"

I blinked, wondering if I'd entered some sort of twilight zone. "I'm sorry, but did you say 'Inked And Fantastic'?"

She doubled down on her Kate-is-an-idiot glare. "The tattoo shop name, Kate. Keep up."

It took every ounce of restraint I had not to double over laughing. And then she kept going. "First they allowed the Beans and Things coffee shop, and now this!" Jackie exclaimed before taking a drink of her pumpkin spice hot chocolate from said coffee shop. I eyed her with suspicion, wondering if there really was hot chocolate in her cup, or if she was drinking an illegal latte. The sip seemed to rile her up even more, which was additional proof for my coffee theory. She continued, "I tried tellin' people that coffee house was a gateway drug. Soon we're gonna have nothin' but crime and immorality all over town."

I raised an eyebrow at her quick judgment and dismissal of things simply because they were out of her comfort zone. "Or you could teach your kids that the world is amazing *because* it's full of all kinds of people from all different walks of life who like a variety of things and forms of expression," I suggested.

A collective hush fell over most of The Ladies and it was clear that my suggestion of tolerance had offended them on a deep level. I accepted their reaction as a source of personal pride.

Jackie's face turned to stone and she pointed at me. "You think you're so smart, Kate. Comin' back here with your liberal ideas and tryin' to make everyone change even though you're committin' all kinds of sins with multiple men." I wanted to correct her on that allegation since one, it wasn't true, and two, my romantic life was none of her business, but she wouldn't listen anyway so I decided not to waste the energy and let her drone on. "Well, I'll have you know that we like who we are *just* fine. We don't have to change and you're not gonna make us!" The Ladies behind her started clapping like she'd given an award-winning speech.

And that right there, the stubborn inability to see things from any perspective other than their own, was what was wrong with the world, and what I'd been trying to help improve when I'd decided to become a journalist. I had no problem with an informed opinion—even if it differed from my own. The problem was that most people weren't informed, and were getting the perspective from social media memes and posts instead of legit news sources and journalists who cared about objectivity. I didn't care what Jackie, The Ladies, or anyone else said; I was still going to keep putting information out there. Someday, having an unbiased view of both sides of an argument might change someone's mind, and that's what kept me going.

Jackie continued, "They're allowin' permanent things to be done to their skin and piercin' all sorts of unmentionable places!"

The piercings in all sorts of places had been one of the major arguments against the tattoo shop being allowed in town. I really didn't think anything other than ears and an occasional belly button or eyebrow would be pierced. Not many people in Branson knew what a Prince Albert was, and even fewer would be interested in it.

"It's a...a..." she seemed to be struggling to find the word,

"Travesty!" Found it. "That this kind of body torture hasn't been outlawed yet," Jackie said, full of righteous indignation—or it might have been surprise at her own vocabulary skills, I couldn't really tell.

I gave her a disbelieving look and did my best not to laugh. "If it had, you and most of your Lady cohorts would be in jail."

Her eyes frosted over. "How do you figure that, Kate?"

I stared at her, wondering how she'd managed to get to this point in life without critical thinking skills. "You're talking about body modification, right?"

She nodded.

"How are tattoos any different from plastic surgery, ear piercings, and permanent cosmetics?" I asked. Utah has one of the highest rates of cosmetic surgery in the nation. It even beats Los Angeles for plastic surgeons per capita. Perfection is a mandate in the Beehive State, and women are held to a very high double standard when it comes to body image. I knew for a fact that Jackie Wall had gotten a boob job, and Amber Kane had her nose redone years ago. Botox parties were more popular in Branson than cake—which is shocking considering how addicted to sugar most Utahns are. The injectable parties were held monthly at the homes of various Lady members.

Jackie, realizing I had a point, ignored the facts and continued anyway. "Because church leaders specifically tell us not to get tattoos. They don't say anythin' about plastic surgery."

That was true, but it was still up to each individual because one of the main cornerstones of the Mormon faith is free agency—the idea that people are free to make their own choices...church leaders just liked to restrict access to things that allowed people to do so. Growing up Mormon in a town where ninety-five percent of residents were all members of the same religion, and then overseeing a newspaper that went out to the majority of them, forced me to be extremely well-versed in their beliefs, despite the fact that I was no longer a part of the religion. "Because your body is a temple and you're supposed to treat it like one and not do anything to disrespect it. But," I said, repeating myself since Jackie had apparently not heard me the first time, "how is altering your skin any different than altering your body with bigger boobs or a nose job? Or even changing your hair color? Or applying fake fingernails or hair extensions? Technically, all of those things fall under body modification. And permanent cosmetics *are* tattoos."

They all stared at me, speechless, like they'd never equated the two or given it any thought. And that was part of the problem. "Maybe you should think about what you're protesting before you start protesting it," I suggested, and walked to the other side of the picket line to talk to the tattoo shop supporters, and Sasha and Axel, the owners of Inked AF.

Axel was lean with spiked hair that had blonde tips and tattoos that covered his arms like sleeves. Sasha was tall and lithe, with bright tattoos down one arm, and hair that frequently changed colors—today it was teal.

"Hey Kate," Sasha said with a warm smile. "Do you want a tour?"

I returned her smile and said, "I'd love one! And some pictures and quotes for the paper." I'd gotten to know Axel and Sasha while they were trying to get approval for their shop to open and really liked them both. They swore, wore tanks tops, drank coffee, and even had wine and beer occasionally. There weren't many of us in a town like Branson

Falls, so when you found a new tribe member, you learned to befriend them fast.

I followed Axel and Sasha inside. The shop walls were painted a deep charcoal and had beautiful, large canvases of artwork on the wall. "Did you paint all of these?"

Axel nodded. "Sasha picked some of our favorite old tattoo designs, and I used them to create a theme for the pieces."

Flowers mingled with geometric shapes, portraits, and landscapes. It all came together in a stunning way that looked almost like wallpaper on the various canvases. "You're both so talented."

Sasha blushed and the look they gave each other radiated love. Axel put his hand on Sasha's back. "She was the master-mind behind the whole design."

I smiled at the intimate interaction. I really admired couples who were clearly in love, gave each other credit, and built one another up.

"I know this has been a long road for you guys and I'm really happy for you," I said. "Has anyone commented on the shop name?"

Sasha laughed. "Most people have no clue, or think it means something else entirely."

I grinned. "From what I've heard, several people seem to think the AF stands for "And Fantastic!"

Axel threw his head back and laughed. "Inked And Fantastic works. We'll let them keep thinking that."

"Have you had any issues with people in town as you've been getting ready to open?" I asked.

Axel shrugged. "A few people here and there. A couple of anonymous notes telling us we weren't wanted here. Nothing too crazy though."

I frowned at the inhospitality. "Some people suck."

"It's a small town where a lot of people already had opinions about us before we even got here, and don't agree with what we do," Axel said, leaning against the front counter. "We weren't expecting a welcome wagon, but we were hoping to open minds. We've already had several people book ear piercings, so that's a start."

I closed my eyes, shook my head, and laughed. Because pierced ears were socially acceptable in Branson, even if they were a body modification. "Of course you have."

"The sad thing is that a lot of people who are against tattoos don't realize the good they can do," Sasha said, grabbing a tattoo book off the table. "A lot of our work helps people heal from something they've been through, whether it's emotional, or physical. The art becomes an outward representation of strength for our clients. Sometimes it's art as a memorial, other times it's to cover up scars from accidents, surgeries, or even domestic violence. Most people don't get tattoos just to get them, there's usually a story behind the art." She flipped through the book, pointing out beautiful work that had been done for the reasons she'd mentioned. It was another side of tattooing that I was certain most Branson residents hadn't considered.

I thought about a friend of mine who'd gotten a tattoo in memory of a lost loved one, and another whose mom had gotten tattoos to cover up the scars from her mastectomy. "I agree completely, and believe you're right that a lot of people don't understand. They think of tattoos as a blanket mistake, not something with meaning. Do you have the names of some of your clients with interesting stories who might be willing to talk to me? I'd really like to include that angle in the article since it's one I don't think many people here have considered."

"Sure!" Sasha said, her smile bright. "I'll check with a few of them and email you some names."

"Perfect." I looked around the shop again and loved the warm energy and feeling of inclusion it represented. It didn't matter whether you were tattooed, pierced, or nothing at all, you'd be welcome at Inked AF. "Do you mind if I get a few photos?"

"Not at all," Sasha said, gesturing toward the main room and the tattoo chairs in the back.

I walked around and got the pictures I needed. A wide shot of the shop, the tattoo stations, and a few with Axel and Sasha. I went outside and got some photos of the front of the building, and talked to a few of the Inked AF supporters. The owner of the antique store next door, Fred Carlson, was standing on the sidewalk, eating a cookie from the grand opening party table.

"Hey, Fred," I said.

He gave me a big smile. Fred and his wife, Molly, had owned the antique shop for years. Fred had worked in the shop as a kid and took it over from his parents when they retired. He should be pretty close to retiring himself. They lived down the street from me and frequently brought me amazing treats. "Hi, Kate!"

"How do you feel about this?" I asked, motioning toward Inked AF.

He shrugged. "It's not somethin' that interests me personally, but I've got no problems with it, or with people who like tattoos."

I smiled. "Can I quote you on that?"

"Sure can," he said with a grin.

I got a few more pictures and quotes as I snaked my way through the crowd, and made sure to give The Ladies a fake smile as I walked to my Jeep. I didn't like them, but I'd jotted down their opinions and would be sure to include those perspectives in my story for objectivity.

As I got in my SUV, my phone rang with the familiar strains of "Brother Love's Traveling Salvation Show." I didn't even have to glance at the phone to know exactly who it was. I'd given Dylan Drake, our local representative in the Utah House of Representatives and resident Branson Falls heart-throb, that ringtone after he'd come over to my house with chocolate covered coffee beans and used his wide chest, full lips, and muscled arm wizardry to try and convince me that a relationship with him was totally doable. It had almost worked. Almost. The ringtone was my personal reminder that despite his arguments to the contrary, and how intrigued I was with the idea of seeing him shirtless—and pantless too— he was a religious politician who was encouraged to date someone with the same beliefs as him, and that meant we could never work as a couple.

And Drake's wasn't the only Neil Diamond ringtone I'd been avoiding. "Play Me" was also on my no answer list. I'd been actively evading both Hawke and Drake for weeks— which wasn't easy in a small town so it had required a few covert maneuvers—and I'd congratulated myself for remaining unseen on multiple occasions.

However, it was painfully clear that I now had feelings for two entirely different men in my life, and I had no idea what to do with that information. I'd been hoping time would reveal the answer. Apparently, time didn't feel the same sense of urgency about the matter that I did, because I'd received no solid answers from the universe, or even Ella—a surprise considering she had an opinion about most things. Her advice about Hawke and Drake, however, had always been, "Do them both—I would." That coincided nicely with what my lady parts were also broadcasting. Luckily, my frontal lobe was still in control...for the moment.

I wasn't sure of my feelings yet, and wasn't ready to explain myself to either one of them. Until I was, I'd keep letting the calls go to voicemail. If I was being truthful with myself I might call that cowardly—but today I called it survival. I put my phone in my purse and drove back to the *Tribune* office.

Chapter Three

I was opening the *Tribune* door when my phone buzzed with a message from my mom. I grinned at the picture of my sweet puppy staring back at me. I'd recently adopted the cute little guy, a tiny pup with a mixed heritage that looked a lot like a terrier. He was black, with a grey and white beard, and I'd immediately named him Gandalf in honor of my favorite wizard. Working as a small town newspaper editor wasn't super conducive to owning a dog, however, because my work hours were so sporadic. Luckily, my mom and dad were close, and my mom had demanded that Gandalf be with her whenever he wasn't with me. I was fine with that, and extremely grateful for the help raising my tiny ball of fur. I adored him and his little grey beard.

In my mom's photo, Gandalf was being a very good boy, sitting and waiting for his treat in his outfit for the day—an adorable little royal blue cape with sky blue colored paws embroidered on the back. My mom had serious sewing skills, and had appointed herself as Gandalf's personal stylist. It was a good thing he liked clothes.

I walked to my desk and put my bag down as another text popped up:

> Gandalf had his afternoon treat. Now we're snuggling!

My mom had recently discovered emojis, which meant that text was followed by approximately seventy-six of them. Several of which were the little poop surrounded by hearts. Given her frequency of little poop emoji use, I had a feeling my mom didn't know what it was. In fact, I was certain of it. I was about to text her back and attempt to explain when I heard Spence's voice, "How was the grand opening of Inked AF?" But he said the full words instead of just the letters AF represented, and that made me laugh and love him even more than I already did.

Spence was tall with dark skin, eyes so clear they could probably see a person's soul, and a jawline that looked like it had been cut from granite. He wasn't interested in girls, or I'd be in even more trouble than I was already in with Drake and Hawke.

"It was good," I said, sitting down at my desk and putting my bag in the drawer. "They had protesters there, of course. Mostly The Ladies, who seemed unable to grasp that permanent make up is a form of tattooing."

Spence rolled his eyes. "Of course they didn't get it. And they're probably told permanent makeup is fine because makeup makes them look more appealing for men and what makes men happy is what matters." Spence was also well-versed in the local religious beliefs, and somehow managed to maintain a life in Branson despite the predominant religion's treatment of LGBTQ+ people like himself. He wasn't out of the closet to anyone in town but me, however. If he ever decided to reveal that fact, people's behavior might change. More than one business had closed when the owners got divorced—because divorce isn't something the church supports either, and townspeople started boycotting the companies, immediately blaming the wives for the failed relationships. The things some people placed value on were often ridiculous.

"Exactly," I said in agreement with Spence's church-related sentiments. "But Axel and Sasha also had a lot of people there supporting them, and they have several ear piercings already booked. I'm certain they'll get more piercing and tattoo appointments as time goes on and they'll do well."

"I hope so," Spence said. "We need diversity here."

I nodded in agreement. It's why I hadn't moved away again yet, and why I hoped Inked AF and the coffee shop succeeded.

"I know you just got back, but I have another story for you."

"What's up?" I asked.

"Betty Turner called. She wants to tell you her potato story."

Both of my brows went up at that. "Potatoes?"

He shrugged. "I have no clue. She just said she wants to talk to someone about it."

I sighed. "She probably found a potato in her garden that looks like Elvis or something."

"That was also my guess. Have fun."

I grabbed my bag and left to uncover the great potato mystery. Sometimes my job was extra glamorous.

I knocked on Betty Turner's door and when she opened it, she was wearing a floral print lavender housecoat, glasses, and holding a newspaper and pencil. The phrase "sweet grandma" probably had her picture next to it in the dictionary. She was around the same age as Ella, and I'd always thought she had a great sense of humor.

"Kate!" she said, full of excitement. "Come in, come in! I was doing my crossword puzzle. Keeps the mind sharp, you know. Though some of the answers are pretty tricky. I didn't even know what a Bluetooth was until I looked it up."

I laughed. "Technology changes fast."

She gave me an overwhelmed look. "No kidding!"

"Spence said you wanted to talk to me about potatoes?"

She nodded. "I sure do!" She waved her hand indicating that I should follow her into the kitchen. She walked over to the fridge and pulled out a creamy potato casserole in one of those disposable aluminum containers with a plastic cover. "This potato casserole was put on my front porch last night!"

I raised a brow. "Someone just left it there?"

She nodded. "I heard the doorbell ring and when I answered it, this package of goodness was sittin' there! Took me a minute to be able to bend down and pick it up—my old bones don't work like they used to, but I managed, and brought it inside."

"Did they leave a note?"

"Nope. It was an anonymous dinner!"

That seemed odd. Maybe they'd gotten the wrong house. "So someone is going around leaving potato casseroles on people's doorsteps?"

She nodded, smiling at her good fortune. "Mine at least!"

"How many of these porch casseroles have appeared?" I asked.

"This is the first, but I hope it's not the last!"

In a big city, random food dropped off on a doorstep without any explanation would immediately make me worried that someone was trying to poison the resident. Branson Falls was a whole different universe though and while arbitrary potatoes and cream could be seen as an act of aggression in other places, here it wasn't the least bit offensive.

"Play Me" suddenly started its seductive melody on my phone and I wanted to close my eyes and think of all the playing Hawke could do. But I was in the middle of interviewing an anonymous casserole recipient, and couldn't deal with that conversation right now. I hit silence on my phone and continued questioning Betty.

I already had a name for the food bandit: the Casserole Caper.

"Did you see anyone run away from the house?" I asked her.

"Nope. It takes me a while to get around though, so I wasn't as quick about opening the door as I used to be."

"Did you try the casserole?" I couldn't imagine any instance in which I'd try a homemade casserole that someone had abandoned on my porch with no identifying information. Abandoned donuts, however, were an entirely different story. I'd eat every last crumb.

"Yes, and that's actually why I called you," she said. "I don't think they used nearly enough cheese and butter."

I blinked. "Cheese and butter," I said slowly, wondering if I'd heard her right.

"Yes," she said, completely serious. "I mean, that's practically a crime in and of itself. I tried telling the police, but they said there was nothing they could do about abandoned porch potato casseroles. But I really think my story needs to be heard and hopefully whoever is leaving the dishes will read it and add some ingredients to make it more tasty next time."

I closed my eyes for a minute, trying to come up with a response. "So you're appreciative of the casserole, but you'd like it to be better built?"

Her smile widened. "Exactly! I knew you'd understand, Kate! Thank you!" She got two plates and put them on the table. "Would you like to try some?" she asked.

Casseroles weren't my favorite meal in general, and I definitely wasn't interested in one that had been deserted. "Thanks so much for the offer, Betty, but I have to get back to the office. I hope you have a good dinner."

"Oh, I will! This casserole is so big it will feed me for a week! I'll add my own butter and cheese."

I had no doubt she would. I waved as I left the house and walked back to my car. Once inside, I dialed my messages. The voice on the other end made my knees weak, and the innuendo in it simultaneously excited and terrified me. "If I don't hear from you soon, Kitty Kate, I'm going to assume it's because you're tied up. And if you're tied up by someone other than me, I'm going to assume that means you need rescue, and show up to take care of the situation. So call me, or you *will* see me."

I took a deep breath and listened to it again before hitting play on message number two. My heart was already racing at Hawke's words, and I knew Drake's message wouldn't decrease my BPM. His voice was deep and just as seductive

THE DEVIL HAS TATTOOS

over the phone as it was in person. "It's me, Katie. Again. We need to talk. And we *are* going to talk. Don't think that not answering my calls or texts will get you out of this conversation—or what will follow the conversation." I frowned. Was that a threat? Because it sounded a little like a really appealing threat.

I bit my lip, then decided if I didn't find something else to bite into, I'd be calling Drake or Hawke back and that would either end with an orgasm or disaster...or both. It was past six o'clock, and it had been a long day. I was hungry, horny, and ready to go home. Cheesy breadsticks with extra cheese and an Oreo shake wouldn't be as good as tasting Hawke or Drake, but it might come close.

I stopped and picked up Gandalf on the way home. I kept his little cape on because it was chilly outside, and he really seemed to like it.

I pulled into the driveway of my cute house with cream colored siding and royal blue window trim. The shrubs and trees in the yard were starting to change into brilliant reds and yellows. They were beautiful, but I wasn't looking forward to cleaning up the leaves. The house had a matching detached garage that I'd started using religiously after my car had been egged.

I unlatched Gandalf from his car seat and he trotted through the back door behind me, into the sunny yellow kitchen. The floor was ceramic, and the countertops were made of square white tiles. As far as décor was concerned, it wasn't my taste, but the house was a well-priced rental and it worked for what I needed. We went through the kitchen and into the living room where I dumped my food on the black coffee table and clicked on the TV.

Gandalf sat on the floor next to me, never more obedient than when food was present. I shared some cheese from my breadsticks with him, and was halfway through my shake when my phone rang. I muted the TV, looked at the caller ID and answered, "Hi, Bobby. What's up?"

"Hey, Kate. The Pope family finished goin' through their house and I wanted to tell you what they're missin' from the robbery."

I grabbed my pen and notebook. "Go for it."

"Well," he said, pausing, "it's a little strange. It was a couple of odd things."

I waited patiently for him to go on.

"They're missin' a book, a remote control, and some VHS tapes."

I gave my phone an incredulous look. "A book, remote control, and VHS tapes? It seems like a lot of work to break into a house for that. What book was it?"

"Some romance about werewolves or somethin' weird." I could practically hear Bobby rolling his eyes over the phone.

"Werewolves are kind of hot, Bobby."

He grunted like he either didn't have a response, or felt my statement didn't deserve one.

"I didn't know anyone even still had VHS tapes or a VHS player to watch them," I said, thinking out loud. "Were they special editions or something?"

"They were those animated ones that are popular with kids."

Interesting. I was fairly certain every household in the

state had owned those VHS tapes, and probably still did. None of the stolen items were remarkable in any way. "Do they have any idea why someone would take those things? Was it an antique remote control, or a rare book?"

"Not that we know of," Bobby said. "The Popes are as baffled as we are."

"Huh. Okay," I said. "Thanks for letting me know."

"No problem," Bobby answered, and hung up.

Robberies usually had a pattern, and a motive. This one made no sense on any level. The perpetrators had stolen a twenty dollar book, a ten dollar remote control, and VHS tapes that I didn't think were worth anything at all, and left a hundred bucks in cash on the counter. I wondered if the Popes had missed something when they went through their house. If so, I was sure Bobby would let me know—provided he liked me that particular day.

I unmuted the TV and settled into the couch with a cuddly Gandalf on my lap to relax for the rest of the night.

Chapter Four

"This is a disgrace! The moral fiber of the community is at stake!" Ned Lemon yelled. The handful of supporters around him cheered, giving him more courage to keep going. I winced, wishing he'd stop.

I'd been called to a protest this morning. At first I thought it was another group having a tattoo tantrum, but this was something different entirely. A group of about ten men were gathered around a statue in front of Branson Falls City Hall, attempting to make a statement about a recent Utah state law repeal. In my opinion—and the opinion of a majority of the state legislature—the law was outdated, ridiculous, unenforceable, and should have never become a law in the first place. Ned and his cronies disagreed, which meant that instead of my morning starting off with a quiet cup of coffee, Gandalf cuddles, and meditation, it had started off with coffee to go, a quick doggy drop-off at my mom and dad's, and a lot of yelling in the park in front of City Hall. I was trying to be objective, but the intrusion on my coffee time alone made me slightly stabby.

Ned had been talking for about five minutes, and judging by the way he hiked his pants up, and waved his arms, he wasn't stopping any time soon—and the crowd of spectators was growing. "I don't know how many of you know all the details 'bout this, but the legislature voted to make sex outside of marriage legal! And people can't be persecuted for sodomy or adultery anymore!"

I wanted to correct him and tell him the word was "prosecuted," because people were absolutely still being persecuted for sodomy in Utah.

A grumble of outrage went through the crowd at Ned's sodomy statement. Because to Ned and his religious cronies, fornication was bad, but sodomy was pure evil. It took a lot of restraint to refrain from rolling my eyes. Ned continued, "This is a blight on our state and everythin' the people who live here represent! We won't stand for it, and won't stand for leaders who support this kind of immorality!"

Sometimes I wondered why I stayed living in Branson Falls, then I reminded myself that if there was no one in town pushing a different perspective than people were used to, then everyone would keep seeing only one side. Still, I squeezed my eyes shut in an effort to head off my deep desire to scream in frustration at Ned's limited viewpoint. The scream was at the top of my throat when I heard Ned say, "Just you wait! Dylan Drake will be here soon to explain himself!"

My eyes popped right open and almost fell out on the ground.

Dammit! Dammit! Dammit! I was actively avoiding Drake and his biceps! I didn't know he was even in town or I would have asked another reporter to cover this stupid story.

Drake wasn't simply one of the men my ovaries were

lusting over, he was also a lawyer turned Utah State House Representative, which meant I had to see him on a professional basis frequently—though I'd deftly avoided him for weeks. Drake was going to show up any minute now with his dark hair, sexy smile, and perfect ass, and I really didn't trust myself to be around for that. Sometimes my work life and personal life had competing agendas. My personal agenda in regard to Dylan Drake was currently "hide and evade."

I looked around the park in front of City Hall and wondered if there was a suitable climbing tree. A good, sturdy oak with leaves that hadn't fallen yet would do nicely to conceal me. That way I could still cover the story without having to interact with Drake—an interaction that had a high probability of ending with gossip and scandal, and I'd had more than enough of those two things since moving back to Branson Falls.

I was still searching for my oak when I felt a hand on the small of my back. I knew that hand, and a shiver—part anticipation, part irrational fear—ran from my toes to my highlights. "Hi, Katie."

I closed my eyes and tried not to let his deep voice ensorcell me.

"What are you looking for?" he asked.

"A tree," I answered honestly.

I wasn't facing him, but could hear the knowing smile in his voice. "That's an excellent idea. Because then you'll be stuck up there and we can have a very long, and overdue, conversation."

I narrowed my eyes, realizing the flaw in my plan, and grateful that I hadn't started my ascent. I turned around to look at him and immediately decided that was a really bad idea.

Drake was dressed in a deep blue suit that was tailored to fit every inch of his impressive form in a very distracting way. His dark hair was perfectly styled, accenting a chiseled jaw, and his bright blue eyes sparkled with interest. His arms looked like they might break through his coat with muscles that had started their journey as a kid hauling hay bales on a farm, and continued as a high school football team hero. Now, he maintained them by lifting weights in a warehouse and throwing around stupidly large tractor tires for funsies. I would have sacrificed a lot of things to see him naked. The problem was he'd happily oblige and then we'd both end up hurt and angry after he felt obligated to propose and repent for his sexy sins when all I'd wanted was to see his twig, berries, and the sculpture they were attached to —not be married to them for time and all eternity.

His eyes met mine and my breath went AWOL. We were stuck in that no-breath-eye-hypnosis for a solid ten years—or at least that's what it felt like, until I heard someone shout, "There he is!"

Drake made a noise that sounded a lot like a snarl. "Saved by the town mob," he grumbled, moving away from me with regret. "Don't think we're done here." He turned, and took several long strides toward Ned and the rest of the group.

I breathed a sigh of relief as Ned launched into his grievances and Drake listened intently. When Ned was done, Drake lifted an arm in the air, trying to quiet everyone down enough for him to speak.

"I did vote to repeal the fornication law," Drake said, raising his hands again to quiet people down when more murmurs erupted at his admission. "It was a misdemeanor that was put on the books decades ago. It was a piece of pointless statement legislation that hadn't actually been prosecuted since it was enacted. The law was absolutely unenforceable and made Utah look foolish. Not only that, but I strongly disagree with big government. This yet another law allowing the government to tell people how to live their lives. I can't support that, and don't think most of my constituents support it either."

He was right about that. If there was one thing conservative-leaning Branson Falls loathed, it was an overreaching government. Still, Ned did not seem convinced.

"It was put on the books for a reason!" Ned raged.

Drake raised an eyebrow. "Do you want the government in *your* bedroom judging *your* sexual preferences?"

Ned's face went bright red and he distinctly resembled a beet. "Ain't nothin' wrong with what I do in the bedroom, and ain't none of your business either!"

"Exactly my point," Drake said without a hint of the smugness I felt he was entitled. "It's not anyone's business, and it can't be enforced, so it shouldn't be on the books, which is why I voted to remove it."

One of Ned's cohorts yelled out, "But it's wrong!"

"In your opinion," Drake answered patiently.

"In God's opinion!" Ned boomed, attempting to make his voice deeper so it would sound like he was receiving direct revelation from the trinity.

Drake took a deep breath. "There are laws on the books about certain sex acts too. Sex acts that I'm certain every one of you has participated in, and I guarantee you wouldn't want to be thrown in jail for. Do you want those prosecuted as well?" It was quiet enough to hear the men squirm. Drake raised a brow and continued, "It's a dangerous thing to use your own beliefs as a barometer for others."

Ned was undeterred. "Laws set a moral standard for the community! It's important!"

I'd heard that argument used by some of the Utah lawmakers who opposed the repeal. Apparently, Ned had seen the same news articles I had.

"Laws and morals are two completely different things," Drake said. "One is enforceable in court. One is not."

I could tell this was going to go on for quite a while, and the argument would continue going in circles. I'd gotten the gist of the debate, so I slowly started backing away, trying to be as inconspicuous as possible.

"Katie," Drake said, turning his attention to me and ignoring all the men around him. "Don't you dare leave."

I gave him a solid glare. "I'm sorry, Representative Drake. Your role does not extend to controlling the press."

"I'm not trying to control you. And I'm not speaking as your politician."

"But you are my politician." And something more, but I wasn't sure what.

"Katie," he said, his voice an interesting combination of growl and plea.

My phone started singing "Forever in Blue Jeans," Spence's ringtone, and I saw it as a definitive sign from the universe and every possible higher power that I should get the hell out of there. "Gotta go, Drake," I said, waving my phone at him. "Work."

I hadn't run that fast since I'd been hiking one afternoon and something much larger than a dog had started chasing me through the bushes. I fully expected Drake to do the same, but

Ned and his cronies were persistent, and they weren't letting him out of their circle until they'd beat the issue of his vote to death.

I answered the phone. "Another robbery was reported, and there was an assault involved," Spence said.

"Oh no," I said, getting in my car. "Where was it?"

"Betty Turner's house."

I froze, stunned. She got the random porch casserole and then her house was burglarized? It seemed like too much of a coincidence. "Betty Turner? Were the casserole capers trying to steal their casserole back?"

"I'm not sure," Spence said, "but get over there as fast as you can and find out."

I was already on my way.

My good friend and EMT, Annie Sparks, was treating Betty and getting her ready to go to the hospital when I arrived. I'd met Annie because she was frequently the emergency responder who managed my mom's adventures. She was Mormon, and one of the few non-judgmental and open-minded people in town. I enjoyed spending time with her and her husband, Rich.

"Hey, Annie," I said.

She smiled at me. "Hi, Kate. We need to get together again soon."

I nodded. "Lunch?"

"Sure," she said. "I'll text you."

"How's Mrs. Turner doing?" I asked. "Is she able to answer some questions?"

Annie nodded. "She's in a little pain, but we've given her some medication. It looks like she has some bruises, and possibly a concussion. We're taking her in for an evaluation to be safe. She probably would have been hurt a lot worse if she hadn't fought back."

The idea of being a grandma who could fight off intruders made me want to cheer. Someone needed to get her a super-hero t-shirt.

Mrs. Turner was propped up on the stretcher in her living room so I stood next to her while I talked. "Hi, Mrs. Turner. How are you feeling?"

She took a deep breath. "Well, I'm mad as a wet hen to tell you the truth, Kate. Those wicked men invaded my home and tried to steal from me and hurt me in the process! What's the world coming to?"

I nodded in empathy. "Being taken from in any way is a violation. I'm sorry that happened to you."

Her eyes softened with my words. "Me too. I can't imagine what they would have wanted."

"It seems weird they broke in and attacked you in broad daylight." Then again, the robbery at the Popes' house had happened during the day as well. "Did you recognize them at all?"

Betty shook her head. "No. They said they were here to treat the house for bugs. I have a company that takes care of spraying several times a year, so I thought they were doing the regular service. But once they were in my house, they started going through my things. I told them to stop. They didn't listen and started calling me the most uncouth names! Like they were raised by beasts! They grabbed my purse and started going through it, so I marched right into my bedroom and got Bambi. That stopped them mighty quick!"

"Bambi?" I asked, confused.

"My gun," she said, like I should have known her gun had a name, and that it was basically a Disney character. "Once I got the gun out, they pushed past me and knocked me over on their way out the door. I bruise like a fruit, and at this age, falling takes more of a toll on me than it used to. Then I called the police."

It took me a minute to recover because I was riveted by the story of a seventy-something-year-old woman owning a gun, brandishing it, and scaring off the criminals who were in her house. I finally came back to my senses and asked, "Did your neighbors see anything?"

Her lips turned down in a frown. "Not that I know of."

"Okay, well if you think of anything else, you have my number," I said. "Do you have someone staying with you when you get home later?"

"My daughter and grandkids will come from out of town to stay with me." I noticed a black sign with white writing in a pretty script that said, *Love, Loyalty, Family* that had fallen on the ground during the fight. I was glad she had family close who could help her. Being home alone after a robbery would be scary.

Annie and some of the other EMTs moved Mrs. Turner out the front door and to the ambulance.

Bobby was standing on the front lawn so I walked over to talk to him. "Were you the first on scene?" I asked.

He shook his head. "I was the second."

"Mrs. Turner said she had a gun. Is she licensed?"

He nodded. "She's had a concealed carry permit for years. Lots of people in Branson do."

Betty wore glasses with frames thicker than rocks, so I was surprised she could see well enough to use her gun. Then again, she hadn't needed to use it this time, only threaten with it. And the robbers were probably more afraid of her possible bad aim than her good aim.

I wrote the info about her concealed carry permit down in my notes. "She said she thought they were her pest control company. Did the neighbors see anything?"

He looped his thumbs into his front pockets. "We're still talking to some of them, but no luck so far," he said.

"Do you think this is linked to the other robberies in town?"

He lifted a shoulder. "Not sure. But seems kinda coincidental for it not to be."

"Is there anything connecting what happened to Mrs. Turner to what happened with the Popes?"

"Not that we can tell, but we're still lookin'."

I jotted down some notes before asking, "Did Mrs. Turner have time to see what they stole?"

"She told us they just took some money from her wallet."

It was weird they were going through her other belongings but only took cash. Maybe they were searching through her things to find her purse though.

"So they only took money from Mrs. Turner, but during the Popes' robbery, the money that was sitting out in the open was left on the table undisturbed."

"I know," Bobby said, pressing his lips together like he was thinking. "It's strange."

That seemed odd to me too. Why would the robbers leave money in one home, but take nothing but money in another?

Another officer called for Officer Bob and he raised a hand indicating he'd be right there.

"Will you let me know if you find out anything else?" I asked.

"Will do," Bobby said, walking away.

I was on my way to my Jeep as my phone rang with "Brother Love's Traveling Salvation Show." I took a deep breath and silenced it. Less than a minute later, a text message flashed.

> Running away isn't going to work. Neither will avoiding me. Or hiding in trees.

For about five seconds, I thought about texting him back something snarky, then decided that after our rendezvous in the park, a text would lead to more conversation and it was probably best not to engage right now.

Chapter Five

"Hey ya, Kitty Katie!" Ella said. She was sitting at one of the extra *Tribune* desks, looking at something on the computer.

I raised a brow at her for the nickname. Drake called me Katie, a name I'd hated until he'd recently explained his reasoning in a way that had made me melt like hot butter under a Tahitian sun and still did. And Hawke called me Kitty Kate. "Have you decided to combine Drake and Hawke's nicknames for me now?"

"I couldn't decide which team to choose, so I thought I'd be on both."

I nodded. It seemed like as good a solution as any.

"Heard you were with Drake this mornin'," she said.

I rolled my eyes and sank into the chair at my desk. It seemed the gossip and scandal bit had happened even though I'd tried to avoid it. "I wasn't *with* Drake. I was covering Ned and his compatriots at City Hall who were protesting the repeal of the law that made it illegal in Utah to have sex outside of marriage."

Ella barked out a laugh. "It don't matter that it's against the church rules. Ned and a bunch of his buddies would've all been in jail years ago if they'd started arrestin' people for breakin' that stupid law. What dummies."

"I agree."

Ella made a squeaking noise and hit a button on the computer.

"What are you doing?" I asked. It sounded like she was playing some sort of game. Ella was willing to try just about anything, so I wouldn't put it past her to be a Fortnite aficionado.

"I'm fightin' for this bid!" She punched a few more buttons with gusto.

I pushed my brows together and walked over to her computer. "Bid?"

"Yep! I want this vase. Looks real old and like it's worth somethin'."

I gave her a sideways glance. "I didn't realize you were in the market for old things that look like they're worth something."

She clicked on another button, upping her bid so she was the highest. "I wasn't, but then I found out about this Not Just Junk site and now I'm obsessed! It's like those people who go to garage sales and wind up with an antique worth a million bucks!"

I gave her a confused look. "But you're not hurting for money." Ella's husband had been a doctor so her family had been well-off, and when her husband died, she'd been the beneficiary of a sizable life insurance policy in addition to their joint assets. She drove around in a convertible sports car that she traded in yearly, gave money to several non-profits, and she only volunteered as the *Tribune*'s archivist because she wanted to be around people and have something to do.

"I don't do it for the money. I do it for the battle!" she said, and the bit of crazy that showed in her eyes made me slightly nervous. "I want to win the bids! And if I find somethin' worth a lot, that would be even more fun!"

"How often do you have to check your bids?" I asked, looking at the website's user interface. It looked a lot like every other bidding type website out there. A headline of the item, description, place for photos, and bid information on the side.

"I get notified every time some nincompoop tries to outbid me. And I can list categories that interest me and get notified every time somethin' new is uploaded to that category."

"That seems like a lot of time and effort."

She shrugged. "I've got the time. I'm gonna be a Not Just Junk legend!"

I laughed. Everyone needed goals and motivations. Becoming a bidding legend on stuff that may or may not be junk, was currently Ella's. I had no doubt she'd find a new motivation soon.

Spence walked in with lunch for Ella and I. He handed Ella her burger, and me a sandwich, fries, and Oreo milkshake. I love Oreo milkshakes with obscene amounts of extra Oreos, but a recent experience had changed how I viewed them entirely. I still enjoyed them, but now I couldn't eat one without thinking of Hawke.

"Thanks," I said to Spence.

He nodded and took a bite of his food. "I stopped to grab

lunch and everyone was talking about the robbery at Betty Turner's."

"I heard all about it," Ella said around a bite of her burger.

"Did The Ladies activate the phone tree?" I asked.

Ella nodded and swallowed. "And a post on the Facebook group so we could discuss it."

The Facebook group was a recent addition to The Ladies gossip arsenal. And Ella was nice enough to inform me that it had mostly been started on my behalf so The Ladies could all keep track of me and my love life. They weren't pleased that Drake seemed to be interested in me, and firmly, and erroneously, believed I was having sex with both Drake and Hawke. It was a good thing that fornicating law was repealed so I couldn't get arrested for it anymore. I had no doubt The Ladies would have turned me in had they known the law existed in the first place.

"Do The Ladies have any theories?"

"Undoubtedly, they're blaming you," Spence offered.

I rolled my eyes. "They could probably find a way to spin it."

"Nah," Ella said. "They're mostly wonderin' what's goin' on with Drake, Hawke, and your lady parts."

"Nothing. And my lady parts are none of their business," I said around a bite of my food. "Who do The Ladies suspect is robbing people?"

"They mostly think it has to do with the tattoo shop. The robberies didn't start until it opened, so they think the shop brought wicked people into town and it's God punishin' us for allowin' miscreants through our borders."

I almost choked on a fry. "I wasn't aware the Branson Falls borders were closed."

"The Ladies think they should be."

I wouldn't be surprised to see them suggest their own version of the Wall of Jericho next.

Spence's phone buzzed. "An emergency town meeting has been called for tonight to address the robberies. People were worried when it happened to the Pope family, but everyone thought it was an isolated incident. Now that someone has actually been injured, it's a problem."

I agreed that two robberies in as many days was probably more than a coincidence, but I wasn't sure how they tied together yet. I couldn't see any similarities in the cases. But a town meeting wasn't a bad idea. Getting people together to form neighborhood watches and be more vigilant couldn't hurt.

"What time is the meeting?" I asked.

"Seven," Spence said.

"I should be able to cover it. Let me text and see if my mom can keep Gandalf a little longer."

I texted my mom.

> I have to cover a story later tonight. I'll probably be done around nine. Can I swing by and pick up Gandalf after the meeting?"

"He's the cutest little guy," Ella said. "Your mom should have an Instagram account with him and his outfits!"

I was surprised she hadn't started one yet. "If she knew how to open an Instagram account, it would have probably happened by now."

My mom texted back

> Of course! And that means I get extra time with my grandpup!

Her text had about twenty emojis attached, including several little poops.

She followed that up with another text.

> I love these fun little texting pictures!

I texted back.

> I know. You keep sending me the little poop.

It took less than thirty seconds for her to reply.

> What are you talking about? What little poop?

I texted her the little poop back.

Her reply came swiftly, and included about twenty of the wide-eyed embarrassed emojis.

> That's a little poop????!!!!! I thought it was happy chocolate ice cream!!!! I've been sending it to people with hearts!!!!

I started laughing and couldn't stop so I sent her several laugh-cry emojis.

She texted again.

> I'm very upset about this!

> About the fact that you're sending people love poops? I think you should be happy. You'll start a trend.

> NO! I was tricked! Why would poop have a smile on it?

> Why would ice cream have a smile?

> Because ice cream is delightful! Ice cream smiling makes sense!

Her reasoning made me laugh even harder.

> I'm just going to have to make my own emojis!

At that point, I had tears running down my face from laughing so much, which meant everyone in the office was interested in what was giving me a giggle attack. I showed the text thread to Spence and Ella, then they were laughing too. Ella asked for a print out of it so she could put it above her desk. Then we all got back to work.

Spence posted some updates to the *Branson Tribune* social media accounts about Betty Turner's attack, and the emergency town meeting. People immediately started commenting that they'd be there because the town was going to the demons, and many blamed the coffee shop, Beans and Things, and Inked AF.

Sasha sent me the information for a few of her tattoo clients who had used their tattoos to cover up scars, and as a way to memorialize loved ones. I called and asked them some questions so I could provide a more balanced piece on tattoos and why people get them. Now that I knew The Ladies were blaming Inked AF for the robberies, it was even more important to me to make sure readers got to see the good that tattoos could do for people instead of automatically assuming anyone who gets tattoos is a bad person because that's what they're told to believe.

I worked on the Inked AF story, the casserole caper who was dropping off anonymous casseroles that lacked the proper amount of butter and cheese, and started the story about the robberies at the Popes and now Betty Turner's house. The *Tribune* is a small town weekly paper, which meant I'd be able to combine both robberies into one story—and frankly, I was fairly certain the two were somehow connected, I just needed to figure out how.

I'd been working all afternoon and knew I'd have a late night with the town meeting, so I decided to take a walk and try to clear my head. It was fall and there was a bite to the air, but the sun was still out and the brisk breeze felt cleansing as I buttoned my coat and made my way to the park a few blocks away. I used to love coming here as a kid, and still sometimes stopped by to swing on the swings, or attempt the monkey bars.

I settled into my favorite swing and pushed off, tucking my feet up so they wouldn't drag on the ground and I could enjoy the ride. The back and forth of the swing let my mind drift, and of course it drifted right to Hawke and Drake. I needed to stop being such a coward and face them both. But what would I say? They were two of the most alpha-y alpha males I'd ever met. I didn't think they'd handle me dating them both very well, but I definitely wasn't ready to make a decision about which one of them I wanted to be with. Hell, I didn't know if I wanted to be with anyone! My last relationship had made me leery of guys who thought they should be in charge. I was not the right woman for that kind of man. I wanted a partner, not an overlord. I needed more time with them both to help me figure out my feelings. I needed to date them and get to know them, and let them get to know me. I had reservations regarding Hawke and Drake, and those reservations included whether they could handle someone as independent and outspoken as me. My last significant other hadn't been able to.

I was deep in thought and hadn't even noticed that my swing had come to a stop until I felt two warm hands grip the swing seat on either side of me, a warm touch that sent electricity straight through my hips. The hands pulled me back, lingering for a moment, then let go. I turned around to see Hawke moving to the side so I wouldn't hit him when the swing came back. He was wearing his regular uniform of charcoal cargo pants, a dark grey t-shirt that was practically painted on and enhanced every giant muscle in his chest and arms, and combat boots that he could easily run in or kick the smiling chocolate ice cream out of someone with. His straw colored hair took on a pretty golden sheen in the afternoon sunlight, and the shadow of his beard only enhanced the strong lines of his sculpted jaw.

He took a seat in the swing next to me and I had to remind myself to breathe.

"So, I see you aren't tied up."

There were so many ways I could answer that I wasn't sure where to begin.

He didn't give me much time to narrow down my potential responses.

"Why haven't you been returning my calls or texts?" he asked.

The man got right to the point. I needed something, anything, to distract him. "Did you know that you have a tongue print? Every tongue print is different, just like a fingerprint." I winced as soon as the words came out of my mouth. I'd recently been reading a book on random unknown facts and that's the first one that came to mind.

Hawke winged a brow at my incredibly useful bit of information. "I don't think that's true. I think we need to do some testing and find out."

My heart started a sprint and I realized I should have chosen a random fact with much less sexual innuendo. "I read a book about it and feel pretty confident science has already vetted the claim."

"Mmmm," he said, grabbing my swing, which had slowed considerably, and moving closer to me. "I don't."

I thought about backing away. I really did. For about one second, the angel on my shoulder had control and reminded me I had feelings for two men and shouldn't be kissing either one of them until I figured things out. And then Hawke's huge hand was in my hair and his other arm was wrapped around my waist, and his soft, full lips were pressed against mine in a searing kiss that immediately made me want those lips other places as well. Hawke kissed like every kiss was his last, and in his line of work—a line of work I wasn't entirely sure of but knew it straddled the line between moral and immoral—it might be. It was easy to get lost in the feel of his hands and the intoxicating smell of salt, soap, and the beach that was one hundred percent his. Reasoning skills came back to me slowly, but eventually they did return and I knew I needed to put some water on this fire immediately or we were going to end up back at my house doing things that until recently, were illegal in Utah.

I pulled away, licking my lips, and was almost drawn right back in when I saw the heat in Hawke's eyes. I shifted my focus, searching for something that might pull us away from the bedroom we were almost headed to.

"You haven't been climbing house walls over on Evergreen Street this week, have you?"

"Not this week."

I gave him a look. "You've been climbing walls on Evergreen Street on other days?"

He raised a brow. "You never know what I'm up to, Kitty Kate."

That was true. And it concerned me.

"You didn't answer my question," he said.

"I know. I was avoiding it on purpose."

"Like you've been avoiding me." It was a statement, not a question.

I looked everywhere but at Hawke. The tennis courts could use a cleaning, and some of the playground equipment needed to be painted. I should do a story on that.

"You know I'm pretty difficult to dodge?" he asked.

I did. That's why I'd been so impressed that I'd accomplished it. I gave myself an inner pat on the back and tried not to let how pleased I was with myself show on my face because I'd been successfully avoiding him for weeks.

"So when you careened around the corner into an alley to try to escape my Mustang coming down the road, leaving a trail of dust behind you, that did not go unnoticed."

My eyes widened. Dammit! I was sure he hadn't seen me!

"And when you hid from me in the grocery store like the kid running from the velociraptor in *Jurassic Park*, I saw every move you made."

My mouth gaped at that bit of information. I thought I'd been so stealthy! "You saw me?" I felt offended and deflated all at once. I'd been running from aisle to aisle like an assassin with a cart and I totally thought I'd kicked ass and could have a second job as a ninja!

"The store has mirrors on every aisle so the cameras can catch people trying to steal things. You were holding bread, milk, cheese, ice cream, cookies, chocolate, and candy. And you kept dropping stuff along the way. There was a literal trail of sugar that led right to you."

I wrinkled my nose, even more annoyed. "I had to abandon my cart when I saw you and only took the necessities."

He arched one brow. "And then you climbed into a freezer. I'm not even sure how you got in there. It was full of frozen vegetables."

It hadn't been easy, and I'd managed to give myself a frozen pea wedgie, which was not the most comfortable experience, and not one I would recommend. Plus, I'd almost frozen my boobs off. "I didn't know where you were!" My exasperation was showing in the pitch of my voice.

"The Farley kid is going to think monsters live in the grocery store freezer section," Hawke mused. "He's going to be traumatized for years."

I did feel bad about that. "I apologized. To him, and his mother. I wasn't expecting a kid to be in the frozen vegetable section. Ice cream, totally, but not frozen veggies. And then I saw you leave so I thought I'd made it through the ordeal without being seen."

Hawke's eyes sparkled with amusement. "I had to leave before you caused a major event. It was like watching your mother."

I gasped, more horrified at the comparison to my mom's disaster tendencies than anything else. "I do not have my mom's catastrophe genes."

He narrowed his eyes. "They might have been sitting dormant for twenty-five years and are now starting to make an appearance—like a volcano."

I gave him a glare that would have shriveled a lesser man.

"Your attempt to escape was better than a movie. I asked the grocery store owner for the security footage."

"You did not!" I said, giving him a playful punch to the arm. It was like hitting a rock. I rubbed my fist to try and soothe it, but Hawke took it instead.

"I think you need some practice in evasive maneuvers. My house, and bedroom, are always open."

I could feel the heat creeping up my face and since I wasn't prepared to have a conversation about sex or our relationship —whatever that relationship was—I decided now would be a really good time to change the subject. "There was a burglary on Evergreen Street. The Pope family. That's why I asked you about it."

"I know." He said it with the confidence of a man who knows everything, and chances were good Hawke actually did.

"And another burglary yesterday at Betty Turner's house."

He nodded at that information too.

"Do you know anything about either of those crimes?"

"Not yet, but I'm interested."

"I think they're connected, but so far I can't see anything that ties them together," I said, going over the details again in my mind. "The police can't figure it out either."

"If they're connected, this won't be the last. More information will come out as more robberies happen."

I nodded in agreement. "People in town are worried and an emergency town meeting has been called for tonight."

"I know that too."

"Is there anything you don't know?"

His eyes darkened and he gave me a look full of heat. "Plenty, Kitty Kate. Plenty. But I'm looking forward to finding it all out."

I turned my gaze away from him because I didn't trust myself to keep it there. A car pulled into the parking lot. I probably wouldn't have noticed if it hadn't pulled in directly across from the swing set. The person inside the car seemed to have a larger head than normal. It took a few seconds for my brain to process what I was seeing, but I realized that I was staring at someone wearing a giant squirrel head looking right at us. I couldn't see the rest of the squirrel's attire, but wondered if he was in full costume, or only wearing the head.

Hawke must have noticed my attention and looked in the same direction I was focused on.

"Is it just me, or is a squirrel driving that Corolla and staring at us?" I asked, still returning the squirrel's attention.

Hawke watched the car with interest. "It's definitely a squirrel."

"Seems strange a giant squirrel would be hanging out in the library parking lot."

"It's October. Maybe he's on his way to a Halloween party and got lost."

That was as rational an explanation as any. The car stayed in the parking spot for a few minutes and then pulled out and drove away.

I glanced at my watch. "I need to get back to work and get some things done before the town meeting tonight."

"I'll see you there," he said.

"Hey," I said as I started walking away. "What are you going to be for Halloween?"

His lips spread into a wide grin. "Anything you want me to be, Kitty Kate."

My heart sped up and heat rose in my cheeks. That was a long list.

"I'm excellent at fulfilling fantasies," he said.

I nodded with assurance. "I have no doubt."

Chapter Six

I got to the meeting early so I could get a good spot to sit and take notes and photos. Half the people in town were already there, speaking in raised voices about what Branson Falls was coming to. The city council members hadn't even shown up yet.

I found a chair and got my notes in order. I was curious how the council and police were planning to address the robberies since the crimes hadn't been going on long. Getting ahead of the problem and making people aware was probably the best course of action, but they had no suspects or leads.

I was reading through my notes when I felt a large form slide in next to me and my body reacted immediately. Drake. He was wearing the same thing he'd been wearing this morning, and this time, I had no convenient tree to climb.

"You've been avoiding me for weeks."

He got right to the point. Just like Hawke had. They were men on a mission.

I shrugged in response. "I've been busy."

He gave me an assessing look. "Not that busy."

I narrowed my eyes. "How do you know?"

"Because I know."

This wasn't a conversation I wanted to have with half the town as our audience. Granted, most of them were otherwise engaged in spouting off theories about who was committing the robberies, but still. The Ladies had sneaky spies everywhere, and I had no doubt there was one in the area listening in.

I sighed, put down my notebook, and met his eyes. "I'm not sure who's been apprising you of my schedule, but I've got a casserole caper dropping casseroles off on random doorsteps, a slew of robberies that make no sense, and people committed to taking down the new tattoo shop simply because the owners are providing a service they disagree with. I'm a little occupied right now. So unless you know something about one of those issues, I don't have time to talk."

"You seem to have plenty of time to talk to Hawke."

I gave him a confused look. That wasn't true. I'd been avoiding Hawke too. Until today.

He raised a brow. "You were with him at the park a couple of hours ago."

Dammit! That stupid Ladies Facebook group was going to be the end of me, and by end, I meant it was going to make me so stabby that I ended up in jail for actually stabbing someone. "Number one, who I spend time with is really none of your business. Number two, I was talking to Hawke about one of the stories I mentioned a second ago."

He narrowed his eyes like he didn't believe that was the only thing we'd been doing. And it wasn't. If he hadn't already been informed about the kissing part of mine and Hawke's rendezvous, it was only a matter of time.

I slitted my eyes right back and dared him to challenge me on it. My glare must have been intimidating enough that he decided to change course. "I know something about one of those issues," he said.

I raised a brow, interested. "You do?"

He raised one back. "I do."

"What?"

His lips slid into a smug smile. "That information will cost you."

My face contorted like I'd sucked on something sour. "I don't like being manipulated."

He put his hands up, palms out in front of him. "I'm not manipulating you. I'm offering information in exchange for a conversation. I'm told that talking is kind of what reporters do."

Okay, he was right about that.

"But," he said, continuing, "I'll add that on a personal level, my feelings are a bit singed. I'm not sure what I did wrong to make you distance yourself from me, but I'd like the opportunity to talk with you about it."

I respected that. A lot. He didn't want to let things sit and simmer. He wasn't afraid of emotion, confrontation, or hearing how I felt. He wanted to talk through it, regardless of what the outcome might be. And he had a fair point. I'd been spineless and avoided the smiling little happy chocolate ice cream out of him. But I still had no idea what to tell him about my feelings, or exactly why I'd been avoiding him because I didn't know what those feelings were. "Okay," I said. "Let's have a conversation about the story issue and I promise we'll get to the personal stuff at some point." When I figured it out. "What do you know?"

His lips tipped up like he knew he'd caught me. And he had—a long time ago, before I even really had boobs, and I'd been fighting his blue eyes and six-pack ever since. "How about I stop by and we can talk about it where there aren't so many ears." He tilted his head in reference to all the people in the room with us.

"Okay," I said. "Unless a story breaks, I should be at the *Tribune* office tomorrow."

He pressed his lips together. "Or I could stop by your house later tonight."

My house had a bed. And a comfortable couch. And a soft rug. And sturdy walls. And really, none of those things even mattered where my willpower was concerned; the bare floor would work just fine. The main issue was that my house had been the location of our last almost-tryst. Therefore, my house was a no-Drake zone. Not to mention the fact that Drake's car at my house at any time of day would illicit an immediate drive-by and discussion from The Ladies, but Drake's car at my house after eight PM would cause a full-on incident. "I don't think my house is a good idea."

His brows rose. "You don't?"

"Nope."

Drake's eyes heated. "Too many memories?" His tone was suggestive and my lady parts responded accordingly.

And bedrooms, I added in my head.

"You could come to my house instead," he suggested.

That was a tempting offer because I'd never been inside Drake's house and wondered what it looked like. He owned it, which meant that unlike my house, he'd been able to decorate it. You can tell a lot about a person by their home—I had strong opinions about countertop stone, flooring, drywall texture, and theories about people based on whether or not they liked wallpaper. The temptation to stop by Drake's house immediately receded when I thought of the number of beds and comfortable couches that probably existed there as well.

I'd recently attended a lecture by a very smart neuroscientist on brain function. He'd explained that every human is born with a limited amount of daily willpower, gifted to each person by their genetic code, and that willpower gets depleted daily as the day goes on by everything from traffic frustrations to what clothes to wear—which explained why so many of my poor choices were made at night. That class had made me realize that I should probably always limit my interactions with Hawke and Drake to daytime, preferably morning when my willpower tank was full.

"I won't get out of here until late tonight and I've been working since Ned and his idiots started their protest at the butt crack of dawn this morning."

"Fair enough," Drake said. "I'll stop by the *Tribune* office tomorrow."

I glanced around the room and caught the eyes of The Ladies huddled together in the back like a nest of vipers lacquered in Aqua Net. Amber Kane glared and whispered something in Jackie's ear. Jackie's gaze darted to me, then to the seat next to me where Drake had planted himself. She slitted her eyes and if I'd been within striking range, I was certain I'd be on my way to the hospital for some Lady antivenom. I knew how much Drake's interest in me irritated her, and I gave her a wink to aggravate her a little more before I turned back around.

The meeting was about to start. I thought Drake might get up and leave, but instead he settled in next to me and I had to use all of my remaining daily willpower to focus on the councilmen seated at the front of the room instead of Drake's mass of muscles in squeeze range.

Councilman Jessie Green called the meeting to order. "We're here to discuss the recent spate of robberies," he said. "I know many of you are concerned. I want to ensure you that we've been in constant contact with the police department and they're keepin' us updated about their investigation. So far, there doesn't seem to be anythin' tyin' these crimes together, but the police have committed to increasin' their patrols and want to encourage all of us as a community to watch out for each other and let them know if anythin' strange or out of place seems to be happenin'."

A voice in the crowd interrupted councilman Green, "The only thing strange and out of place is that new tattoo shop. No one was gettin' robbed until they came into town."

Another voice chimed in, "That's what we get for allowin' sinful things in our town. They bring the wickedness with them."

That started a whole new contingent of smaller arguments among citizens and the cacophony of anger was making it hard for me to hear all of the various complaints, let alone write them all down. I was recording the meeting so I'd have to review the audio later to make sure I got everything correct.

As I looked around the room, I caught the eyes of Axel and Sasha. Axel looked upset, and Sasha looked defeated. I felt bad for them both. They were being attacked simply for being different, and people in small towns with a rigid set of beliefs tend to fear difference more than anything. It's that kind of attitude that leads to mob mentality.

Councilman Green held up his hand and started speaking loudly to try and get people to quiet down. "I know we all have a lotta opinions about this, and I want to hear them. But to do that, we need some semblance of order. If you want to talk, get in line and use the mic."

A line formed almost immediately with people expressing anger and fear over what was happening in Branson Falls. Some were mad that the town had changed and wasn't safe like it used to be when you could leave your door unlocked all night and never have to worry about a thing. Those people were all older than my grandparents. Others were worried and concerned for Mrs. Turner and wanted an update about her health. The idea that someone would come into an elderly woman's home and attack her was unsettling for many. I took notes as each person spoke, and kept my recorder on so I could go back and review any quotes I used. The line of people was almost done when Fred Carlson stepped up to the mic.

"I don't think the tattoo shop is the problem," Fred said. I'd seen Fred at the Inked AF grand opening and talked to him a little bit. His business was right next door and he hadn't seemed concerned about having a tattoo and piercing studio as a neighbor. He'd even given me a quote supporting them.

"And you're some kind of authority?" Another town member yelled from the crowd.

Fred gave an exasperated look. "My antique shop is in the building next to them. I haven't noticed anything strange, and everyone who stops in to Inked AF seems nice. Some of them have even come over to my store and bought things after getting their tattoos. I really like seeing the artwork and hearing the stories behind the design they chose."

Another person in the crowd spoke up, "That doesn't mean some of 'em aren't the ones robbin' people! These robberies didn't start happenin' until the tattoo shop opened."

A hush fell over the room as Sasha made her way through the crowd of people and stepped up to the mic. "As most of you know, I'm one of the owners of Inked AF. First, I want to thank Fred for his kind words. We love having him as a neighbor and have enjoyed visiting his shop. I know there's a lot of concern around our tattoo shop, but I want to assure you that any connection between our shop opening and the robberies is one-hundred percent coincidental. We were horrified to hear about Mrs. Turner and hope she'll be okay. Our clients are good people who have a variety of reasons for getting their tattoos. I know the *Tribune* has a story coming out about some of them and I'd encourage you to read it before you pass judgment on people who make choices you might not agree with. In addition, we want the Branson Falls community to be comfortable with us, and we want you to know our doors are open to you any time. Feel free to stop in, get to know us, and ask us questions. We'd love to get to know you too, and we'll continue to try and be good neighbors to you—like we hope you'll do for us in return."

The crowd was completely silent as Sasha stepped away from the mic. I looked around for Axel, but couldn't see him. I wondered why he'd left. Maybe he was upset and needed some air. I knew what it was like to be the subject of gossip and disdain in town and totally understood the inclination to either get out of the area or murder someone. Leaving was a better choice…usually.

The last person in line was a woman with dark hair and a wide smile that dimpled her cheeks. She had kind eyes and looked like she was in her fifties. "I'm Betty Turner's daughter. I want to say thank you to everyone who has called and stopped by to check on my mom. She's doing fine and is mostly just angry that someone dared to beat her up. She'll be carrying her gun, Bambi, around more often now. We've got family members staying with her, but thank you all for your concern. It's nice to know she's well-looked after here, especially since most of her family members live at least an hour away."

Councilman Green turned things over to the Branson Falls Police Department, who basically reiterated everything the councilman had already said about increasing patrols, and needing everyone to keep an eye open and report suspicious things immediately. The meeting adjourned a few minutes later.

As I stood up, Drake said, "I'll see you tomorrow, Katie."

His eyes glinted as he said it and I wondered what else he thought he'd be seeing. "At the office," I verified.

"Sure," he said with a wink.

That sounded ominous. I thinned my eyes as I walked out of the room and left the building. As I made my way to the car, I saw Sasha standing with Axel about fifty yards away. I couldn't hear them, but I could see Axel's face was full of anger, and Sasha seemed to be trying to soothe him. My heart twisted for them and I really did hope people in town would open their minds, and read the article in the *Tribune*. Maybe it would make some people reconsider their viewpoints.

I got to my Jeep and found a giant made of skin, muscle, and not much else, leaning against it. "I think these robberies are connected, but I'm not sure how yet," Hawke said.

"Same page," I said, gesturing between us.

"I'm going to have my guys look into things."

I narrowed my eyes. "Who exactly are your "guys"?"

"People who know how to find out things other people don't." His expression gave nothing away.

Hawke always answered my questions by not really answering my questions. And that was one of the things I worried about in a relationship with him. I was a reporter. I needed transparency and information. If he wasn't willing to share with me, or if he couldn't, then how could we have an open, meaningful, and deeper relationship? Bonding required vulnerability and trust.

"How do they find out those things?" I asked. "Is it a series of questions? Do the questions involve some form of torture?" I tried to put a playful tone in my voice, but I wasn't kidding.

"They use a variety of methods," he said.

"That's still not really an answer."

"You never answered my question about why you've been avoiding me."

"Nice misdirection," I drawled.

He lifted a shoulder and grinned.

"I was hoping you forgot about it," I said.

He licked his lips slowly and my eyes snagged there, wanting. "I don't look forward to much, Kitty Kate, but you're one of those things. I notice when you're not around. Don't make the mistake of thinking otherwise."

My heart sped up and I seriously considering pushing him against my Jeep and kissing him for the second time today. "Noted," I said, my voice more breathless than I'd intended.

He eyed me, assessing my full lips and pulse fluttering at hummingbird speed on my neck. "I understand you're trying

THE DEVIL HAS TATTOOS

to figure things out. I'm okay with that. I'm patient. Just don't keep me in the dark."

And that was another reason my heart was having difficulty listening to my head. There was something attractive about a man who paid attention, and Hawke was the most detail-oriented man I'd ever met. He knew exactly what my problem was without me even having to tell him. When I'd first met him I'd been annoyed by his perception because it made me think I was easy to read. Now I knew it was that Hawke was even more exceptional at profiling a person than social media and big data.

"I'll do my best," I said. I got in my car and left to pick up Gandalf.

I pulled up in front of the gray brick house I'd grown up in. The weather hadn't turned cold enough yet for the flowers to die, so my mom's red petunias were bright and cheery as I made my way to the front door. I opened it and Gandalf came careening around the corner wearing his little blue cape. He was moving so fast it looked like he might be flying.

I couldn't contain my smile and immediately dropped to the floor to give him hugs and pets. He tolerated it for about ten seconds, then ran to the other side of the room and brought me one of his toy balls. I threw it and almost hit my mom as she came in from the kitchen wearing jeans and a pink and green floral blouse. Her deep brown hair was pulled back into a twist, and she had her hands on her hips, looking as exasperated as ever.

"I'm *mortified!*" she said, her tone almost as embarrassed as her red cheeks indicated.

I knew she was probably referring to the little poop/heart incident, but it had been several hours since I'd talked to her last and that left endless possibilities of events that might have occurred since so I thought I better clarify. "About?"

Gandalf brought me his ball back. I threw it and watched as he disappeared down the hall.

My mom looked at me like I'd lost my mind. "The happy chocolate ice cream with hearts! What else?"

I gave a little shrug. "Well, I wasn't sure. You're usually involved in a plethora of incidents by noon so it's sometimes hard to keep up."

My mom rolled her eyes and swatted me across the back with the towel she kept perpetually over her shoulder when she was home.

"I just can't believe anyone would think that's a poop! It's *smiling!*" she said, exasperated. "Why would poop smile?"

She'd asked the same question this morning, which meant she'd thought about it all day and was still confounded. "To make it more enjoyable for people to see?" I offered. "Or maybe it's for passive aggressive people who want to call someone a bad name but this makes it seem cute."

She scrunched up her nose. "That's a dirty trick."

"It's hard to read real intentions with texts and emojis," I said, playing tug of war with Gandalf and a toy rope. "You're the perfect example. All these people think you've been telling them you love their poop and really, you've been saying you love happy chocolate ice cream."

She stomped her foot. "It *is* happy chocolate ice cream, and I'm standing by that!"

I liked that the great little poop/happy chocolate ice cream debate was the hill she'd decided to die on. "Well, *you* can think it's happy chocolate ice cream, but everyone else who gets that emoji from you will think it's a little poop. So keep that in mind."

She put her hands on her hips, irritated at technology and the world. "This is almost as bad as the time my stupid phone sent the nice neighbors the F word! I didn't type that word. I've never even used that word in my life! It was totally unauthorized!"

I widened my eyes at that and was surprised I hadn't heard about it on the town Facebook page. The F word was a big deal, especially coming from my mom. I didn't know that she even knew the word, or how to use it properly. "What did the neighbors say?"

"Oh," she said, swinging her towel in a negating gesture, "they texted me back and let me know I'd typed the wrong thing, but I've never been so humiliated in my life! Me! Using the F word! Can you even imagine?!"

No, I couldn't. I still got in trouble for swearing around her—even lesser swears. And I was annoyed that her phone knew that word. Mine usually autocorrected it to 'duck'.

"Or the time I asked you about shrimp for dinner," my dad said, coming around the corner with Gandalf in tow. My dad was tall and built like a tank. My tiny little dog looked even smaller next to him.

My mom's eyes got wide and murderous. "I told you we were *never* to talk about that again!"

My dad held up his hands in front of him like they might be some sort of defense for my mom's glare. I'd been the recipient of that glare more times than I could remember and knew hand shields did nothing. My dad should have been aware of that fact as well. "Kate's here, and I have witnesses. Plus, you wouldn't want to try murdering me in front of Gandalf. It would traumatize him forever."

"What happened with the shrimp?" I asked, genuinely curious.

"Your mom started a commotion, that's what," he said.

Mom's mouth was puckered and her eyes were so narrow I thought she might do my dad bodily harm. "It was *not* my fault."

My dad raised his eyebrows and started laughing.

"It all started because I got a new fancy phone. I usually love Cyrus because he answers all of my questions and sends people nice texts when I tell him to."

My mom had changed her voice assistant to speak in a male voice with an accent because she thought it was exotic and "liked having James Bond in her pocket." That was a direct quote. I'd never asked my dad how he felt about having James Bond in her pants. Since the voice was now an exotic man, she'd decided it needed a new name, and had spent an inordinate amount of time coming up with the Cyrus moniker. I wasn't sure what Siri/Cyrus had to do with shrimp but I was going along for the ride.

"But," she continued, her tone dark and foreboding, "this time, Cyrus failed me horribly."

"So you told your phone to send a text about shrimp?" I asked.

My dad shook his head. "She was texting me about dinner using the voice-to-text feature. Apparently, when she says shrimp, your mom's phone thinks she's saying another less palatable word—one that many people use the little poop emoji for."

"How did your phone even know that word?" I asked, baffled. My mom was not a swear fan.

She was working herself into even more of a huff. "The phone heard wrong! I DID NOT swear!"

I eyed her suspiciously. "Your phone has to know a word for it to show up, even as a mistake, which means your phone learned the word from someone." Which also applied to the F word, but I decided not to add that fuel to her current bonfire.

She thought about that for a minute. "I was in the car and it must have listened to music from the car next to me and translated the lyrics while I was trying to text your dad!" She said it with the enthusiasm of someone who'd solved the mystery of where Jimmy Hoffa's body was located. "For the record, I NEVER swore! And Cyrus is a pill."

"You're blaming this on a song? In an entirely different car?" I gave her a look that was echoed by my dad and basically conveyed disbelief at her expert justification level. Our reactions seemed to make my mom even more affronted.

"The only explanation I could come up with was that the phone had a bad chip in it, and liked to make things up on its own. That little chip monster gets me in a lot of trouble." Her lips were pressed into a pucker indicating she was highly perturbed.

"This is going to turn into the Branson Falls Sophie Saxee Shrimp Scandal," I said. "SSSS for short. It even sounds like hissing."

"That's pretty accurate," my dad said. "Because every time I bring up the shrimp incident, your mom sounds like a snake about to strike."

She shook her head. "More like shush, shush, shush, shush," she said, then paused. "I would say Shh, Shh, but I know where that got me last time."

"Swearing at your husband?" I offered.

She swatted me with her shoulder towel again.

"Be grateful you were saying shrimp and not another word like witch, duck, or truck," I said.

She pressed her lips together. " 'Truck' has been a problem before."

Gandalf brought my dad a ball to throw. He faked throwing it about three times before tossing it down the hall and watching Gandalf take off after it. "She took the phone back and demanded a new one because of the shrimp situation," my dad said. "She was adamant it had hearing issues."

"Did they give you a new one?"

My mom gave a little self-satisfied smile. "Did they have a choice?"

If I knew my mom, that answer was most definitely no. Most people would do anything to avoid becoming collateral damage in one of her catastrophes.

Gandalf came over and pawed at my mom's legs. She sat in one of her uncomfortable living room chairs that felt like you were running butt first into a rock every time you moved, and picked Gandalf up. He snuggled right up in her lap and gave a contented little sigh. "What's going on with the robberies?" she asked, trying to change the subject. "Did they tell you anything new at the town meeting?"

I shook my head. "Not really. The police are increasing patrols, and asking residents to keep them informed if they see anything strange. Most people are blaming the tattoo shop, which is ridiculous."

"The robberies didn't start happening until the tattoo shop opened," my dad said.

"It's a pretty shaky argument. I don't think the shop is involved. I've gotten to know the owners and correlation is not causation."

"What does Hawke think?" my mom asked.

I gave her a look. She'd grown exceptionally fond of Hawke and seemed to respect his opinions above all others—mine included. I'd recently been made aware of the fact that Hawke sometimes stopped by to visit with my mom, and help my dad with his Mustang. "He thinks the same thing as me. That the two robberies are connected to each other, but we aren't sure how."

"So you've seen Hawke lately," she asked, trying to be sneaky with her prying.

"I see him a lot. He lives in Branson…most of the time."

"I don't see him as much as you do," my mom noted with a lilt to her voice.

"I wasn't aware you were trying to," I said.

"Me either," my dad said, one brow arched.

My mom rearranged Gandalf's collar. "I'm simply saying that I think Hawke likes seeing you and probably puts himself in your path frequently."

I gave her a look. "He has resources I don't, so I often end up working with him. That's all."

She gave me a look right back. "The position Ella and I found you two in during the UFO investigation says otherwise."

I thinned my eyes and my voice dropped an octave in warning. "I tripped."

She rolled her eyes. "And fell on top of him?"

I lifted my shoulders. "He broke my fall. I could have been hurt."

My mom shook her head, a little smile playing at the corners of her lips. "I think you might be in denial, Kate."

I scooped Gandalf up. "Probably in the same way you're in denial about how your phone confused a swear word with a crustacean."

My dad laughed and my mom's lips pressed into a perturbed line. "Thanks for taking care of Gandalf," I said, giving my mom and dad both a hug. My dad petted Gandalf's little black head and my mom kissed it. "I'll bring him by tomorrow morning on my way to work," I said.

"I'm baking him probiotic and vitamin infused pumpkin cookies shaped like little bones. He should be excited!" mom said.

I laughed as I went out the door and on the way home, I had the fleeting thought that my dog probably ate better than I did.

Chapter Seven

Gandalf and I had a yummy breakfast. I got peanut butter toast and coffee. He got freeze dried raw food and goats milk with vitamins. His food cost more than mine on a weekly basis, but I'd done my research and knew how much better Gandalf's health would be and how much longer he'd live on a specialized diet. The freeze dried raw option made it much more pleasant than feeding him actual raw meat.

After we both finished eating, I loaded him up and secured him in his car seat in my Jeep, and dropped him off at my mom and dad's house before heading into work. My mom had still been horrified over the little poop and shrimp situations, but I had no doubt she'd find something else to concern herself with shortly.

I checked my phone as I got out of my Jeep and saw a text from Annie. I texted back and we set up lunch.

I hadn't even made it three steps into the office when Ella accosted me in front of the water cooler. "I heard if that fornication law was still in force, you and Hawke would both be in jail for defilin' the kids' swing at the park."

I rolled my eyes and moved past her to my desk, putting down my coffee thermos—which I wasn't afraid to say contained actual coffee, unlike most people in town who lied and said they were drinking "hot chocolate" because they didn't want to be judged for their sinful hot beverage choices.

"You've got to be kidding me," I said, trying very hard not to want to boob punch some nosy Ladies. "Hawke and I were just talking. In a totally public place."

One of Ella's eyebrows arched like she didn't believe a word I'd said. "I heard there were all kinds of acrobatics happenin' and Hawke was diddlin' you in the swing."

My mouth dropped open. "That is patently false. And I'd need a much more private place than a park, with far more surface area than a swing, for what I'd want to do with him." Though a swing could probably be worked nicely into that fantasy.

Ella's eyes widened to the size of saucers, and then she hit her hand on her leg. "Hot damn! I knew you two were doin' it!"

I closed my eyes and sighed. "No, we aren't."

"But you want to?" she asked with interest.

"Have you seen Hawke," I asked incredulously. "Who wouldn't want to see him naked?"

She gave me an appreciative look and I had a feeling she'd considered the same thing herself. "What about Drake?" Ella asked. "He's still mighty interested in you. The Ladies said you were all over each other at the city council meetin' last night."

I took a deep breath and counted to ten. "Drake sat next me at the city council meeting and talked to me about a story I'm working on. We didn't even touch."

"But you want to," Ella hinted, wiggling her eyebrows.

"Drake is very nice to look at as well," I said, trying to give a noncommittal answer because I *did* want to see them both naked, but I didn't want the baggage that came with their nudity, or the choices I'd have to make after the liaison.

Ella's phone chimed and she squeaked as she looked at it. "I won a bid! I'm gonna need a new room with lotsa shelves for all these treasures I'm findin' on Not Just Junk!"

"What did you win this time?" I asked.

"A stuffed animal!"

I gave her a look. That didn't seem worthy of celebration.

"You know you can get stuffed animals at pretty much any store in town or online?"

Ella shook her head so fast it looked like she was trying to evade a spastic wasp. "Not like this," she said. "This is the super special batty-bat-squeak-and-scream edition. They only made five thousand! It was danged hard to get too, bein' that Halloween is so close. Everyone wanted it for their Halloween displays!"

That did not surprise me. Utah is well-known for its Halloween obsession, ghostly décor, and some of the best haunted houses in the United States. In some towns, Halloween decorations are more popular than Christmas decorations.

"Well, I'm glad you got it."

"It wasn't cheap, but it'll be worth it when I post to Snapchat showing it off!"

I gave her a look. "You have Snapchat?"

"Sure I do! Only old people still use Facebook. I'm hip to all the new social."

I didn't doubt it. She probably knew more about those

apps than I did. And I couldn't wait to find out what new groups The Ladies were forming to troll me on them all.

A scratchy voice on the police scanner startled me. I listened as the dispatcher relayed a vandalism report and that police were being requested at the scene. When I heard the address of the property that had been hit, I was out the door before I even had a chance to see what Ella bid on next.

I got out of my Jeep and saw the eggs covering the side of the house. Having been the recipient of a car egging recently, I knew what a royal pain it was to clean the slimy yoke and whites off of paint, and did not envy the job that awaited the homeowner—who was now rounding the side of the house and walking straight for me. "You must have really wanted me to come to your house, Drake," I teased. "But this seems a little extreme, even for you."

He looked at me like I was nuts as he stopped a few feet from me. "As much as I want to see you, I wouldn't have vandalized my own house to make it happen."

I made a tsk tsk noise. "I guess I know where I am on your priority list."

He leaned in next to me, his breath hot on my neck as he whispered, "I don't think you do, actually. Why don't you come inside and I'll show you exactly where you stand, and where I brace you against a wall as I kiss you breathless."

I could feel the heat rising in my cheeks but decided I would not let him win. I smiled sweetly and held his eyes as I said, "It's adorable you think you'd be in control in that scenario."

His lips slid into a slow and sensuous smile and I decided I needed to stop the sexy banter immediately or we'd be inside trying every one of the positions he'd considered and more. "I've never seen your house before," I said, changing the subject.

Drake lifted his brows. "You haven't even driven by?"

Okay, so I *might* have found his address, memorized it, and driven by repeatedly, but I'd never done serious reconnaissance. And I'd certainly never seen his house with him around, and I'd never looked at the interior. "I'm sure I've driven by it for a story at some point."

His eyes sparkled. "You should come in. Let me show you around."

I gave him a look. "Oh no. I won't be coming inside."

Drake's eyes darkened and he looked almost predatory. I'd seen him look that way before...when he was about to tackle someone on the football field, or tempt a cheerleader.

I took a step back to get out of pheromone range. "I'm definitely *not* coming inside," I said, just to make it clear that the double entendre wasn't on purpose.

"Inside. Outside. I'm not picky."

Neither was I. And that went for both Drake *and* Hawke. It was a problem.

"Scared?" he asked.

"Terrified," I answered. "You've probably got some Mormon missionaries inside there waiting to accost me."

He rolled his eyes and I redirected the conversation back to the current situation. "When did this happen?" I asked, gesturing to the wall of breakfast on his house.

"Sometime after midnight, when I went to bed, and before seven in the morning, when I woke up."

"And you have no idea who did it?"

He shook his head.

"Pissed anyone off recently?"

He laughed. "It would probably be easier to list who I haven't pissed off."

We had that in common. "What about security cameras. You threatened to install them at my house, so I assume you have some here?"

"I do, but whoever egged the house knew the cameras were there and chose angles the video didn't cover."

"That's frustrating. And interesting. It means it's probably someone you know."

"Or someone who has been watching the house." He pointed to the cameras on the roof at each corner of the home. "The cameras aren't hidden, and the range isn't far. It wouldn't be hard to figure out the line of sight and stay out of it."

That was true, but it didn't feel totally right. "It's eggs. On your house. Dripping disaster onto your flower beds. That seems kind of personal."

He shrugged. "At least that's all it was. I'll get the pressure washer out and clean it off. It will be fine."

"Hopefully it's an isolated incident."

"Fingers crossed," he said, holding up his entwined fingers. "I—"

The romantic strains of "Play Me" started coming from my bag and Drake stopped talking mid-sentence. "Whose ringtone is that?" he asked with narrowed eyes.

I pulled my phone out and hit the button that sent the call to voicemail. "I don't really think that's any of your business."

He eyed me for a minute, trying to decide if he wanted to

push the issue. He decided to go with a different tactic. "What's *my* ringtone?"

"It's "Brother Love's Traveling Salvation Show"," I answered without apology.

His eyes widened in offense. "The song about the traveling preacher?"

"Yep."

"Why in the world would you choose that song for me?"

"Because every time you call, it reminds me that you're a religious politician and both of those things complicate other things."

A muscle worked at his jaw. "I disagree. And I think you need to choose a better ringtone for me."

"I think this one is perfect. You should be happy about it. You used to not even warrant your own ringtone at all."

He gave me a very dissatisfied look. "And a traveling preacher convincing people to blindly follow him and do dumb things is supposed to be an upgrade?"

I looked at him like he'd lost his mind and seriously needed an attitude adjustment. "It's basically the most fun song in the history of music to sing along to! It's *definitely* an upgrade!"

I got the feeling he didn't agree by the way the vein in his forehead was popping.

"You need to work on being more grateful," I said, pointing at him. "Your life would be so much better for it." I poked him in the chest as I spoke, and as a zing of electricity pulsed through me at the contact, I realized touching him might have been a bad idea. I snapped my finger back and discreetly checked to see if it was smoking before glancing up at Drake. Judging by the look in his eyes, he didn't seem to think touching had been a bad idea at all. I needed to get both of our thoughts off the front door that was only thirty feet away and the house that contained comfortable beds and very sturdy walls. "You said you had some information for me? Why don't you tell me now since I'm here. It will save you a trip into town."

"Are you ready to have a conversation about what's happening between us?" he asked.

I pursed my lips. "No, not really."

"Why?"

I took a deep breath and blew it out. "Because I don't have any answers, Drake," I said, exasperated. "I'm still trying to figure it out." I was annoyed that I had to explain it. Hawke had just understood me and my mental state. Probably because he undoubtedly had a file on me bigger than Cambridge Analytica's, but still. I didn't have to explain myself with Hawke, and that was nice.

Drake considered me for a moment. "What can I do to help you?"

I shook my head and sighed. "See, this is the thing dudes get wrong. You want to fix things and move forward, but that's not what I need. I don't want you to fix this. It's not something you can fix anyway, it's something I need to work through on my own and make some decisions about. Some things take time and can't simply be dealt with and moved on from. What I need is for you to be there for me while I figure it out. If I have questions or need something in the meantime, I'll let you know. But I'm confused and still processing. Until I work through my emotions, I can't tell you anything."

For a few seconds, I thought for sure the lawyer in him was going to try and fight me on my assessment. He even opened his mouth like he was about to launch into a defense, but then he closed it, pulled back, and nodded. "Okay. I'll be here if you need me."

I blinked, wondering if I'd somehow entered an alternate universe. Our entire relationship, or whatever it was, ran on banter. I was surprised that not only had he listened to me and wasn't trying to argue his point and get what he wanted, he was also agreeing to give me space. I was about to say thank you when he continued, "The thing I was going to tell you is that I saw Scott Pope at the grocery store."

"The first robbery victim?"

Drake nodded. "He was telling me about the robbery and mentioned that their four-year-old, Theo, blamed it on his imaginary friend, Speckles."

"Speckles? Interesting name."

Drake nodded. "Theo said he looks like he's covered in paint speckles, so that's what he named his friend."

I raised my eyebrows. "I'm not sure that a four-year-old is the best source of information. The six-year-old kid across the street blamed it on a superhero climbing walls."

"That's the thing," Drake said. "Theo says Speckles has special powers."

I grinned at that. "Did Theo mention what Speckles's powers are?"

The corner of Drake's lips lifted slightly. "Fighting crime and telling stories."

I folded my arms across my chest. "Fantastic. So we've got an imaginary friend that may or may not be real, who fights crime and tells stories. I'm sure that will turn out to be an excellent lead."

Drake lifted his shoulders. "You never know. Maybe you'll

make a connection later and it will all make sense. I thought I should let you know though."

I wasn't under the illusion that Speckles would provide me with the robbery smoking gun, but I was in the business of information and the more I had, the better. Even if it sometimes seemed ridiculous. "Thanks for letting me know, Drake."

He nodded. "Wanna stick around? I could use some help cleaning this off, and I probably won't be wearing a shirt."

That offer was mighty tempting. Luckily, the universe knew I had no self-control and gifted me with my phone buzzing and a text from Spence. It wasn't anything urgent, but I was absolutely going to use it as an excuse to avoid Drake temptation. "I have to get back to the *Tribune*, but I'll talk to you later." I tried not to sound too disappointed at not getting to watch him scrub down his house sans shirt, but I was. "Good luck with your house omelet."

He gave me a look. "Ha ha."

I laughed and waved as I walked away, trying not to think of Drake hosing down his house shirtless. If I'd known he was going to be half-naked, I would have egged it myself, and then come back to watch the clean-up.

I got in my Jeep, put my bag down, and pretended to play on my phone for a few minutes while I inconspicuously watched Drake and his abnormally large arms and inhuman abs obliterate the breakfast on his house. I grabbed a pen and put eggs on my shopping list.

On my way back to work, I saw Betty Turner coming out of Get Crafty, the local craft store. She was with a pretty woman wearing an adorable sweater, scarf, boots, and oversized beanie cap that covered her whole head. Sweaters, fuzzy socks, and fall colors were my favorite parts of autumn in Utah. I was happy to see that Betty was out of the hospital and back to herself. I'd hoped she wouldn't let the robbery scare her into not living her life and it seemed like she hadn't.

A white sedan pulled up next to me at one of the town stoplights. Both the driver and passenger turned to stare at me. One was wearing a moose head, and the other appeared to have whiskers, cat ears, and a little pink nose. I stared back, trying to figure out what in the world required a costume mid-morning on a weekday. The car made a right turn, screeching around the corner.

What was up with all these costumes? Were they appearing because Halloween was coming up, or was there a full-on furry convention happening in Branson Falls that I hadn't been made aware of. Surely, there would have been a news release of some sort. And people in Branson would be far more upset about some of the things that happen at furry conventions than they were about the opening of a tattoo shop and coffee house.

Given the robberies and two separate kids who seemed to think outfit-wearing superheroes and imaginary friends were hanging around their neighborhoods, I felt like I needed to do a little digging into this costume situation. I checked my rearview mirror and then made a right turn in pursuit of the potential furries.

I saw the white sedan about a half a mile in front of me and pushed on the gas to catch up. The sedan must have seen me as well, because they put their foot on the gas. I pressed harder on the gas too, but this was a residential neighborhood with lots of kids. I didn't want anyone to get hurt in my chase, and also didn't want to be reported to The Ladies, or the police, so I went as fast as I thought I could get away with. The white sedan had no such scruples and went as fast as they wanted.

The moose and cat careened around a corner. I followed, but the street branched off into three directions and by the time I got around the corner as well, I couldn't see the white sedan anywhere. I'd lost them, and I was annoyed with myself. I was going to have to ask around and find out if anyone else knew who these people were, and why they were showing up all over town like they were doing a live action version of an animated fairy tale. Maybe it had something to do with the robberies? Or maybe it was that Halloween wasn't far away and people were excited to show off their outfits. I wasn't sure, but I'd find out.

Chapter Eight

I grabbed some lunch and went back to the office. I worked on the layout of the upcoming paper, and edited a few articles between bites. I was almost done editing the community news —reports of all the things happening in the smaller towns around Branson Falls that usually included what people had for dinner and who won the most recent family board game— when I got a phone call from Bobby. "Hey, Kate. We had another robbery. You should get over here."

I knew it was serious when I was getting a personal call from the police and not hearing it over the scanner. "Where are you?"

"The Collins' house over by your mom and dad's. I'll text you the address."

I hopped in my Jeep and sped to the scene of the latest crime.

Bobby was standing outside with a frantic woman who was waving what appeared to be photos in front of his face. Bobby was dodging her in an attempt to avoid a paper cut on his nose. As I got closer, I recognized the woman as Trina Collins, a stay-at-home mom with a slightly eccentric side.

"I can't believe you're still here!" she yelled, her tone frantic. "Go! Look for Selma!"

My eyes widened. Who was Selma? Had the robberies escalated to kidnapping? If so, that would explain why I'd gotten a personal invitation to the crime scene from Officer Bob.

"We're doin' our best," Bobby said. "Let us do our job." He turned to me. "Hey, Kate."

"Who is Selma and what was stolen?" I asked.

"Selma is my baby!" Trina screeched, her eyes wide with worry.

My gaze shot to Bobby. "A baby was taken?" I looked around, wondering why there were only two cop cars on the scene if the robberies had intensified to abduction.

Bobby heaved a long-suffering sigh. "Selma is her favorite house plant. A wood sculpture was also stolen."

"I don't care about the sculpture!" Trina yelled. "I care about Selma!"

I blinked. "A plant?"

Bobby nodded, his eyes closed like he couldn't believe house plant recovery was part of his life.

"I tried to make a missing person's report, but the police said no." Trina's voice was full of fury as she glared daggers at Bobby.

Bobby put his hands up in defense. "We talked about this, Trina. Repeatedly. A plant ain't a person."

"Maybe not to you!"

Bobby expression shifted to sympathetic. "It's listed with all the other stolen items. We have pictures of it, and I'm sure Kate will put the photos in the paper for you too so everyone can be on the lookout."

Ah, that's why he'd called me. He was trying to calm Trina down and thought offering to have house plant Selma spotlighted in the paper like a kid on a milk carton would be a good way to do that. I was annoyed at being used for half a second, then remembered that Bobby helped me all the time and I should return the favor. I probably would have put the photo in the *Tribune* anyway.

"We'll find your plant," Bobby said.

"You better!" Trina said. Anger warred with sadness and made her voice break. "She needs to be home before she misses her next dose of fertilizer! And what if the person who stole her doesn't know the proper watering procedure?"

I'd had a lot of house plants in my life. Some of them I'd even managed to keep alive, but none of them had offered me a relationship like Trina seemed to have with Selma. "I'm sure someone will find it," I said. "I'll even post a photo on the *Tribune* Facebook page today."

"Thank you," Trina said, blinking back tears as her neighbor came over to console her.

Once she was out of earshot, I turned to Bobby and asked, "Was the wood sculpture valuable?"

Bobby motioned me over to his patrol car. "Yeah. It was done by a famous Branson wood carver, Ron Storm. The piece was of the Teton Mountains. Most people from out of state wouldn't know what it was, or that it was by Storm, but a lot of people who live in Branson would have recognized it and seen the potential value."

I raised a brow. "This is the first robbery where something of value has actually been taken."

"That we know of," Bobby amended.

I gave him a look. "I don't think anyone is fighting over the Pope family's TV remote."

Bobby shrugged. "You never know."

"Are you planning to search for the sculpture locally?"

He nodded. "Yeah, but stolen items like this are always hard to find. A lot of times thieves will take the item out of the area and sit on the item for months before selling it so they're less likely to get caught."

"Where do you look for something like that?"

"Pawn shops mostly. And we list the items in a database that all Utah law enforcement has access to. But a lot of stolen items are never recovered."

Before I'd moved back to Branson Falls, I'd done a story on art thieves. Ron Storm's sculptures were part of the art world. Big ticket and famous items were hard to sell, unless you were selling them underground and on the black market—which was rather lucrative. A Ron Storm sculpture wasn't a DaVinci, but they were all western cowboy and landscape themed pieces, and they were definitely popular with a segment of Utahns, western art fans, and collectors. But trying to track down one piece when there were other similar pieces done by Storm, was going to be a challenge. Maybe I'd ask Hawke if he had any resources that could help. Because Hawke always had resources—legal or not, and there hadn't been a time he'd been unable to offer me assistance yet. I'd get ahold of him and find out.

"Thanks for letting me know about the robbery, Bobby. And for throwing me under the bus with the Selma situation."

Bobby's lips spread into a wide grin. "I figured you would've posted the story with a picture of the plant anyway. Now you can add some info on contactin' the police if someone sees Selma."

"Glad I could help," I said dryly.

He laughed.

I finished scribbling some notes, borrowed a photo of Selma from Trina, and waved at Bobby.

A text buzzed as I was getting in my Jeep.

It was from Drake.

> I've decided I'm fine with your ringtone since the song opens with the words "Hot August Night," and that's pretty indicative of a recent night we had.

I could feel my cheeks heating as I read the words. It had been close to August. It had definitely been hot. And I'd stopped things before they hit scorching. And now I was going to think of that night every time Drake called. I scrunched up my nose at that. I probably needed to find him a new ringtone.

Since I was in the area, I decided to stop and give Gandalf some cuddles. His happy face, unconditional love, and kisses, always made my day better.

I knocked as I opened the front door and went inside. The house smelled like cinnamon and happiness and I wondered

DESTINY FORD

what delightful thing my mom was concocting. I found her in the kitchen, her shoulder towel in place, hair a frizzy mess, and she was frantically breaking up what looked like pumpkin dog treats. As I got closer, I realized some of them didn't look like dog treats at all. Some of them looked a lot like penises. I had zero interest in my mom and dad's sex life, but I was suddenly very curious about these cookies. "Soooo," I said, pointing to the countertop, a multitude of questions clear in my eyes.

She glanced up at me, a wild look in her eyes. "I tried a new recipe for these dog treats and the dough didn't hold together as they cooked. One end of the bones broke off! On every cookie! Instead of thirty little bones, I got thirty very *naughty* little treats!" She said it all so fast and frantic that it came out like one long, high-pitched, run-on sentence.

I couldn't hold back my laughter and burst into a fit of giggles. It took me several minutes to compose myself enough to speak. "That might possibly be the best story I've heard in weeks. This could be your greatest Catasophie ever!" My mom had a tendency for getting into crazy situations and causing disasters. The frequency of her incidents had led people around town to merge the words "catastrophe" and "Sophie Saxee" and call them Catasophies. She was not a fan, but I thought it was an apt description.

She pointed a cookie at me without realizing she was using an excited bone end to make her point. "My adventures don't need to be ranked."

"You're right. It would be an exercise in futility anyway since it's a constantly evolving list."

If her eyes had been lasers, I'd be mostly dead.

"What did Gandalf think of the cookies?" I asked, picking

one up and smelling it. It smelled like a dog would like it fine, penis or no penis.

"Well I certainly didn't give him any! They look like porno cookies, Kate! *Porno!*"

That explained why Gandalf was sitting patiently next to the island, kinking his neck to look up in hopes that one of the broken wieners would drop. "I suspect Gandalf doesn't care in the least about the shape of his treats. He just wants to eat one."

She looked at me like I'd lost my mind. "What kind of grandma would I be if I gave penis cookies to my grandpuppy?!"

"An epic one," I offered.

She glared at me. "No! Horrible, Kate! I would be horrible! I have to fix this and make them random shapes. He can have some once they're not X-rated anymore."

I laughed at her insistence and discreetly pulled out my phone to snap a photo for my scrapbook. This was an event I never wanted to forget. "I mean, it should make you feel pretty good to know you've already done some accidental testing and could easily open an erotic bakery."

She threw a set of bone balls at me and I deliberately let them fall to the ground. Gandalf was pleased and scarfed the treat right up without taking even a millisecond to consider the shape of what he'd eaten.

"Gandalf loves them!"

My mom huffed an exasperated sigh. "What are you doing here anyway?" She asked. She was obviously trying to change the subject so we weren't talking about her pumpkin penises anymore.

"There was another robbery around the corner." I tilted my head in that direction. "The Collins family."

"What?" My mom's eyes were huge, like she hadn't anticipated that a robbery might actually happen in her own neighborhood. Given the frequency of the thefts—and my mom's luck—I was wondering if she'd be next. "When did this happen? And why didn't I know about it?"

"I'm not sure. I'm surprised you didn't hear the sirens."

She glanced down at the cookies and frowned.

"Then again, you were pretty distracted with your wiener treats."

She threw her shoulder towel at me. "Stop saying that!"

I giggled and gave Gandalf another piece.

"Tell me more about what happened at the Collins'?"

I told her about the wood sculpture and the plant. "Oh my," she said with serious concern. "Trina will not handle it well if she doesn't get that plant back."

"She seemed to be having a bit of a fit," I agreed.

My mom shook her head in disbelief. "I can't believe someone is invading homes this way and taking personal items with so much meaning. What if we're next?" she asked, her voice going up an octave.

"It would require a pretty brave thief to take you and your reputation on. They'll probably avoid your house because proximity to you alone could be a trap."

She stuck her tongue out at me. "I think we're all at risk, and something needs to be done."

"The police are doing their best, and I'm trying to find some connection but haven't yet. Lots of people are working on it, though. Speaking of which, I need to get to the office." I bent down and gave Gandalf a few pets and a little kiss on the top of his head. He tolerated it—mostly because I think he was under the impression I had more erection cookies for him. I grabbed some balls off the counter and handed them over, thinking I'd get a reprimand from my mom, but I didn't. Instead, I found her blankly staring at the wall like she was concentrating really hard.

I snapped my fingers. "Mom, are you okay?"

She glanced over at me and waved her hand in front of her like the spontaneous meditation hadn't been odd. "I'm fine, but until this town is safe and sound again, I'm going to be on watch."

"That sounds ominous."

She didn't reply and went back to breaking up her bones. I waved and yelled "I love you" on my way out the door.

As I drove by Inked AF, I saw Sasha and Axel outside. Axel was waving his arms in the air, his face screwed up in anger and Sasha looked like she was on the verge of tears. They were clearly arguing and I felt for them both. Relationships were hard enough as it was, but add in a business partnership to that and both could quickly fall apart if they weren't managed separately. Good relationships embraced conflict and pushed through it instead of pretending it didn't exist, or would magically go away. The key was good communication and a willingness to listen to one another, understand, accept responsibility, and compromise. I hoped they would be able to work out whatever it was they were going through.

I got back to the *Tribune* and dropped my bags in my desk drawer before sinking into my chair.

"Hey," Spence said from his office. "I wondered where you went off to."

I woke my computer up so I could write down the notes about the Collins robbery, and post Selma's photo on the *Tribune* Facebook page. "Someone egged Drake's house."

Spence's brows rose. "Any idea who it was?"

"He says it could be anyone. My money is on Ned and his buddies who were upset about his vote to legalize sex outside of marriage."

Spence rolled his eyes. "It was such a ridiculous law."

I nodded in agreement. "We could have both been thrown in jail for that one."

"I think I would have been in more trouble than you," he mused.

"Probably. Anyone in particular you'd be in trouble with?" I asked nonchalantly.

Spence had been sneaking off randomly and giving overt hints that he might be seeing someone for a while. I wondered how serious it was. I didn't want to push him, and knew he'd introduce me when he was ready, but I was super curious.

Spence's eyes sparkled at the question. "There might be."

I arched a brow. "Any chance I'll get to meet the special someone soon?"

Spence chewed on his bottom lip. "I would say there's a good possibility."

I grinned and went back to the summary of my day so far. "After Drake's egg situation, I got a call from Bobby. There was another robbery."

"Where?"

"The Collins family, in the same neighborhood as my parents."

"What did they take?"

"A Ron Storm sculpture, and a house plant."

"A plant?"

"Mrs. Collins was far more upset about the plant than the art. Though Bobby tells me the art is worth significantly more."

Spence whistled like I'd made a massive understatement. "An original Ron Storm sculpture is definitely worth some cash. It seems like the thieves are taking really random things."

"I know," I said, nodding. "And at first it seemed like they were taking things that were worthless. It makes me wonder if the victims don't realize everything that has actually been stolen from their houses."

"It's a possibility," Spence said. "I don't think I'd be able to pinpoint exactly what was taken in my house after a robbery. Is there anything tying the robberies together yet?"

I shook my head. "Not that I can see, but I have a theory." It's one I'd been considering since I left the Collins' house. "All of the people who have been targeted so far are transplants to Branson Falls. They didn't grow up here." Spence looked at me thoughtfully and I continued, "The Pope family moved to town recently, Betty Turner moved to Branson years ago from California, and the Collins family has only been here for about ten years."

Spence tilted his head, considering. "So you think it's someone who doesn't like new people moving to town?"

I shrugged my shoulders. "Maybe. Ella mentioned The Ladies not wanting new people in the area. Maybe they're not the only ones. I know there have been a lot of people upset about the tattoo shop and coffee shop opening. They're blaming outsiders for everything that's happening. Maybe the robbers are trying to make sure nothing else new and unfamiliar is brought into Branson Falls. They could also be trying to get rid of the stuff that's already here. I think Sasha and Axel are having a hard time and they've only been officially open for less than a week. The coffee shop seems to be doing okay, but I'm sure that's because they sell non-coffee sugary drinks too. But I'm going to talk to Sasha and Axel tomorrow and see how things are going and if they have any more insight."

The back door chimed and Ella sauntered in. "Howdy," she said, grabbing a donut from the treat counter. I didn't even know the donuts were there. Clearly, my treat radar needed an adjustment. I got up and grabbed a glazed and thickly frosted chocolate donut with peanut topping for myself. It tasted like heaven.

"Did anything else happen while you were out and about?" Spence asked.

"I saw a car with two people in full costume get-ups on my way back here. A moose and a cat. I followed them but they turned into a neighborhood and I lost them there."

Spence stared at me, his own donut halfway to his lips.

And I wasn't done. "There was someone dressed up as a squirrel sitting in their car and watching me and Hawke at the park the other night too. It was weird. Have we had any other reports about costumed creepers lately?"

"Not that I know of," Spence said slowly.

"It's the superheroes!" Ella exclaimed.

Spence and I both looked at her like she'd suddenly sprouted turnips from her ears. "What superheroes?"

"You know!" she said, her voice going up several exciting octaves. "Those people who like cosplay so much that they decide to wear it all year. They go around towns dressed up in their outfits and they watch for criminals. They're basically a neighborhood watch, only they have secret identities."

I wondered if she'd hit her head or something at home and was suddenly delusional. I subtly checked her pupils to make sure they were the same size. They were. "I've never heard of these people."

"What?" she exclaimed like she was affronted. "They're everywhere! Look 'em up!"

So I did. And my mouth fell open in shock as my search results brought back about a thousand stories of these real-life vigilantes who were often mistaken as suspicious people, and rightly so if my experience with them so far was any indication. "I had no idea this was a thing."

"There are lots of organizations people can sign up to be superheroes with," Ella said.

"So someone started a chapter here?" Spence asked.

"Yep!"

I glanced up from scrolling through an article about one of the organizations in Salt Lake City. "Do you know who the organizers are?"

Ella gave me a look. "That there is privileged information. I can't reveal my sources."

I gave her a look back. "Well do you think you could get me a meeting with them? I'd like to talk to them and see if they have any more information about these robberies." I also wanted to question them about the robberies since I had two kid witnesses who had pinpointed some sort of costumed hero in relation to the Pope robbery.

"I can't make no promises, but I'll see what I can do."

"Thanks, Ella," I said. I finished my donut and spent the rest of the day editing until it was time to pick up Gandalf.

Chapter Nine

I stopped by Beans and Things, the coffee shop, on my way to work the next morning. Gandalf was with me, so I grabbed him a little puppuccino, which was essentially a shot of whipped cream and would make him extra hyper for my mom. She'd think he was just really excited for more of her erotic dog bones. The thought of her accidental naughty treats made me giggle all over again.

If the line at Beans and Things was any indication, they definitely weren't having problems getting customers. The non-coffee drinks they offered that weren't against church rules helped that. Sasha and Axel would have a hard time making a living giving people non-permanent tattoos.

I finally found a spot at a table outside. I sat with Gandalf on my lap, enjoying the crisp autumn air. I gave him some treats to go with his drink and he thanked me with a wet kiss across my cheek. I laughed and snuggled him closer.

"I can't believe I'm about to say this, but I'm a little jealous of your dog."

Hawke slid into the chair beside me and gave Gandalf his

hand to smell. Gandalf had met Hawke previously, and knew who he was, though even if he hadn't, Hawke could have easily charmed my dog into submission in seconds. "Your hands are all over him and his tongue was all over you," Hawke said.

I'd never heard of someone able to turn a dog snuggle and lick into something sexual, but Hawke was a master of most things. And I thought it was probably best not to respond to that particular statement because that banter would likely end with me seeing Hawke's real life naughty bone, and I had too much on my agenda for today to fit in a quickie. Plus, since Hawke and I hadn't had sex at all yet, I knew that when it happened, nothing about that experience would be quick.

"What are you doing here?" I asked, shocked to see him, and the large cup of coffee in front of him. Hawke did not seem like the flavored coffee type. In fact, I'd pinned him as the type of guy who took his coffee black, with a side of gunpowder.

He held up his coffee in response. "It's morning. I needed coffee."

"You don't have coffee at your house?"

"I do, but you're not at my house."

Okay then. It was time to change the subject. "Have you heard back from your people about the robberies?"

Gandalf was pawing at Hawke's leg, trying to get his attention. Hawke reached out to pick him up and held him while he scratched under Gandalf's chin. I swear I heard Gandalf sigh and I completely empathized. I'd be sighing if Hawke was petting me too.

Hawke shook his head. "I'm still working on it, but there's

not much tying things together, and I've been dealing with some other situations."

I raised a brow. "What kind of other situations?" I asked. I always asked. He rarely answered, but I was ever hopeful he'd eventually open up.

"Some things."

"Involving?" I led, hoping he'd answer.

"I'm not sure yet, but I believe some politicians are in the mix."

I raised my other brow at that. "Interesting. Is Drake helping you?"

He gave me a look like I was on something seriously impairing my cognitive abilities. "I don't need Drake's help."

"Do you need mine?" I asked, always willing to extend a hand, especially when it might tell me a little more about Hawke and his business.

He eyed me speculatively. "Maybe. We'll see." He took a drink of his coffee and then asked, "What about you? Any other leads on the robberies?"

I told him about the Collins robbery and my theory. "I think they're targeting people who moved into Branson Falls and didn't grow up here. So you should watch out."

Hawke's lips spread into a terrifying grin and his eyes flashed with challenge. "I dare them."

Something fluttered in my stomach at his expression and subsequent threat. "I'd kind of like to be there if they did try it."

His lips slid into that slow, sexy grin that made me think he probably got as excited about murder as he did about sex. And that worried me.

I checked the time and realized I needed to go or I'd be

late. "I've got to get Gandalf to my mom and dad's house. Let me know if you find out anything else and I'll keep you in the loop."

Hawke nodded and tipped his coffee in my direction. "Nice ass," he said as I walked away.

Heat flushed my cheeks as I rolled my eyes, a smile spreading across my lips. I buckled Gandalf into his car seat, and drove to my mom and dad's.

My mom opened the door looking more wide-eyed than usual. I was suspicious immediately. "Heyyyy," I said, eyeing her and trying to figure out what was going on. "Did you have an extra shot of espresso this morning?"

She gave me a strange look. "No. I mean, I had a couple of cups, but what does that have to do with anything?"

I examined her again. "You seem...over-stimulated. And you're acting kind of weird. Are you sure there's nothing going on?"

She rolled her eyes and waved me off. "Don't be silly," she said, taking Gandalf from me. He was squirming like crazy, probably because the amount of whipped cream he'd consumed was the equivalent of giving a toddler an entire vat of cotton candy. "He's a little hyper today," I explained. "You might want to let him run around in the backyard for a while."

"Why is he hyper?"

There was no need to admit to the shot of sugar, or the lecture I'd get in response. I shrugged. "He's a puppy. Puppies have a lot of energy."

Now she was the one eying me with a suspicious expression. I kissed Gandalf on the top of the head. "Enjoy the penis bones grandma made you, little buddy!"

My mom gave me a solid glare and swatted me on my butt on the way out the door. I laughed all the way to Inked AF.

I walked into the tattoo shop. It seemed pretty slow and no customers were in sight. That wasn't a good sign.

Sasha came out of a back room looking haggard. Whether from worry, lack of sleep, or relationship issues, I had no idea. But something was up. Her smile brightened a little when she saw me. "Hey, Kate," she said, coming over to give me a hug.

"Hey!" I answered, trying to be as upbeat as possible.

"What are you doing here today?" She motioned to the couch in the front of the store. A coffee table covered in books of artwork done by her and Axel sat next to the couch.

"I wanted to stop by and see how things are going. I know that city council meeting was rough, and totally uncalled for. They're blaming you because you're new in town and an easy target. Don't let them discourage you. You haven't been here long and things will get better."

Her eyes started to shine and she looked down. "It's been harder than we were expecting," she said, "and we haven't even been open that long."

I reached out and touched her hand. "I'm sorry." I felt bad for her. I knew what it was like to come to a new place and try to convince people that despite your differences, you were still worthy of their kindness and respect.

"Some people have been really supportive. Others, not so much."

I nodded, understanding. "Do you think anyone might be targeting you with these rumors about the tattoo shop and the robberies?" I asked. It was a theory I'd been considering. People loved to gossip in small towns and there were enough people who didn't want the tattoo shop in Branson that I wouldn't put it past someone.

Sasha's eyebrows went up. "You mean someone robbing people on purpose and trying to blame it on us or our clients?"

I lifted a shoulder. "That, or maybe someone who doesn't want you here so they're telling people it's your fault. I know there were several people at the city council meeting who were speaking along those lines. Can you think of anyone who has been particularly vocal?"

Sasha gave a humorless laugh. "I could list the people who have been supportive more easily than the ones who haven't. It seems like most of the town wants us gone."

Based on the city council meeting, I didn't blame her for feeling that way. "What about the anonymous notes you said you got before the opening. Do you still have them?"

She shook her head. "I wish we'd kept them, but we threw them out. We knew they were from people upset that we were different, and didn't see a need to keep the notes, or that kind of energy, around." She paused, pressing her lips together as she thought. "Now I wish we had kept them."

"Do you remember what the notes said?"

She took a deep breath. "They were standard anonymous notes. One said to get out of town. Another said we'd regret being here. One was left on our door. Another came in the mail."

Both of those sounded like threats to me, and I wished she

still had them so I could compare the wording and see if the notes sounded like the same person. And if they'd kept the envelope, I could check the postmark to see if it came from Branson Falls. "If you get another note, will you let me know?" I asked.

"Sure," she said, the corners of her mouth turning up slightly though the smile didn't reach her eyes.

A noise came from the back and Sasha and I both looked up to see Axel, messy hair, disheveled clothes, and looking like he was in desperate need of a nap, walk out of the back room.

"Hi, Axel," I said.

"Hey, Kate." He gave me a tight smile, like he had other things on his mind and pleasantries were an afterthought.

"I have to go run an errand," Axel said, his eyes going to Sasha. "I'll see you both later." He touched Sasha's shoulder as he walked by, his skin pulled back in a worried expression as he opened the door. Everything from his reactions to his body language seemed way off.

"Are you okay?" I asked Sasha once Axel was out the door. "You seem a little frazzled."

She twisted her hands together, her knuckles going white with the effort. "I'm stressed. And Axel is too, but he seems more stressed than usual. And he's been acting this way for months. I don't know what's going on, but I'm worried."

"What do you think he's stressed about?"

Sasha gave a short, exasperated laugh. "Everything. Money mostly. Money affects everything else. We put all of our savings into the tattoo shop, and we haven't had as much business as we thought we would. It's early, but still. He's worried the shop won't take off and we'll lose everything."

I understood money problems. Being a small town newspaper editor certainly didn't make me a millionaire. "Money can affect everything. Have you talked to him about it?"

"I've tried, but he doesn't really want to talk."

"That makes things hard," I said. "Maybe you should talk to someone…a counselor or financial planner? Maybe both?"

She picked at a piece of fabric in her torn jeans as she thought about it. "Yeah. Maybe."

"There's a good counselor I went to high school with over in the Branson Peaks office park. Her name is Debbie Jacobs." I pulled out my phone and found her contact information. "I sent you her info if you decide you want some outside help."

Sasha nodded. "Thank you. I really appreciate it."

"Of course." The conversation lulled for a minute as I looked at the beautiful and intricate art pieces on the wall.

"You need to come in and get a tattoo," Sasha suggested.

I stopped short, surprised by the offer. A tattoo was something I'd always been interested in, but I was worried about what it would look like when I was eighty. Since eighty wasn't guaranteed for anyone though, I kind of thought it might not be a bad idea. I'd just have to get something I wouldn't regret. "I might have to do that sometime," I said.

Sasha smiled, and I gave her a hug before I walked out the door. On my way to the *Tribune* office, I couldn't help but think about Axel's strange behavior at the city council meeting, the argument I saw him and Sasha having when I drove by the other day, his quick departure when I arrived today, and Sasha's revelation that they were having financial problems and had been for a while. Maybe there was a chance Axel was trying to supplement their income with the robberies. It didn't make much sense since a lot of the items being stolen had been insignificant, but things didn't add up. As much as I didn't want the robber to be Axel, I wasn't going to rule him out either.

I got to the office and immediately bumped into Ella.

"Hey," Ella said. "I got you a meetin' with the superheroes."

I blinked, in awe of her connections. I still had no idea who the superheroes were. "How did you manage that?"

She stared at me. "I know people."

Clearly.

"Be at the library park by the tennis courts at six tonight."

I gave her an impressed look. "I'll be there. Will they be in costume?"

She shrugged. "Probably. But they'll find you. Be by the tennis courts."

I nodded, wondering what exactly I'd gotten myself into and if I should bring some back-up to the meeting.

Spence came out of his office and grabbed some Halloween candy out of the dish at the front desk where our part-time office assistant worked. "I got word that another casserole was dropped off last night," he said, unwrapping a mini candy bar and popping it into his mouth.

I raised a brow. Another casserole? That was odd. "At Betty Turner's again?" I asked.

"No, I imagine whoever dropped it off the first time probably wasn't pleased with her cheese and butter critique and took her off their anonymous food delivery service list."

"I could see that," I agreed. It was still odd that Betty had been robbed right after the casserole delivery, but I hadn't been able to find a connection there yet either.

"This was at Delia Dole's house."

"Interesting," I said. "Another widow."

Spence nodded. "I thought the same thing."

"I'll go check it out." I grabbed my bag and went to find out more about casserole caper number two.

Chapter Ten

Delia lived across the street from the first robbery victims, the Popes. Brandy Pope was outside loading something in her car when I got out of my Jeep. She waved, and yelled my name, "Kate!"

She started toward me, so I met her halfway. "Hey, Brandy. How are you doing?"

Brandy lifted a shoulder. "Okay. Still a little freaked out, but Scott installed every camera and security system known to man on our house so that gives us a little more peace of mind."

I understood that. I'd had someone break into my house before and the sense of unease and vulnerability that followed wasn't something I'd been prepared for. I'd thrown a fit when Drake threatened to install cameras and a security system at my house, and Hawke had started tracking my car, but security measures really did make me less paranoid. "The security system will help for sure."

"I know you were asking about what items went missing in our robbery."

I nodded. "Bobby said a remote control, VHS tapes, and a book." I still had no explanation for the items, or how they related to the robberies at Betty Turner's or the Collins' house.

She nodded in confirmation. "I was cleaning out my office the other day, and noticed I was also missing a couple of stuffed animals."

I raised a brow. "Stuffed animals for kids?"

She laughed. "I know it seems silly, but I collected them growing up. I thought they were going to fund my retirement. I wasn't the only one with that plan, and the collectors market for them was flooded so I never made anything off of the toys. But I've kept them for sentimental reasons."

I remembered the toys she was talking about. They'd been all the rage when we were kids, and everyone had bought them up like the toys would be the next gold rush.

"Maybe the robber thought they'd be worth something too?"

"It's possible," Brandy said. She pulled a photo out of her wallet. "I took some pictures of the room for insurance purposes last year, and these were the animals that were taken."

The photo looked like it contained the image of every stuffed animal this particular company had ever made. Brandy had circled an octopus and a flamingo.

"They only took two?" I asked.

She lifted a shoulder. "From what I can tell. I didn't take inventory of the toys often, and there were a lot of them."

"Can I keep this photo?" I asked. I wanted it for reference in case any of the stolen items started turning up.

"Sure," she said. "It's a copy."

"Thanks, for letting me know. I hope it will help us figure out who's committing these crimes."

"Me too," Brandy said. "Have a good day, Kate."

"You too." I turned around and went back to Delia Dole's house.

Delia had seen me pull up and was waiting for me at the door. "They left me mashed potatoes!" Delia said with a wide smile as she opened the storm door and ushered me inside her house.

"Plain mashed potatoes?" I asked. Betty Turner's dish had been a full-on casserole.

"Well," she said, motioning for me to follow her into the kitchen, "I think they tried to make it into a shepherd's pie of some sort since there were some veggies and meat on the bottom, but it was mostly potato."

I'd always thought shepherd's pie looked like someone mixed all their food groups together and then frosted the whole thing with potatoes. I'd never seen the appeal, but some people were fans. "Shepherd's pie isn't a common casserole in Utah." The most popular casserole was the one Betty Turner had received: a version of funeral potatoes. It usually consisted of potatoes with copious amounts of cheese and butter, topped with a variety of odd items from bread crumbs to potato chips, or my dad's favorite: Cheetos.

"It's not," Delia exclaimed! "That's why I was so excited to try it."

All of these women getting casseroles dropped off and eating them willy nilly was making me nervous for Branson's widow community. They were risk takers for sure.

"Did you like the casserole?" I asked.

"I did. And there's plenty left over if you want some!"

I smiled. "No thanks," I said, trying to be polite and not insinuate that a person anonymously gifting food shouldn't be trusted. "I'm meeting a friend for lunch and don't want to spoil my dinner."

She gave me a thousand watt smile. "Isn't that special! Well thanks for stopping by. I admit, when I heard about Betty's casserole, I was a little jealous. Now I'm so excited to have one of my own!"

I smiled at her. "Let's get a pic of you and the casserole for the *Tribune*."

I snapped some photos, finished writing down some notes and quotes, and checked my watch. If I hurried, I'd be right on time for my lunch with Annie. I said good-bye and then left to meet my friend.

I walked into the Mexican restaurant and Annie was already sitting in a booth. Unlike a previous visit I'd had there, this was not the corner booth, and it didn't contain both Drake and Hawke, so I felt pretty safe that this particular lunch wouldn't end up on The Ladies "stalk Kate" social media pages, but I could never be sure.

Annie waved, her jet black hair tinted with a dark blue looked stunning as I slid into the booth across from her. "Hey! Your hair looks great" I said, genuinely happy to see her. It wasn't easy to find accepting friends with an open mind in a place like Branson. I was grateful I had her in my life.

"Thanks," she said. "I decided to try something new."

Mormons were discouraged from dyeing their hair "unnatural colors." Annie was Mormon, but she wasn't afraid to push the limits and I loved that about her. "Did you get pushback for the color at church?"

"Not yet," she said with a wicked little grin. "But I just colored it so we'll see what happens on Sunday."

I laughed.

"How's your day?" she asked, taking a sip of her water.

"A little hectic, but that's pretty normal," I answered.

"I haven't heard any crazy stories on the scanner lately so your mom must not be the one keeping you busy."

I gave her a look. "My mom's always keeping me busy, but not today," I paused, and added, "yet." Then I told her about the pumpkin penis bones and we both laughed until we were in tears.

Our server came over and took our order. As she walked away, Annie's expression turned curious.

"What's that look for?" I asked.

She grinned like she had a secret. "I've heard some things..."

I raised a brow. "That sounds ominous." Frankly, I wasn't surprised. I was the subject of most of the posts on The Ladies secret Facebook page, a fact I knew only because Ella had let it slip, and then Hawke had confirmed it. I still wasn't sure how Hawke had gotten access. I'd tried to sneak into the group so I could keep track of the fake life of lies The Ladies were building for me, but I'd been denied under every name I tried. Hawke was a wizard though—and probably a merce-nary, I wasn't sure—so he had access to all kinds of magic that I didn't.

"The rumor going around is that Drake spent the night at your house last month."

I almost choked on the red cream soda our server had dropped off. "What?" I asked through my coughs.

"Someone saw his truck parked at your house late at night and people started talking."

Oh good grief. I rolled my eyes. Drake and his dumb giant yellow Hummer that looked like a school bus on steroids. It wasn't very stealthy, and I'd told him so. Repeatedly. "I can think of two times that might have happened. The first was during the cookie debacle. After I left your house that night, I got home and ate more cookies, and then I apparently called Drake and invited him over. I have no recollection of the cookie eating, or invitation. It seems when I eat a lot of pot-laced cookies, I get horny and have temporary memory loss."

Our server brought our food and it smelled heavenly. I was glad they were fast so I didn't have time to fill up on tortilla chips and their delicious salsa.

"Blackouts are fun," Annie said, her eyes twinkling with mischief as she cut into her food. "Did Drake come over when you called him?"

I swallowed a bite of cheesy goodness before answering, "He did. He thought I sounded strange on the phone. And he told me he only stayed long enough to make sure I was fast asleep. He even tucked me in."

She raised her eyebrows at that. "Is that *all* he did?"

I nodded. "The sexy lingerie and robe I'd apparently put on for him were still firmly in place when I woke up. He's not the womanizer everyone thinks he is. He just has women throwing themselves at him all the time. It seems I was one of them that night, but he would never take advantage of a female who wasn't an active, and more than willing, participant. He left after I'd fallen asleep, and he locked the front door on the way out."

"And the second time his truck was recently at your house?" she asked.

"He came over to check on me after the shoot-out last month because he was in Salt Lake when the incident occurred. He brought me chocolate covered espresso beans from my favorite coffee shop and told me we should date. Again. This time, he almost convinced me."

"Almost?"

I nodded, and played with the straw in my glass.

"Have you been one of his active and willing participants?" she asked, point blank.

"No," I said. I didn't add the "not yet" part of the sentence that continued in my head.

She eyed me for several seconds. "Do you want to be?"

I pressed my lips together. "That's a complicated question."

She took a bite of her food before pressing on, "Is Hawke as complicated?"

I sighed at that. "He might be even more complicated."

Annie pushed her brows together like she was confused. I didn't blame her. If I were standing on the outside looking in at a woman with two of the most eligible bachelors in the state interested in her, I'd also be befuddled at the woman's lack of decision making skills. "What are the issues with them both?" she asked.

I took a couple of bites of food and used the time to collect my thoughts before responding. "Hawke's job is dangerous. I'm still not even exactly sure what it is, but I think he might be a mercenary and I'm not sure how I feel about that, or the fact that his work constantly puts him in danger." A feral part of me that I didn't even know existed until recently got a little turned on by the fact that Hawke could kill people with his bare hands, and likely had—more than once. "Plus, he's gone a lot for his job, and his schedule is chaotic. I never know when he's going to be in town and when he won't be. Add to that the fact that he can't really talk about what he does and all of those things would make a relationship with him problematic. Not being able to share things with your partner makes it difficult to build and maintain a bond."

Annie considered all of that for a few minutes. "And what about Drake?"

I sighed. "Drake is every girl's high school fantasy. He was definitely one of mine. It was easy to keep him at arms-length when I thought he was an egotistical, womanizing, patriarchal asshat. Now I know he's not. But he's also a Mormon—which complicates things because we don't even come close to sharing the same beliefs and we both have vastly different ideas of what is right and wrong. Plus, he's a politician in a state that expects him to act a certain way, and be with a certain type of girl. I would not excel at being arm candy. Arm candy isn't supposed to have opinions or ask questions—I'm paid to ask questions for my job! I also have a metric ton of opinions that would not play well in the Utah political arena. And I'd cause quite a fuss when I showed up next to him in my "Feminist is my second favorite F-Word" shirt."

"People here would think 'F-Word' stood for 'family' or 'faith.'"

I laughed. "That's probably true."

"Have you talked to Drake about all this?"

I moved my head from side-to-side in a wishy washy gesture. "A little. He says he doesn't give a damn what my religion is, or what people think. But his work as a politician is literally to care what people think. He still practices law and could go back to doing it full time—and he told me he would —but I think he has aspirations to move higher in the political spectrum and I worry he'd resent me in the future for affecting that. So despite what he says, I still feel like our religious differences and our jobs would make a relationship problematic. And," I paused, realizing a hesitation I didn't even know I'd had until right then. "What if he doesn't live up to my fantasies?"

Annie's eyes sparkled as her lips tipped up. "Or…what if he's better than them?"

Her words hit me like a ton of bricks. I'd never considered that a relationship with Drake might work, and not only work, but be even better than I'd ever imagined—because I had a pretty damn good imagination. I'd given weight to every con, but hadn't let myself consider the possible pros. I felt like I'd blown a romance fuse and couldn't even really process it. "I don't think I'm ready to consider that question, or the answers." If he was better than the fantasy I'd constructed around him, I had no hope. And so far, he'd been better than anything I'd ever dreamed. If he was even better with his clothes off, I was in real trouble.

She laughed. "So you care for them both?"

"Yes." I admitted it like I'd just eaten something raw and slimy. "It seems I've caught feelings. I wish there was a vaccine for that."

"It would solve a lot of problems," Annie agreed, taking one last bite.

Our server brought our checks and boxes for our leftovers.

"I have to get back to work," I said, trying not to splash

enchilada sauce all over the place as I transferred my food from my plate to the box. "But I'm so glad we did this! We need to do it more often. And next time, I want to hear all about what's going on with you and Rich." It drove me nuts when people only talked about themselves. Conversational narcissists were real, and I made a point not to be around them—or be one of them.

"I was far more interested in what was going on with you this time around, but we definitely need to get together more," she said. "And if anything happens with your love life, you better text or call me immediately."

I laughed. "The Ladies will probably report it before I do."

"True, but they're liars and can't be trusted."

I wasn't going to argue with that.

Chapter Eleven

It was six-thirty. I'd arrived at the library park fifteen minutes early to ensure I didn't miss out on the superheroes. I was waiting patiently on a bench by the tennis courts and scrolling through my emails to get some work out of the way.

I heard a chirping noise and looked up to see what I can only describe as a cosplay gang making their way across the park. The squirrel was there. So was a raccoon, a fairy, and someone dressed in spandex and a cape wearing a unicorn mask that covered his eyes and forehead, complete with a horn. I imagined the cape would be cumbersome in hand fighting.

"Hi," I said, standing up to greet them. I wondered if they'd communicate with words, or as the characters they represented. If it was as characters, we were going to have a real problem because I didn't speak fairy or raccoon.

"Hi, reporter lady!"

We were four words in and I had already identified the unicorn. My good friend, Keanu, who got his name because he reminded me of Ted from *Bill and Ted's Excellent Adventures*, had been helpful on a couple of my investigations since I'd moved back to Branson Falls. I knew it was Keanu under the unicorn mask because of his distinctive voice and speech, and the fact that he never actually called me by my name, he always used the nickname, 'reporter lady'. I wasn't certain he even knew my real name. To be fair, I didn't know his either and he would always be Keanu to me.

"Hi," I said to unicorn Keanu, trying not to give away the fact that I knew who he was. "Doesn't your cape get in the way when you're trying to fight crime?"

He looked at me like I might not be the smartest person he'd ever encountered, and given that he was either drunk, high, or both most of the time, I kind of took offense to that. "I don't use my hands to fight! I use my powers."

Ah ha. "And what are your powers?"

"Intimidation."

Alrighty then. I wasn't going to tell him I thought his powers might work selectively because with his shiny green cape and glittery blue horn mask, I was more likely to ask him to accompany me to a dance club than a crime scene.

"This is Nut Man," Keanu in a cape said, gesturing to the squirrel.

"Nut Man?" I repeated, certain I'd heard wrong.

"We're the Vendetta League," Nut Man informed me.

I scribbled that bit of information down. I'd hate to get the name of their franchise wrong. "So does everyone in the Vendetta League have to be dressed as an animal?"

Nut Man shook his very large head. "Well, they don't have to. We've expanded to include anyone who wants to dress up and stop crime."

"Is there a name for the organization you work with?" I asked.

Nut Man nodded and his head almost fell off. He reached up to steady it and prevent it from Godzilla-ing any stray bugs on the ground. "The Speedy Superheroes."

I wrote that down. "Are you the person who organized this chapter of the Speedy Superheroes?" I'd looked up several of the real superhero organizations around the country so I knew there were a lot of them the Vendetta League could be operating under.

"I'm one of the founders."

"What exactly is your mission?" I'd read about some of the superhero organizations online and they were all similar, but I wanted to know what the Speedy Superheroes were supposed to be doing specifically.

"To help. In any way we can."

I narrowed my eyes. "That's kind of a broad definition. What does it mean?"

He gestured with his hands and the oversized squirrel paws distracted me. "We have people doing neighborhood watches in places that have had crimes. And we patrol the city, especially at night when bad things are more likely to happen. We also do charity work and visit kids in the hospital. It really perks up their spirits."

"How do people find you?" I asked.

"Anyone can submit a request on the Speedy Superhero website. Needs are matched with the organization closest to the person making the request."

Interesting. "Do you partner with other Speedy Superhero groups? Have Superhero parties maybe?" If anyone else had been listening to my conversation, they would have thought I was making a joke, but my questions were totally serious.

"Sometimes. There are occasionally get-togethers in bigger cities like Salt Lake. Everyone comes in costume and uses their alias."

That seemed like it would be hard to manage. Hundreds of people known only by costume and fake names? It could be a security and liability nightmare. "Do you personally know all of the members of the Vendetta League?"

"By costume."

Okay then.

While I liked the idea of the Speedy Superheroes in theory, its organizational structure seemed problematic. The secretive nature of the group required superheroes to stay anonymous and that could be a catalyst for all kinds of nefarious things and situations. "How do you know that the people in your group are actually working to stop crime and not performing crimes themselves?"

Nut Man, and at least one more superhero—I think it was the fairy—gasped. "Because that would violate all of the superhero codes!"

I wasn't sure if codes were really that important to all of the Speedy Superhero members. A group like this that allowed for complete anonymity would be a fantastic networking tool, and hunting ground, for a full-on psychopath. I was surprised the Speedy Superheroes organization hadn't thought of that, or the nature of playing God and judging good verses bad by their own personal barometer instead of the law. I pressed them on it. "But there are a lot of superheroes that aren't looked on fondly by the police. Take Batman for example. He was doing things in the name of good, but he was dishing out punishment based on his own judgments of right and wrong. It undermines the entire concept of justice. That's the debate: are these people superheroes or vigilantes? And where do you fall on that side of the argument?"

Nut Man shook his head. "We respect the law and would never do anything that might cause problems. We're here to be an extra watch dog. We let the public know they're being looked out for, and let criminals know they're being watched. When we see something happening, we call the police."

"So the costumes are some form of coercion?"

"No, but we tend to get more attention in costume and our presence can be a deterrent for people looking to commit a crime."

I could see that.

"How are people chosen for the group?"

"They submit an application."

"And you don't ever know who they really are?"

Nut Man threw his furry arms up and seemed incensed. "No! That would violate the superhero's right to be anonymous!"

Far be it for me to out a superhero.

"I've only seen the superheroes recently. How long has the Speedy Superhero Vendetta League chapter been open in Branson?"

Nut Man thought about it for a beat. "Since the beginning of summer...so about five months. At first it was only me and four other people. But we've been adding members as more people find out about us and want to join."

"Do you, or any of your superheroes, have additional

insight about the robberies that have been committed around town?"

Nut Man shook his head in a slow, sad way. I'd never seen a more somber squirrel. It's like he'd had his cache of nuts stolen. "None of our people were near the scenes when the robberies happened. We're getting new members all the time, but right now we're small, and we have to balance our super-hero work with jobs and families and life. We do what we can, but we haven't caught the robber yet. We're looking though!"

It was good to know the superheroes were on the case.

"Okay, I think I have enough for now. Can I get ahold of you if I have any more questions?" I'd found out why I was being followed by costumed citizens, and discovered more information about the Speedy Superheroes that would help me in my additional research.

"Sure," Nut Man said. He handed me a card with his name on it, complete with a tiny cartoon of a squirrel, and his email address.

Uni-Keanu piped up, "I told them you were a cool reporter lady and would do a super nice story about us! That's why they agreed to meet."

I nodded. "I'll do my best."

Uni-Keanu gave me a huge smile.

I'd do a story, but I'd remain objective in the process. I was also going to look into whether these superhero groups around the country had ever had issues with people joining who were using the group as some sort of cover. If that was the case, then maybe I needed to be watching the members of the group more to see if any of them were involved in the robberies.

The superheroes fanned out, leaving for their respective

assignments. I put my notebook back in my bag and looked up to see Hawke walking toward me, his attention on the costumed superheroes. He was watching with a combination of interest and suspicion. "What's up with the animal gang? Is there a furry convention?"

Funny, since a furry convention had been one of my first thoughts as well.

"Apparently, they're part of a group of real superheroes. They patrol cities and fight crime."

Hawke winged a brow. "Interesting."

"Not unlike you," I pointed out.

He tilted his head in acknowledgment. "I have more of a specialized skill set."

That he did.

"Did they seem normal?" Hawke asked.

I scrunched up my nose. "I'm certain one of them was Keanu, so define normal."

A smile spread across his perfectly shaped mouth and I had to pull myself away from the image of where I wanted those lips because Hawke had decided to start talking and I needed to pay attention. "So they're a bunch of civilians who think they're legit superheroes cosplaying all over town trying to stop crime. Maybe they're helping, maybe they aren't."

He summarized the situation well. "Seems like it."

"Did they have any information on the robberies?"

"No, they didn't. They're not a huge group so they can't be everywhere. At least, that's what they said."

"But you don't believe them?"

I paused a minute thinking back to everything they'd told me and my suspicions. "The superheroes are anonymous. It seems like people masquerading as superheroes could be used as a vehicle to commit crimes."

Hawke scrubbed a hand over his chin that was currently sporting a tiny bit of very sexy scruff. "Didn't the kid who saw the robber at the Popes' house describe the person breaking in as a superhero climbing walls?"

"Yeah. It might be nothing but I'm going to do some more digging into the superheroes and see if there's a connection between them and the robberies." I paused, remembering the Collins' robbery. "Speaking of robberies, do you have any contacts that might be able to help me search for a specific stolen item?"

Hawke's eyes got slightly wider, which I'd come to realize was a sign of interest from him. "Depends on the item."

"Trina Collins is the latest robbery victim. They took her house plant, Selma, and a valuable wood sculpture of the Teton Mountains done by Ron Storm."

Hawke tilted his head to the side. "I don't think there's much hope for the house plant."

"Don't tell Trina that. She was far more upset about it than the Ron Storm sculpture and the sculpture is worth a lot more, and should be easier to identify if someone tries to sell it."

Hawke nodded his agreement. "The problem with a Ron Storm sculpture of the Teton Mountains is that a majority of Ron Storm's sculptures feature the Teton Mountains."

"I've noticed," I said. "I always thought he must be obsessed with boobs."

"Most men are," Hawke said, his eyes glittering and falling to my chest before coming back to rest on my face. "The French trappers who named them were."

I was surprised he knew that bit of Teton Mountain info. "I guess I shouldn't play trivia games with you because you might win."

He grinned. "I know things."

"Probably a lot of things that are classified and illegal."

He grinned wider and kept quiet in the way that cops and people who routinely keep a lot of secrets do. "It kind of annoys me that you don't feel compelled to respond to my statements and questions."

"I keep secrets for a living."

"And I ask questions for a living."

He shrugged.

"It complicates things."

"Life is complicated, Kitty Kate. We figure it out."

I sighed. This conversation was not going to end today and I had a feeling we'd be having some version of it for years to come, especially if we tried to have a romantic relationship. I moved the subject back to the Collins robbery. "Trina had a photo of the sculpture so it should be easier to identify. Is there a way to put an alert out on it and get some sort of notification if that particular piece ends up for sale somewhere?"

Hawke thought about it. "If it's sold online, it's easy to track. Offline and to private sellers is a different story. Send me the pic and I'll see what I can do."

"Thanks," I said, pulling my phone out and texting him the photo. I sent it, then realized he'd followed me to the park, which meant he'd checked the tracker he had on my Jeep and he was probably here for a reason. "What are you doing here anyway?" I hadn't heard his 1967 Shelby Mustang or his Harley pull up, and they were both loud enough that I would have been able to identify them from blocks away. Then again, I'd been distracted with the costume brigade.

"I was actually looking for you."

I raised my brows with interest. "For?"

"I have an event in a few days. It has to do with something I'm working on, and I'd be less noticeable and threatening with a beautiful woman by my side to take attention off of me. You asked if you could help the other day. This would help."

I'd asked, but didn't think he'd actually follow through and enlist me for assistance. Maybe this meant he was willing to open up more and wanted to include me in his life. "Okay," I said, trying not to let my overeagerness show, "do you want to tell me more about the event?"

He pursed his lips. "I actually can't. Everyone invited is sworn to secrecy or they lose their ticket."

That seemed sketchy. I'd heard about events like that before. They usually included sex swings and orgies. "I'm not into the *Eyes Wide Shut* scene, so if that's the kind of event you're attending, you'll have to find another beautiful girl." It wouldn't be hard. I was certain his little black book was the size of Mount Everest.

Hawke's eyes sparked with amusement. "So you don't like sex?"

I held up a finger. "Point of clarification: I don't like sex with an audience."

His lips spread into a sly smile that promised all sorts of carnal things I'd probably never even considered or heard of. "The goal is to have sex so good that you don't care whether or not you have an audience."

My eyes widened thinking of every person on the planet,

and even some animals too, that owned cell phones with cameras. "I will always care about an audience."

"Not with me, you wouldn't."

My cheeks immediately pinked. Was the park getting hotter all of a sudden? Because it felt like it was getting hotter. Global warming was going to kick our asses.

Hawke laughed. "This event isn't like that," he said in a reassuring tone, "though you will require a specific wardrobe. I'll send something to your house."

"Okayyyy," I said, letting my trepidation show. I wanted to help him, but I hated putting myself in positions where I didn't know all the details and didn't have a fully formed plan. Plus, I needed to know what the outfit was so I could coordinate, and decide what body parts needed to be shaved.

Hawke grinned. "Don't look so scared. It's not a big deal and I think the reporter in you will find it intriguing."

I raised a brow. "That does make me more interested."

"I guess all I had to do to get you to go out with me was dangle some mystery."

I made a noise between a grunt and a snort. "All you've been dangling since I met you is mystery."

He grinned. "And you're still here so I guess it's working."

I sighed. "It would work better if you'd open up once in a while. Bonding with someone I know very little about makes it hard to form a connection."

His eyes held mine, sparks arcing between us so aggressively that I thought we might cause an electrical storm. He leaned over, pressed his lips into my own and I could feel his hardness everywhere. His tongue tangled with mine until I was lost in his lips, his touch, and promises of more to come when he pulled back and gave me a slow smile. "I think we connect just fine, Kitty Kate. And when we do finally have sex —and we will—I promise you won't care where it happens, or who sees it." His hand dropped from my waist and his sudden lack of touch felt like I'd lost something vital. "I'll text you the time to be ready, and send over your outfit."

As he started to walk away I managed to gather my brain cells again and yelled, "It better not be a costume!"

He laughed and I wondered what I'd gotten myself into.

Chapter Twelve

I went into work early because I needed to get some things done before I had to leave for Gandalf's afternoon puppy training class. He'd been going to training for a few weeks and was doing really well. He'd already mastered basic commands, but today's lesson was on "leave it" and he wasn't the best at leaving things alone that he really wanted. It wasn't lost on me that that particular trait was one Gandalf and I shared. Only Gandalf's "leave it" challenge usually came in the form of food left on a sidewalk or dropped from my counter, and my challenge came in the form of two very large and attractive men.

I was editing some articles when Ella wandered in around ten with donuts and handed me a napkin as she opened the box. I selected one that was glazed and frosted white with sprinkles on top. "Thanks for the donuts," I told her, taking a bite. She sat down at an empty desk with a computer that some of the freelance reporters used when they were occasionally in the office.

"You're welcome," she said, sounding distracted as she logged on.

I watched her for a minute, noticing her lips pulled back in either anger or anxiety, maybe a combination of both. "What's going on?" I asked.

Her nose scrunched up in annoyance. "I'm fightin' for this bid and some dummy keeps pushin' the price up!"

"What are you trying to buy?" I asked, getting up from my desk and going over to look at her screen.

"A bunch of those old animated fairy tale VHS tapes."

I raised an eyebrow. This was the second time I'd recently heard about animated fairy tales on VHS—the first time was when they were stolen from the Pope family. "VHS tapes?" I asked, confused. "I don't even know where you'd find a VHS player to watch them. There are adults alive now who wouldn't even know what those are. They're basically a relic."

"I know!" she said. "That's why they're highly collectable!"

"Seriously?" My mom had an entire cabinet full. I'd have to go raid it and see if any of them could be sold.

"Yep! Pristine copies can go for thousands."

I stared at the bid on her screen, watching the price for the VHS rise by the minute. "I had no idea. How long until the bidding is over?"

"Twenty minutes. And this AllTheGoodStuff nincompoop isn't going to steal it from me!"

I watched her, laser focused and answering each bid with one of her own. At this point, I wasn't sure if Ella really wanted the VHS tape, or if the appeal was now about winning the bid. I had a feeling it was the later.

As I sat there watching, a thought clicked in my mind. "Where's the pic of the little stuffed bat collectible you won the bid for?"

She showed it to me.

"Can I get a copy of the photo?"

"Sure," she said, texting it to my phone. "What do you need it for?"

I looked at the bat and the VHS tapes on Not Just Junk and wondered if they were the same things stolen during the robberies in Branson. Brandy hadn't circled a bat on her photo, but she'd told me she hadn't taken a stuffed animal inventory lately either, so she might have missed it. Granted, those stuffed animals and cartoon VHS tapes had been owned by almost every household in the United States, but I thought it was strange both of those items had been stolen from Branson Falls in the past week, and now they were both on the Not Just Junk site. There could be a chance that the items being sold and the items stolen were one and the same. "A hunch," I said. "I'll tell you more if it's what I think it is." I watched her scroll through the site as she waited for her bid time to tick down.

"Does the page show who the seller is?" I asked.

"Yeah," she said, pointing to the name Carzo39.

I wondered if that was a last name or a screen name they made up. "Is that the same person who sold the bat you bought?" I asked.

She tilted her head, thinking. "I can't remember."

"Can you still check and see who the bat seller was?"

"Maybe..." she said, distracted. "But not until I make sure I win this bid."

I nodded. Winning the bid was very important.

"Do I need an account to see what's for sale, or can I get on Not Just Junk and scroll through the site?" I asked.

"You can get on and scroll."

I went over to my desk and started scanning the site. I was

looking for other items I might recognize that had gone missing from the robberies. There were a lot of categories and items for sale, with hundreds of pages in each category. I started looking through the pages and then sighed; it would take me forever to sort through them all. I needed to refine my search.

I decided it would be better to look at newest items first, in categories where I knew something had been stolen. So I checked the art category and the sub category of sculpture first, then, after being shocked to find a house plant section, I checked it next. I didn't find Trina's plant, Selma, or their Ron Storm sculpture, but I decided I'd keep an eye on the categories I thought might list potential stolen items. I signed up for an account and put a watch on those categories so I'd get a notification any time something new was posted.

Ella made a loud whooping noise from across the room. "I got it! I won! Take that, AllTheGoodStuff! Who's got all the good stuff now, huh?"

Ella was trash talking an avatar on a computer. We'd officially entered into some strange dimension.

I searched around my desk until I found the photo Brandy Pope had given me of her stolen stuffed animals. She'd said an octopus and flamingo had been stolen, but I wondered if she also had a bat and hadn't noticed it was missing as well.

I picked up the photo and compared it to the one Ella had sent me. Sure enough, Brandy had a bat in her collection just like the one that had been sold. I wondered if she still had it.

I saw the shelter owner, Michelle James, at the front desk as Gandalf and I wandered around the store. Michelle had been the one who encouraged me to get Gandalf and I'd always be grateful to her for that. She had eight kids and an army of animals. I wasn't sure how she did it all, but she managed, and she did it well.

"Hey, Kate!" Michelle said. "Glad you could make it."

"Me too." There was always a chance that a story would interrupt puppy training. It had already happened once and my mom had taken him instead. It wasn't a bad thing. We were basically co-parenting the little guy so it was good for him to learn to listen to commands from my mom and dad too, but I knew it was important for Gandalf to see me as his alpha and being at the trainings was a big part of that. "How are you doing, Michelle?"

"Pretty good. Trying to figure out Halloween costumes is rough."

"Kids are hard to please."

"So are the dogs," she said and we both laughed.

"We're almost ready to start if you want to go to the back," she said.

I walked into the room, prepared to let Gandalf greet his friends, and stopped in my tracks. It seemed we had a new addition to the class. Gandalf was pulling at his leash, trying to get over to the toys. I narrowed my eyes, unfroze myself, and corrected Gandalf as I continued to glare at Drake, talking to someone on the far side of the room. Drake finished up his conversation and came over to give Gandalf a pet.

I eyed him suspiciously. "You do know this is a puppy training class?"

Drake glanced up at me between rubbing under Gandalf's chin and then his belly. "I do."

"Have you acquired a dog that you haven't told me about?" I asked.

"No, but you did and I thought I should get some tips in."

I wasn't sure if I should think that was cute, or stalkery. My eyes managed to narrow even more. I could barely see out of them at this point. "You're taking time out of your day for puppy training when you don't even own a dog?"

He pressed his lips together. "I might have one someday."

I gave him a look. "A dog of your own?" Because I was not prepared for the insinuation that he might one day be Gandalf's puppy dad.

Drake grinned. "Sure."

Good grief. Not only did most of Branson already think we were dating—or more than dating—a mutual puppy training class would make them all certain of it. Someone had probably already snapped a photo. I fought back a sigh. I needed to take control of this situation.

"You grew up on a farm," I reasoned. "You know how dogs are trained. I think you're totally fine."

He leaned against the wall, his eyes lighting. "Worried someone's going to see me here with you?"

Yes. That's exactly what I was worried about. "No. But I'm aware that your time is valuable."

He gave me his thousand-watt politician's smile. "Which is why I'm spending it with you."

"We could do something another time," I offered.

His lips curved. "Okay, do you want to come back over and watch me take my shirt off while I clean more stuff off of my house?"

Dammit! I thought I'd been so sneaky with my stares! I tried to smooth my expression to something blank and vague. "Has someone been throwing things at your house again?"

His lips spread into a huge grin as he totally ignored my question. "Despite the fact that you said Spence urgently needed you at the office the other morning, you sat in your car for a good ten minutes doing nothing."

"I wasn't doing 'nothing'," I defended. "I was answering some messages." From my mom. I'd been replying to her pictures of Gandalf. And I'd made it seem like my work situation was more serious than it was because it gave me an excuse to leave when what I'd really wanted was to drag Drake into his eggy house and help him out of his clothes.

"Next time, get out of the car and come inside. You could see a lot more that way."

I slitted my eyes...had he been reading my mind? Add black magic to the list of reasons I probably shouldn't get involved with Drake—probably.

He continued, "I'd even make you breakfast."

I gave him a look. "There won't be a next time."

He looked at me like I was nuts. "I'm a politician and a lawyer. This isn't the last time my house will be egged."

"Maybe I'll be the one egging it next."

He grinned. "You'd do it on purpose so you could see me without a shirt."

He was not wrong.

My lack of an answer was all the answer he needed and his lips tipped up in a knowing smile.

Michelle came in and we started the training. We placed a treat on the floor with our hand over it and let the dogs try to get the treat. As soon as they stopped trying to get the treat, they'd get praise and the reward of another treat from our other hand. Once they'd mastered leaving the treat alone with our hand on top of it, we were supposed to remove our hand, leave the treat on the ground, and tell them to leave it. As soon as they looked away or showed disinterest, they got a reward. Then we were supposed to increase the time they had to be patient and keep repeating that process. Gandalf did okay the first time, but after that, he sat there looking like I was keeping the crown jewels from him. He waited all of five seconds before he pounced on the treat.

"Let me try," Drake said.

I gave him the treat and he put it down in front of Gandalf. "Leave it."

Gandalf sat there happily, listening to Drake and completely ignoring the food in front of him.

Drake gave him a pet and a treat. "Good boy! You're such a smart dog!"

Drake went through the sequence again making Gandalf wait longer. And again, Gandalf sat there, tongue lolling out of his mouth in a happy little smile, waiting for Drake's command.

My jaw went slack.

Drake kept going and got to a thirty second pause before I grabbed Gandalf's leash back from him.

"This is madness! He's *my* dog!"

"He likes me." Drake's face was positively beaming and I kind of wanted to punch his perfect nose.

"Don't flatter yourself. He likes everyone."

"But he *listens* to me." Drake bent down and nuzzled Gandalf's nose like they had a little secret noseshake.

"Hey!" I said to Gandalf, incensed. "You're supposed to be

helping me smash the patriarchy, buddy! Not contributing to it."

"This is a sign," Drake said. "Your dog *loves* me. Now we have to be together or it will break Gandalf's little heart."

I rolled my eyes and picked Gandalf up, then went back to trying to get him to listen to me—his actual owner. We practiced "leave it" for another fifteen minutes and brushed up on some tricks we'd learned at previous trainings before the class ended.

I said goodbye to Michelle and some of the other puppy parents and dogs before I left. Drake followed me out.

"I have another question for you," Drake said as I let Gandalf smell every tree, stick, and weed on the way to the car.

"You charmed my dog and I think you might be a dark wizard or something so I'm pretty sure the answer is already no."

"If I were a dark wizard, I would have charmed you by now."

"Maybe you're a bad dark wizard."

"But my black magic works selectively on dogs?"

I pointed at him. "Exactly!"

He laughed. "I was wondering if you'll go to the fall carnival with me."

My eyebrows shot up way past my forehead and probably straight into the stratosphere. "That's a very, very, *very* public event." All of The Ladies would be there. All of them. Probably my mom and dad too. It was a huge town party.

His lips tipped up. "I know."

"If we go there together, everyone will think we're dating."

"Everyone already thinks that. Most of them think we're engaged. And some even believe we secretly eloped."

My jaw hung open. "Who thinks *that?*"

He shrugged. "People. I've had some questions about it."

I folded my arms across my chest and gave him a look. "Who started that rumor, Drake?"

He lifted his arms in the air. "I honestly don't know."

"Because I heard that people were talking about how you were sleeping over at my house a couple of times and I can totally see you or someone on your political team spinning it like we're already married so you wouldn't get in trouble with the morality police."

He ran his tongue over his lips and it was almost enough to distract me from my irritation. "That's a lot of assumptions, Katie. Let's break them down. Number one, I certainly wouldn't start a rumor like that, and I wouldn't let my team do it either. Number two, if we'd had sex, everyone would know about it because they would have heard you screaming my name. Repeatedly."

I gave him serious side-eye. "That's presumptuous."

He leaned in, his face inches from mine. "I dare you."

Yes! My lady bits screamed. My brain was still there for back up, however, and reminded me Drake was close enough that you couldn't even fit a scripture page between us, let alone the whole Book of Mormon like the Branson Falls dating rules decreed. I backed up to a suitable distance of about ten feet. My brain only had so much control and I couldn't guarantee I wouldn't climb him otherwise. "You know, if we ever do get to that point, you're going to have a lot to live up to."

He grinned and tugged on his full bottom lip with his teeth. "Oh, we'll get there. And I fully intend to."

And my cheeks were flaming hot again. Someone really needed to do something about climate change because we absolutely weren't going to survive it.

"You wouldn't break the rules and have sex outside of marriage," I said. It was one of my hesitations about Drake. He talked a lot of game, but I didn't know if he actually had some. He was Mormon and no sex before marriage was a serious rule.

"There's a lot I would consider doing for you."

I eyed him with a trunk-full of suspicion. I knew how guilt and manipulation worked and religions were experts at both. I really didn't think he'd break those rules, and if he did, I had a feeling he'd regret it. I didn't want to be the cause of that.

This conversation was getting deeper than I had time for at the moment. I needed to change the subject and fast. "I'm already going to the carnival. I have to cover it for the paper."

"Great! What time should I pick you up."

I shook my head. "I'm working, Drake. And I'm on call. I need my own car."

"Okay, then I'll see you there."

The fact was, I really did want to see him. I'd thought about my talk with Annie regarding the men in my life, and running from the situation wasn't helping my head or my heart. I needed to get to know Drake and Hawke better, push the relationships forward, and make a decision about what I wanted from there. Doing that meant spending more time with both of them, and having those deeper conversations to see if we actually could make something work. "I'll see you, and if I have time after I'm done getting photos and notes for stories, maybe we can get a hot chocolate or something."

He grinned. "I'll take whatever you're willing to offer."

I nodded and strapped Gandalf into his car seat. "I'll see you at the carnival then."

Drake leaned into the car and petted Gandalf goodbye, and as he did it, he discreetly slipped his hand over my ass and bit his bottom lip. "I can't wait."

Sparks coursed through me at his touch and my mind immediately went to the other places I wanted his hands.

He grinned, then turned and walked down the street to his car. I swore I could feel his hand on my ass all the way to mom and dad's house to drop Gandalf off.

Chapter Thirteen

I grabbed a donut from the treat table, went back to my desk, and called Brandy Pope.

"Hi, Brandy, this is Kate Saxee at the *Tribune*."

"Hi, Kate," she said, "What can I help you with?"

"I have a quick question for you. I was looking at your stuffed animal photo and noticed you had the special edition bat in the photo. Do you still have it, or could it have been taken during the robbery as well?"

"Hmm," she said, "let me check."

I heard her walking and after a couple of minutes she gasped. "Kate, it's gone. I can't find it. There are so many of the toys and I rarely take stock of them all so I must have missed it when I was going through the stolen items. I'll have to let the police know."

It wasn't concrete evidence that the robberies and the items on Not Just Junk were connected, but it was a lead, and one I definitely wanted to follow up on.

"How did you know about the bat?" she asked.

"I saw someone selling one and thought it might be

147

connected. I'm still getting the information, but I'll let you know if I find out anything."

"Thank you!" she said.

I hung up and realized I was probably going to have to ask Hawke for assistance on this one.

"I found the name!" Ella said as she wandered in from the back entrance. "I emailed it to you."

"Name?" Spence asked.

"I asked her to look something up for me on her Not Just Junk bid site," I explained.

"The seller of the stuffed bat isn't the same as the seller of the VHS tapes."

Spence's eyebrows shot up. "VHS tapes?"

"A lot happened while you were gone this morning." I paused, "Speaking of that, where were you?" I'd been in early, and hadn't seen him all day.

He looked like a deer in headlights. He paused like he was trying to come up with an activity. "Errands," he sputtered, and then started rearranging things on his desk in an attempt to take my attention away from where he'd been.

"Errands?" I asked, my tone doubtful.

"Yes," he said, this time more confident in his lie.

My reporter instincts were buzzing off the charts. "You know my job makes me really good at reading people, and I can usually tell when they're lying, right?" Body language betrayed an incredible amount of information and the ability to read it had helped me on multiple interviews and investigations.

He pursed his lips, totally aware of the B.S. detecting talents I'd developed over the years.

"I'm also paid to be observant," I said, grabbing Ella's donut box and offering him one. He took it and I leaned in so Ella couldn't hear me. "You have a button undone."

Spence's cheeks pinked and I laughed. I'd actually made him blush. While I was training Gandalf, Spence had been in bed—and he hadn't been alone. "I need to meet your friend," I whispered.

Spence smiled. "Soon."

I pulled up my email from Ella. The bat seller's username was Milkshake4. That didn't provide me with an abundance of information either—other than a preference for ice cream. So the bat and VHS sellers weren't the same—that put a wrench in my theory that the items were stolen from Branson. Then again, there was nothing stopping a person from making multiple seller accounts. The two sellers might still be the same person. I wasn't ruling anything out at this point. However, finding the real names behind Carzo39 and Milkshake4 would require more searching power than my *Tribune* background checking tools offered.

I texted Hawke.

> I need some usernames tracked down to find out who they are in real life. Can you help me with that?

He texted back.

> I can help you with all kinds of things.

I had no doubt. I texted him the names Ella had given me and the Not Just Junk website.

He texted back.

I'll get on it.

My mind immediately thought of all the things I wanted him on. It had been a really long time since I'd had sex—*really* long. That had to be the explanation for my overactive hormones and it had nothing to do with the fact that Hawke and Drake were two of the hottest men I'd ever seen and it was deeply appealing that they were both interested in me.

My phone buzzed again.

Or you could get on me.

Geez! It was like he was reading my mind too! Drake and Hawke were both dark wizards! Though I had a feeling Hawke was significantly darker than Drake. It didn't seem like there was much Hawke couldn't, or wouldn't, do.

The scanner erupted with noise. It sounded like another robbery. I grabbed my bags and finished typing out a text on the way to my Jeep.

Tempting, but I have a story to get to.

I pulled my phone out again and saw the last text from Hawke.

I'm always available for a ride.

That was never a question in my mind.

I put my phone in my purse and tried not to think of the images Hawke's message conjured up in my head as I climbed the steps to the Nesson house.

Bobby opened the door as I was about to knock.

"Hey, Bobby," I said, pulling my camera out. "What's the story? Do you know what was taken yet?"

Bobby shook his head and chuckled. "False alarm."

I tilted my head to the side. "So there wasn't really a robbery?"

Bobby hooked his thumbs into the loop on his belt buckle. "Nope. Gil Nesson came home from the store and heard strange noises comin' from down the hall. He grabbed an axe as defense—

"An axe?" I asked, sure I'd heard wrong.

"Yeah, he's been practicin' axe throwin' in his backyard."

That seemed dangerous. "Is that legal?"

Bobby snorted. "Sheesh, Kate. We can't regulate wood choppin'!"

I guess that was true, but I hadn't considered random flying axes to be a threat up until this point in my life. I'd be on the lookout now.

Bobby continued. "He had his axe and went down the hall to investigate. He found his bathroom door closed and some-thin' bangin' inside. What with all the robberies in the news, he thought he'd maybe captured a thief. The knockin' and poundin' noises made it seem like whoever was in there was extra trapped. Gil didn't want to do a solo battle with the robbers if he didn't have to. So he grabbed his phone, ran out of the house, and called 9-1-1."

"But you didn't find a robber?"

Bobby grinned. "No siree. We found one of those magic vacuum robots."

I blinked. "A Roomba?"

He lifted a shoulder. "Or somethin' like it. Somehow it got itself stuck in there. Must have knocked the door shut and then couldn't get out so it just kept bangin' around."

I gave him a suspicious look. "This sounds like something that would happen to my mom."

Bobby laughed. "That's what I said. She doesn't have one of those robot vacuums, does she?"

"No, she doesn't." And I'd make sure she never got one because she could cause all sorts of chaos with it. The police would be over there constantly. We hadn't let her get a digital voice assistant for the same reasons. She'd attempt to put flour on her grocery list and accidentally order a live camel—and then she wouldn't want to send it back.

Bobby shook his head. "That artificial intelligence is gonna be the end of humans, I'm tellin' ya."

Most of the time I thought Bobby's theories and opinions were a little out there, but I was kind of in agreement with him on this one.

"Did Gil not know that he owned a Roomba?"

"It was new. His wife bought it last week and it was still learnin' the terrain when it got stuck. Next time it'll know not to go in the bathroom."

I was pretty sure there was a setting for that.

Gil came out of the house and I went inside to get a picture of the vacuum criminal.

"That's gonna be a pretty funny news story," Gil said.

I nodded, thinking it would probably be picked up and mocked on social media. I didn't control the news though, I just reported it.

I put my camera back in my bag and then caught Bobby's expression. His eyes went wide and his face took on the look of someone that had seen something they couldn't quite comprehend. "What in tarnation?" he said, his voice getting louder with each syllable.

I turned and saw what I can only describe as the impossible.

A dragon. And it was stomping toward us. The ensemble was dark purple with sequins in various shades of purple and silver on the front. It had little triangular fabric peaks going down the back of it from the top of the head to the tip of the tail, and those peaks were adorned with gold filigree that shimmered in the afternoon light. There were claws, also sequined, on the hands and feet, and a dark purple sequin mask covered the dragon's eyes. It stood a little over five-feet tall, and from the moment I'd seen it coming, I'd recognized the stride. I would have known who it was regardless, but her matching dragon sidekick that was the same height as my dog, gave it away.

"Never fear! I'm here to help!" my mom said, hands on her hips and tail swinging in a manner that some might find threatening.

I stared at her outfit, completely dumbfounded. "What is..." I raised my hand up and down, gesturing to her very elaborate costume, "this?"

"It's my crime fighting costume!"

I blinked, realization dawning all at once. "You joined the Speedy Superheroes Vendetta League?"

She nodded. "Call me Cuddles!"

I blinked. "Cuddles?"

She flashed a smile indicating she was very proud of her naming abilities. "Isn't it a super cute dragon name?"

I closed my eyes and fought the urge to give up. After a few deep breaths, I was ready for more questions. "How did you know about the Speedy Superheroes?" I asked. The story hadn't hit the paper yet.

"Ella, silly."

Of course.

I had no idea how my mom had passed the Speedy Superheroes background check. You didn't even need a background check service to search Sophie Saxee's name and find out she'd broken the Utah law of not committing destruction on a mass scale multiple times. I had Speedy Superhero research on my list of things to do, and now I was going to make sure I crossed it off as soon as possible.

"With all the robberies, I'd been considering starting a neighborhood watch of my own when Ella told me about the Speedy Superheroes," she explained. "Considering my sewing skills and crime fighting abilities, I felt uniquely qualified to join." Her tone beamed with pride.

I raised a brow. "Crime fighting abilities?"

She put her hands on her hips. "I always know when something's not right. My superpower is intuition."

I gave her a look. "I'd argue your superpower is creating chaos."

She glared.

At least I knew she wasn't scaling walls. That wasn't in her human skill set, and her dragon costume was far too bulky to make an ascent.

"Did Gandalf want to be your sidekick, or did you enlist him?" I asked.

She gave me an affronted look. "Of course he wanted to! He wouldn't like missing out on all the fun!" She bent down and scooped him up. His little purple costume with matching dragon peaks, sequins, gold filigree, and threatening tail matched her outfit perfectly. He was smiling like he was the happiest dog in the world.

"Where's the criminal?" she asked, her tone no nonsense and ready to work. "How can I help?"

"There was no criminal," I explained. "It was a robot vacuum misunderstanding."

She looked at me like I was crazy, and I felt like that response was ridiculous considering her current getup and most of her life in general.

"I missed it?!" she cried, sounding seriously disappointed. "I came as soon as I heard the police scanner!"

I made a note to text my dad and have him hide that sucker. This whole situation had trouble written all over it.

"If you came as soon as you heard it on the scanner, your response time isn't great because I've been here for fifteen minutes."

She stomped her foot. "Oh, fooey."

"How long does it take you to get into that costume?" I asked.

She tilted her head, her eyebrows coming together as she thought. "I haven't timed it, but it's not quick."

I was sure of that. If I were trying to get into it, I'd need a team of people and some tools.

"I'm not sure you took speed into account during your design process."

She pressed her lips together. "This was my first case and a trial run. I've learned a lot, including the fact that I need to get Gandalf's costume on first because it's too hard to maneuver once I'm in all my glory. I will make some outfit adjustments for future calls."

I caught Bobby's eye and couldn't tell if he was worried or amused that she might be at future crime scenes.

"I can't believe you got him to wear that," I said, pointing to Gandalf. He didn't mind capes and clothes, but he was a full-on baby dragon that looked like a tiny version of my mom only with more fur. I was certain that if I'd tried to put him in that outfit, fits would have been thrown. My mom probably bribed him with treats.

"I bribed him with treats," my mom said.

Gandalf wagged his tail, and with it, the dragon tail wagged too. I had to admit, it was pretty cute.

I looked at my watch. The day had been long and it was winding down. I was ready to go get some super cheesy breadsticks with ranch dressing and relax at home with my dog and dinner.

"I'm almost done for the day, so I can take Gandalf off your hands."

"Oh, that's good," she said. "We had to walk here because I couldn't fit in any of our vehicles and it's a long way for his little legs."

She turned on her claws and made her way back home.

Bobby laughed. "Your life is one entertainment after another."

I nodded. "Boring isn't even in my vocabulary."

I took Gandalf, put him in his car seat, and then ordered our food.

The breadsticks smelled like gooey cheese and bliss, and I couldn't wait to get in the house and eat. Gandalf's tongue was hanging out of the side of his mouth as he stared longingly at the box and I knew he felt the exact same way.

As I pulled into my garage and unlatched Gandalf from his seat, I noticed two guys walking on the sidewalk in front of my house. They were tall and big, like linebackers, and one of them had a tattoo sleeve visible on his arm. They were watching me as they walked, and they weren't being sneaky about it.

Gandalf noticed them too, and started a low growl in the back of his throat. Every hair on the back of my neck stood up. I'd gotten a strange vibe from them, but Gandalf had too, and that made me even more concerned.

I checked for my stun gun in my purse and walked toward them to see what they needed. As I moved in their direction, they hurried their pace and walked away. That was weird. What were they doing? And what did they want?

I turned to go inside the house and saw my older neighbor, Phyllis, outside putting some gardening items away before winter. "Hi, Phyllis," I said, walking toward her. Gandalf took the opportunity to chase some leaves in her yard.

"Kate! So good to see you!" Gandalf ran over and she gave him a little pet. Gandalf and Phyllis were good friends. They'd forged a bond during our weekly date where we watched bad reality TV shows together. There had been a few occasions I'd had work calls during times my mom and dad couldn't take Gandalf and I'd been able to drop him off with Phyllis instead. I suspected she spoiled him as much as my mom. It was adorable.

"I'm excited for a new season of *Strangers in Love.*"

Her face lit with excitement. "Me too! I've been reading about it and this season sounds crazy!"

"Crazy is fun," I said, bending down to take a leaf from Gandalf's mouth. "Speaking of crazy, did you happen to see those two guys walking down the sidewalk a few minutes ago?"

She nodded. "Yes. They've actually been by twice today. I thought maybe they were with the city because they seemed like they were looking closely at the homes and yards in the area."

"Were they looking at all the homes and yards, or ours specifically?"

She thought about it. "I couldn't say, I only noticed when they were by our houses, but they seemed very interested. It was odd."

"Did they come and talk to you?"

"No. But they did wave when I saw them."

Hmmm, maybe they were criminals with manners. Or maybe they were trying to blend in and not succeeding. I'd never seen them around town before though, and I would have remembered the tattoo sleeve because other than Axel, not many people in Branson had one. "And you didn't recognize them?"

"Nope. Not at all."

"Okay," I said, grabbing Gandalf from where he was chasing another leaf around the yard. This time of year was like dogapalooza and every fallen leaf became a toy. "Let me know if you see anything else strange."

"I will."

"I'll see you for *Strangers in Love*! I'll bring the caramel popcorn."

"I'll make the cheese dip!"

I smiled and waved as Gandalf and I walked into my house. I put the breadsticks on the counter and then got Gandalf out of his leash, harness, and dragon costume. I pulled the breadsticks out and ate my dinner, all the while wondering who those guys were, and why they'd been prowling around my house and street all afternoon.

Chapter Fourteen

It was a good morning so far. Gandalf was safe with my mom…well, as safe as he could be, my coffee was hot, and I'd already crossed multiple things off my to-do list. The carnival was tonight, so it would be a long work day, but I was excited for carnival treats. I was also looking forward to seeing Drake, which kind of surprised me, but now that I'd accepted I couldn't keep running from my emotions, I felt lighter. Embracing the path forward instead of staying stalled was good. The idea of The Ladies and entire town being there to witness our not-totally-a-date date did not excite me, but I'd learned that there were some things I couldn't control and other people were one of them.

Next up on my list was contacting the Speedy Superheroes main office. I looked at their website, found a main office phone number, and dialed.

"Speedy Superheroes," a perky voice on the other end answered.

"Hi, I'm Kate Saxee, editor of *The Branson Tribune* in Branson Falls, Utah. A chapter of your organization was recently opened here and I was wondering if I could ask someone a few questions for a story I'm writing?"

"Sure," she said, a smile in her tone. "I'm Emily Brown and I help manage the various superhero chapters. How can I help you?"

"Hi, Emily," I said, my voice friendly. "Can you tell me how chapters of the Speedy Superheroes are organized?"

"Of course. Once a group has at least five interested parties, they can submit an application to become a chapter. We do a background check on the individuals and if the background checks are approved, the chapter pays their application fee and they're listed on our website and searchable for new members and people who want to enlist their help."

"There's an application fee?"

"Yes," she said. "It helps cover the administration of the website, staff payroll, background checks, and making sure the chapters are organized and managed, and that people in need of help are connected with the superhero organization closest to them. It doesn't seem like much, but there's a lot of work behind the scenes and our headquarters staff is small."

"How much is the application fee?

"One thousand dollars."

My eyes widened. "That seems high. Is it pretty comparable with other organizations?

"It is," she said. "There's a lot of work that goes on at the headquarter level to make sure each chapter runs efficiently."

"Is that a one-time fee, or is it annual?"

"It's an annual fee."

That was a lot of money. Even if there were ten superheroes, they'd still all have to pay a fee of a hundred dollars a year. And they were volunteers. I'd have to ask our Vendetta

League how many members they had, and who put up the money for the initial application.

"From what I can tell, it seems like anyone can be a super-hero—" my mom included— "even someone who might not have the best intentions. Can you tell me how the background check works?"

"I can assure you, our superheroes are thoroughly vetted for exactly that reason. They're required to fill out a lengthy application including all of their identifying information. Then a full background check is done through a third party security company. For liability reasons, we don't keep the applications on file, but the security company does and the information can be used in case of legal issues. The security firm passes along any pertinent information before we make a determination about whether or not the individual is allowed to join."

"Have you had any problems with people joining without a background check?"

She paused on the other end. "What do you mean?"

I'd been thinking about this ever since my mom had threatened to start her own furry neighborhood watch. "Well, someone could simply put on a costume and start running around town saying they're a member of the Speedy Super-heroes even if they haven't filled out the application or had the background check done."

She paused on the other end. "I guess that's always a possi-bility. But I've never heard of it happening, and that's really something that would be out of our control."

She was right. She couldn't control someone lying about their involvement and pretending to be part of the team even if they weren't. Still, that seemed like a legal liability.

I asked her a few more questions about the organization, how many chapters they had and how long they'd been running, and took notes.

"I think that's all I need. Thank you for your time," I said.

"You're welcome. Let me know if I can help with anything else."

I hung up the phone and added the new information I'd learned to the Speedy Superhero story I was working on.

My phone buzzed with a text from my mom.

> I'm making Halloween sugar cookies and grilled cheese if you're free for lunch.

I was definitely free for cookies, grilled cheese, and some mid-day puppy snuggles. I grabbed my jacket and purse and told Spence I'd be back later.

My mom and dad's house smelled like sugar and heaven.

"Hi, Mom and Dad!"

Gandalf came running over to me, his tongue hanging out, and he spun so fast I thought he might catch a case of vertigo and fall over. He brought me a toy and we played for a few minutes.

"Your dad's in the garage."

I eyed her. "What have you done?"

She gave me a wide-eyed innocent look. "Nothing."

My dad had bought a silver 1966 Ford Mustang as a project car a while ago. He worked on it a lot as a coping mechanism for my mom's adventures. I hadn't heard of any Catasophie's recently so she was either keeping them a secret

—which wasn't an easy task in a small town where her daughter was the newspaper editor—or my dad was working on the car because he wanted to work on the car.

"The cookies look good," I said, picking up an intricately decorated little ghost with piping, sparkly sprinkles, and cute silver eyes. She also had orange pumpkins, black cats, and spiders. I stayed away from the spiders—I wasn't a fan. I took a bite of the cherry frosting flavored cookie and it was almost as good as an orgasm...or maybe I hadn't had a really great orgasm in so long that I'd forgotten what they were like.

"Your sugar cookies are my favorite."

She beamed at the compliment. "Your dad likes them too."

"I could live off of them."

She poured me a glass of milk and I sat at the table while she made me a sandwich. It was like being ten all over again, and I was totally fine with it. I could make my own grilled cheese but for some reason, my mom's always tasted better.

Gandalf brought me a toy and I threw it. Then he brought it back and I threw it again. I knew this game and it would go on until I stopped it. He'd trained me well.

My mom's phone buzzed and she grabbed it from her apron pocket, then made a funny sound and laughed.

"What is it?" I asked.

She waved a hand in front of her. "It's silly."

"What?"

"Well, for the life of me, I can't figure out why people keep texting me boobs."

I pushed my brows together. "People are texting you boobs? Like pictures of boobs?"

She pursed her lips and narrowed her eyes. "Not real boobs, but it's implied." She put my grilled cheese down in front of me and I pulled it apart, gooey cheese stretching over the plate. I was practically drooling, and Gandalf, who sat below me with his nose twitching at the delightful smell, definitely was.

"Implied boobs?" I asked. "What are you talking about?"

She put her own sandwich on the table and sat across from me. "Ever since the happy chocolate ice cream—"

"—You mean the little poop."

"I *mean*," she said, giving me a solid scowl, "the chocolate ice cream with hearts situation, I've told people that I'm not using the little text pictures anymore because their interpretation can't be guaranteed. And ever since, people keep sending me texts with this symbol <3." She held up her phone to show me. "It looks like boobs wearing a dunce cap. I giggle every time I see it."

I shook my head and laughed out loud. "It's not boobs, Mom. Turn it to the side and look at it. It's a heart."

She turned the phone to the left and gasped. "Oh my stars! You're right." She paused. "What does :-O mean?"

"That's expressing surprise."

"Oh dear. I really need to apologize to your dad. I thought that was something else entirely," she said, pressing her lips together. "I'll have to make him more cookies, maybe even a pie."

I had a good idea of what she thought :-O meant and was not interested in discussing it.

"How are things going at work?" she asked.

"Good. We're still trying to figure out what's happening with the robberies."

"There hasn't been one for a couple of days. Maybe the

robbers thought there was too much heat on them and decided to stop their criminal ways."

I paused mid-bite. "Heat?"

"You know! Cops, and now the Speedy Superheroes. It's dangerous to keep committing crimes when so many people are watching for you to make a wrong move."

She had a point about that, but my gut feeling was that the robberies weren't over. Also, she'd undoubtedly been watching detective and cop shows on Netflix again.

"I wrote a story about the Speedy Superheroes for the next *Tribune* issue."

My mom's smile widened and she clapped. "That's fantastic! The superheroes are so fun! I've been getting to know them and I'm really happy to be part of their group."

"You do things other than fight crime?"

"We work on assignments as a team. We're mostly supposed to be around and be a presence so people know we're there."

That was the same thing Nut Man had told me, but I had two robberies where a possible superhero might be involved, so if that was the case, the robbery superhero was probably working alone.

"Some of us will be at the carnival," she said.

I raised a brow. "In costume?"

"I believe so. I have to help the food pantry with their booth so I won't get to be a dragon tonight. But I'm sure Cuddles will be out again soon!"

I had no doubt about that.

"Thanks for lunch," I said, giving her hug.

"You're welcome."

I grabbed the plate of cookies my mom had made for me

to take back to the office to share—I was still undecided about the sharing part—then gave Gandalf some pets and went out through the garage to say hello and good-bye to my dad. The Mustang hood was raised and he was standing over it, a towel laid out over the body of the car, protecting the paint while he tinkered.

"Hey, Dad," I said, coming over to look at what he was doing. The car had been in great shape until my mom recently took it for a soggy drive straight into a very wet pond.

"Hey, Kate," he said, putting his wrench down and giving me a hug. "How's work going?"

"It's going," I said. "These robberies are strange. Nothing really ties them together, but they keep happening. The police don't have any leads, and even Hawke and I haven't been able to come up with something yet. I hope we turn up some new information soon."

He leaned against the car and picked his wrench back up. "I heard about the Ron Storm sculpture being stolen from the Collins family."

I nodded, watching him tighten a bolt. "It's the first stolen item with real value."

He looked up, his eyes bigger than usual, like he was surprised. "It's actually not the first Ron Storm sculpture to be taken.

"It's not?" I asked, curious.

"I know of three others in the area that have gone missing during the past year."

I shook my head, stunned. "Why didn't Bobby mention that to me?"

He lifted a shoulder. "Most of them went missing before you moved back here. I'm not sure that all of them were even reported to the police. I know about it because I'm friends with Ron's son, Aaron. Ron's been sick the last few years and isn't able to work on his art much anymore. Ron and his family view Ron's work as his legacy and they like knowing who has his pieces so they keep track of them. The whole family was pretty upset about the missing artwork."

My reporter instincts were jumping around and they were almost as hyper as Gandalf waiting for pumpkin penis cookies. "Do you have the names of the people with missing sculptures?"

My dad thought about it for a minute. "I could probably get them."

"That would really help me out. If other people had pieces lost or taken, I'd like to talk to them. Thanks, Dad."

"No problem, sweetheart. I'll let you know when I find out more."

I couldn't help but think these missing Ron Storm sculptures were also related to the robberies that were happening now. I had no idea how, but I was going to find out, and I was excited to have a lead to chase.

I texted Hawke.

> In addition to the Collins' sculpture that was just stolen, three other Ron Storm sculptures have gone missing in the past year. I don't think this is a coincidence.

He texted back.

> I don't think so either. What do you know about the other pieces?

I texted.

> Not much yet. But I'll let you know when I find out more.

I put my Jeep into drive, rounded a corner, and saw a cop car with its lights flashing pulled over in front of a house. I hadn't gotten a message from Spence that another robbery or some other incident had occurred, but since I was right there, I decided to stop and check it out anyway.

Two girls, one with blonde braids and another with a dark ponytail, stood behind a small card table that held cups and two pitchers. The sign on the front said: "Spiked Cider and Hot Chocolate $1 a cup." The 'spiked cider' part would explain why the police had been summoned. A woman, who I assumed was the mother of the girls, was standing next to them.

Officer Bob and Officer Chase Burton, one of the other Branson police officers, were standing in front of the table, drinking out of two cups.

"Hi," I said.

"Hi!" The little girl with blond braids said, flashing a giant smile. "I'm Kara, and this is Kenzie."

"Do you want a drink?" Kenzie asked. She had the same disarming smile as Kara, and that coupled with the fact that they both had names that started with a K—naming kids with the same first letter of their name was popular in Utah—made me assume they were sisters.

"Sure," I said. "I suppose I should get the hot chocolate since I'm driving." I glanced at Bobby and Chase.

"The cider is pretty good," Bobby said, tipping his glass back.

"The *spiked* cider?" I asked, putting emphasis on the 'spiked' and arching a brow.

Kara giggled, a light chiming noise, and pointed to her sign. "It says: "Spiked with Love", the 'with love' part is just super tiny."

I looked down at the sign and sure enough, 'with love' was written below 'spiked' in super tiny letters. I laughed and looked up at their mom, who was also smiling. The kids were excellent little marketers.

"Well then, I guess I'll have a spiked cider instead since Officer Bob recommends it so highly." I handed them a dollar and they worked as a team with one holding the cup and the other pouring the cider, then they handed the cider to me. I took a drink and the cinnamon and apple flavors were as delightful as Bobby said they would be.

"Were you out on patrol and saw their drink stand, or did someone call and turn them in?" I asked Bobby and Chase.

"Oh, multiple people called and asked us to do a check," Bobby said.

I was certain of that. Most of those calls were probably from people concerned for Kara and Kenzie's souls. They were also people who had no sense of humor and didn't know how to mind their own business. I guessed many of them were members of The Ladies.

"I also got calls from neighbors," the little girls' mom said. "I'm Cindy."

I rolled my eyes as I shook my head. "Of course you did. It's nice to meet you, Cindy."

Bobby shrugged. "We stopped to see what was happenin'. Some people were yellin' about child abuse in their calls. But the girls aren't breakin' the law. They're not even doin' anythin' wrong."

Cindy shrugged. "The girls came up with the idea and I thought it was hilarious, and smart. They're making a killing from people who think it's as funny as I did."

"We're going to do it all next summer with root beer!" Kara said.

They had a good marketing strategy and I had no doubt they'd continue to do well with it. I felt like it was worthy of a story in the paper, and one that might be picked up by the Utah broadcast news stations. I took a couple of photos of the adorable girls and their sign. I was in the middle of taking some notes when one of my least favorite people, Mrs. Olsen, flew up in a full-fledged tizzy with her arms waving. I was surprised she didn't arrive by broom. She was wearing a big brown overcoat that was probably very fashionable in 1963, a yellow scarf, and a hat that stuck up on both sides of her head in a way that resembled horns—a similarity I felt was rather fitting. Mrs. Olsen had declared herself the local morality manager years ago and made a point to give her opinion about right and wrong whenever possible. She and I didn't get along.

"I can't believe this," she huffed, gesturing toward the table and the sign. "These sweet little girls selling alcohol! This is horrible! Just horrible!"

Kara flashed her a bright smile. "Do you want some?"

I laughed and was impressed at Kara's ability to not be

intimidated by a woman many people in town were terrified of.

"I most certainly do not, Kara!" she said. "This isn't the kind of behavior they teach you in church!"

Kenzie blinked and flashed a smile. "We're donating half of our profits to the food pantry," she said, flashing a smile of her own.

Mrs. Olsen sputtered, not knowing what to say to that. Because according to her moral and religious foundations, supporting charities was good, but alcohol was bad. Giving money from alcohol profits to the needy was something Mrs. Olsen absolutely couldn't reconcile. Her face contorted and it was like I was witnessing her blow an actual brain fuse.

I decided I should step in before Mrs. Olsen said something even more stupid than usual. "Read the sign, Mrs. Olsen. There's not alcohol in the cider."

Mrs. Olsen squinted, then stood up like she'd never been so offended in her life. "Spiked with *love?*" She turned her judgy gaze on the little girls' mom. "You know well and good that God wants us to avoid the appearance of evil, Cindy," Mrs. Olsen said. "Wait until I tell our bishop about this!"

Cindy gave a sweet smile in return. "It's not evil," Cindy said patiently—much more patiently than I would have managed. "It's a joke."

"You're teachin' your girls horrible things," she hissed. "And you," Mrs. Olsen said, pointing at me. "This is your fault."

I stared at her, my jaw slack. "How in the world did I get roped into the blame?"

She scrunched her face up into an expression I'd only seen in movies—on an orc. "You drink coffee, wear tank tops, and do the good Lord knows what with multiple men. You're settin' a bad example for our youth and Heavenly Father will remember." She pointed her finger at me to give that last part extra emphasis.

Mrs. Olsen was the type of person who loved playing the victim, and always needed someone to blame; I was an easy target. I tried really hard not to laugh. I did not succeed. "Well, if me introducing new ideas to people is enough to sway them from their own beliefs, I imagine their faith wasn't too strong in the first place."

Mrs. Olsen gave me a solid glare and stomped off down the street, her urine colored scarf swinging in the breeze.

I turned to the girls and whispered, "She's just jealous she didn't think of it first." I gave them a wink. "The story should be in the next newspaper," I said to Cindy.

She thanked me, and I left for the office. I had some articles to write and edit before the carnival tonight.

Chapter Fifteen

I walked into the main gate, and made my way down a long walkway of intricately carved pumpkins, their faces glowing in flickering candlelight. There were carvings of favorite book characters, movies, cityscapes, and pretty much every other possible thing you could think of. The people who carved the pumpkin art were seriously talented and always impressed me. The fall Halloween carnival is almost as popular of an event as the Branson Falls fair—which is saying a lot. Everyone comes to get their fill of candy, cute costumed kids, and socializing.

The smells of garlic, fresh cheesy bread, and baked sugar hit my nostrils and the scent took me right back to a childhood full of caramel apples, friends, and carnival games. I glanced around at the tents. There was always a plethora of yummy food options to choose from, and I was starving. I really wanted to sit down and have a meal, but I needed to get more pictures, quotes, and cover the carnival first. Luckily, there were plenty of snacks available and I stopped to get one.

A little girl who couldn't have been more than eight stood

behind the counter wearing an apron and a blue and white paper hat that made her look like a pirate. "Hi," she said with a wide smile.

"Hi," I answered back, flashing a smile of my own. "I want to get a treat. What's your favorite?"

Her eyes brightened at the question and her smile got even wider. "The chocolate and candy covered Rice Krispie pop!" she said with excitement.

A Rice Krispie pop sounded as good as anything else, and it would be quick and easy to eat. "Great! I'll get that."

"It's two dollars."

I handed her the money and then waited as she left her post and went to an area I couldn't see. When she came back, she was holding a triangular Rice Krispie the size of a New York pizza slice that had been impaled with a wooden stick, drenched in chocolate, and covered in crushed candy. I had no idea what I was going to do with it.

"Thanks," I said, trying not to look overwhelmed. I pasted on an excited smile and hoped she wasn't good at reading expressions. "I can't wait to try it."

She grinned and I turned around, attempting to eat the treat. The chocolate had solidified, which was in my favor, but as I attempted to eat it, I found that the candy pieces had not all been securely attached and I was leaving a trail of treats. Tonight would be a bad night for me to start a life a crime since I'd be relatively easy to find. I also couldn't easily take notes or pictures since one hand was currently occupied holding my pizza sized pop. So I meandered around looking at the various booths while I ate, and listening to the happy, and very loud, screams from kids playing carnival games.

Drake's deep voice managed to slice through the noise. "Hey, Katie."

"How did you find me?" I asked around a bite of krispie.

"I followed the trail of candy."

I narrowed my eyes. "I don't really think that's fair. I'm not the only one with candy around here."

He gave me a look. "You seem to be the only one dropping it."

I glared.

"What is that anyway?" Drake asked, pointing to my snack.

"A Rice Krispie treat," I said, taking another bite. At this rate, I'd be eating it all night and not getting any of my work done.

"On a stick?"

I thought that was pretty obvious. "Yes. On a stick. Treats on sticks are all the Halloween rage this year." Really, I'd been as surprised about the stick addition as he was, but I wasn't admitting that to him.

He leaned over and licked a piece of candy off the krispie that was about to make an escape, then he took a bite and so help me, it was the most seductive Rice Krispie eating I'd ever experienced. He saw my reaction and grinned, slowly licking his lips as he did so. "Well, it tastes good."

While I was waiting for my common sense to return so I could form sentences, another piece of candy fell down my shirt. Fantastic. "Can you hold this for a minute," I asked him, holding out my cereal stick.

He took it from me and watched with a high level of amusement as I reached my hand down my shirt.

"Do you want some help?" Drake asked, his eyes on my chest.

177

I rolled my eyes. "I've got it."

"Because I'm more than happy to help. Really."

And I wouldn't mind him helping. But not here. In this very public place, where all the people were and plenty were undoubtedly watching us—including my mom and dad over in the food pantry booth. I gave them a wave with the hand that wasn't digging around in my bra. My mom's expression reprimanded me from all the way across the room. I fished the candy out of my cleavage and threw it in a nearby trash can before Drake handed my treat back.

"Seems like a shame to waste that candy."

"There's plenty more on the stick if you want it."

"I want it on you," he said in a low voice. And that's when I tripped, Rice Krispie and candy pieces going in every direction. It was an impressive maneuver considering I'd barely been moving. At least I didn't have to worry about the Rice Krispie treat inconvenience anymore. I picked up the remaining pieces and threw them in the trash.

I turned to Drake and hissed, "You can't say stuff like that here."

"Sure I can."

"No!" I said, eyes wide. "You can't."

"Why can't I?"

I waved my arms around. "Public! People! Phones! Cameras! Everyone! Earlobes!" I was so flustered that I couldn't make sentences and was just spouting words—all relevant words, but lacking sense-making modifiers, verbs, and conjunctions.

Drake looked at me, amused. "Your life would get so much easier if you stopped caring about what people think."

"Says the politician who has to worry about what everyone thinks."

"No, I stopped doing that a long time ago. It's the only way to survive politics."

I had no response. And it seemed Drake had decided to keep me company and was going to follow through with his whole go-to-the-carnival-with-me plan. We walked and I took pictures and stopped at various booths to talk with people and take notes. We said hello to my mom and dad as we passed. My mom gave Drake and I both a sweet smile that I knew from experience was anything but sweet. I'd surely hear about her opinions on my boob chocolate retrieval methods and mine and Drake's lack of discretion later. We were almost through the entire carnival when we got to Axel and Sasha's booth. Kids had been running around the carnival all night with the most detailed face painting I'd ever seen. Now I knew why. Axel and Sasha were doing it. "Hey!" I said with a smile. "How are you guys?"

"Good," Sasha said, her smile wide. I hadn't seen her this happy since they'd opened Inked AF. "All of these kids are adorable."

"I've been watching your line all night," Drake said. "You've been busy."

Sasha nodded. "It's been good."

"If only the shop was this busy," Axel said, disappointment lining his face.

"Things still haven't picked up?" I asked.

"No." There was an entire world of meaning in that one word.

"We've been talking about adding some other options," Sasha said. "Ways to expand and offer things people in

Branson might be more inclined to try. We're going to start offering face painting all the time. Cosplay is big here and we think we could tap into that market as well by doing makeup and temporary body art.

I nodded, thinking that was a really good idea. "Targeting cosplayers is smart. Face painting will be good for Halloween too. I'm sure you'll get a lot of business from that."

"It's a lot of work for something that gets washed off though," Axel said, his tone despondent.

I could see his point. I wouldn't want someone to take my hard work and wash it off either. "That would be frustrating."

"But it helps pay the bills so that's what matters," Sasha said, giving Axel a look.

"How is the piercing side of the business going?" I asked.

"It's keeping us above water. People love their pierced ears here," Sasha said. "And we're talking about doing some retail sales with makeup and jewelry as well."

"I think cosplay is a good idea," Drake said. "I know the people who run a few of the popular comic conventions in Utah. Let me introduce you and see if you can work together somehow."

Axel's face brightened at that. "That would be amazing. We would really appreciate that, Representative Drake."

"Please, call me Dylan," he answered. "And it's my pleasure. I like to see good people succeed."

"That would…" Sasha paused, her voice cracking. "That would mean a lot to us. We're very grateful," she said, her eyes watery.

"Happy to help," Drake said. "I'll get in touch with you next week."

"Hey," I said, "You don't happen to remember a client with

a full tattoo sleeve around town this past week, do you? A big guy, at least six-foot-three or taller and strongly resembling a linebacker." The guys who had been wandering around my neighborhood were still concerning me and I wondered if Axel and Sasha had a connection to the one with a tattoo because my house wasn't too far away from the tattoo shop. Very few people in Branson had tattoo sleeves, so I thought the guys might be there supporting Axel and Sasha. I hadn't recognized either of them, and neither had Phyllis.

Sasha and Axel both thought about it. "I can't think of anyone who fits that description," Sasha said.

"Me either," Axel agreed.

"Okay, well let me know if anyone comes to mind."

They both nodded.

The next kids in line were anxiously waiting their turn and I didn't want to deprive them of the masterpiece Axel and Sasha had in store for them.

"I'll talk to you both later," I said, giving Sasha a quick hug and then walking away with Drake.

I leaned in so my voice wasn't too loud. "Thanks for doing that for Axel and Sasha. It's been a struggle since they opened, and I've been worried about them."

He lifted his shoulder in a negating way. "I don't like to see anyone suffering, especially when there's something I can do to help."

"I know they appreciate it, and I think it's really admirable of you."

He flashed his perfect smile. "Anything to make you happy, Katie."

I frowned. That "anything" part is what worried me.

We started to walk to another booth when I saw Jackie

Wall in line for Inked AF's face painting. I was surprised to see her there since she'd literally been holding the largest, and most glittery, protest sign during the Inked AF shop opening. "Hi, Jackie," I said.

She looked at me, then at Drake standing next to me. Realization that we were there together flitted across her face and I swore I saw murder in her eyes before she pasted on the fakest smile I'd ever seen. Like, so fake that she probably deserved some sort of award for it.

"Kate," she said, trying to keep the distaste for me from her tone. I found her dislike of me amusing. She was a bully and when I had interactions with her, I refused to let her BS slide. She resented me for speaking up and calling her out, so I tried to do it frequently. I read a quote once that said, "Some people won't like you because your spirit irritates their demons." I kind of wanted to high-five my spirit for being so antagonizing. She turned her attention to Drake and her entire demeanor changed, her face softening into a sweet facade that concealed a slew of razor sharp teeth. "Drake, it's *so* good to see you," she said, taking his hand.

I rolled my eyes. I knew Drake had no interest in Jackie Wall, though she'd been throwing herself at him for years.

"Good to see you, too, Jackie." He noticed her spot in line and gave her a quizzical look. "Are you here to get your face painted?"

She threw her head back in an exaggerated laugh. "Oh no, I'm holding a spot for my daughter while she's over at the dart booth."

"You're letting your daughter get her face painted?" I asked, confusion showing in the angle of my brows.

She moved her gaze to me slowly like she was deigning to give me attention. "Of course I am."

"You realize it's Inked AF doing the face painting? And you've been one of their loudest protesters."

She rolled her eyes. "This is paint, Kate. Not a tattoo. I fail to see how the two compare."

Jackie failed to see a lot of things.

"Will we be seeing you at the trunk-or-treat this year, Dylan?" Jackie asked.

I had strong opinions on trunk-or-treats and firmly felt that kids, especially kids in small towns where everyone knows everyone, should have to work for their candy not simply wander around a parking lot.

"Maybe," Drake said. "I'll have to see how my schedule lines up."

"Well," Jackie put a hand on his forearm and squeezed a little, "I really hope you're there. I always love seeing what costume you've chosen."

My eyebrows went up at that. I didn't realize Drake frequented the trunk-or-treat, or that he dressed up.

"What will you be going as?" I asked Jackie. Because I had some suggestions.

She batted her eyelashes at Drake like she was trying to be demure—that was not an easy feat for her. "It's a surprise."

"Well, you should definitely check to make sure your costume can accommodate an entire flock of flying monkeys," I said with a sweet smile, then took Drake's arm and walked away.

Drake managed to hold his laugh in for about five seconds. "You know you're making her hate you even more."

DESTINY FORD

I shrugged. "She's a manipulative bully who refuses to take responsibility for her actions and loves to play the victim. Most people are too afraid to stand up to her or call her out on her behavior. I have no problem being the person who pushes back."

Drake put his hand on mine, his eyes soft. "It's one of the things I admire most about you."

My heart did a little flip flop as Drake steered me toward a booth with freshly caramelized nuts. It smelled like paradise and I closed my eyes, letting my olfactory receptors bathe in joy, and in the process, I almost ran straight into a giant squirrel. "Sorry," I muttered, trying to steady us both. At first I thought it was another kid in a costume, but then I realized I'd seen this particular squirrel before. Nut Man. "Hey, Nut Man!" I said, happy to see him. "I've been working on the story about your Vendetta League and the Speedy Superheroes."

"Thank you," he said, putting his hands together in a praying gesture and giving me a little bow.

I'd never been bowed to before and it made me slightly uncomfortable. I put that aside and continued, "How many members does the Vendetta League have now?"

He thought about it for a minute. "Over thirty."

That was more than I was expecting. "You said there were five of you in the Vendetta League to start. Did you all split the cost of the application fee?"

Nut Man shook his head. "No, one of the members covered it."

"The whole thing?" I asked, surprised. It was a thousand dollars. That wasn't cheap. I could pay my rent for two months with that.

"Yeah," Nut Man confirmed. "They said they could take care of it. None of us argued."

"How long ago was this?" I asked.

"We put the application in and paid the fee around six months ago."

That coincided with everything the Speedy Superheroes spokesperson had told me about the chapter approval process. But I was still curious about the person who had bankrolled their application.

"Any chance I can talk to the person who paid for the application fee? I'd like to know more about how they got involved with the Speedy Superhero organization and why they're so passionate about it." Passionate enough to drop a grand on an extracurricular activity.

Nut Man shook his head slowly. "I wish I could help, but that superhero hasn't been at any of the gatherings recently."

That seemed odd. They paid a thousand dollars for an organization they weren't even planning to continue participating in? "How long has it been since you've seen them?"

"A couple of months at least."

But the chapter had only been around for six months. "Any idea why this person stopped attending?"

Nut Man shook his oversized head again. "We only see each other when patrols are assigned and that's all done through the website. Available superheroes join the patrols. The person who paid the application fee for us hasn't joined patrols for a while."

Interesting. "Okay, well if they come back or you see them anywhere, let me know. I'd love to talk to them more."

Nut Man nodded and Drake and I walked away.

"Nut Man?" Drake asked, bemused.

"You can read all about it in the next issue of the *Tribune*."

He chuckled. "I thought I met some pretty interesting people in my line of work, but I think you have me beat."

"You have no idea," I said.

My phone started belting out "Forever In Blue Jeans," Spence's ring tone. Drake tried to hold back a laugh. He thought my Neil ringtones were hilarious. Except for his.

"Hey," I said, answering. "I'm at the carnival. What's up?"

"Another robbery," Spence said.

My eyes went wide. Now would be a perfect time for a crime since almost everyone in town was at the carnival and a criminal would have their pick of almost any house on any street.

"Where at?" I asked, grabbing my keys and hurrying toward the door.

"Inked AF."

My eyes went wide and I raced to my car, Drake close on my heels.

Chapter Sixteen

I pulled up to Inked AF to see the front door smashed open. It looked like someone had thrown a very heavy rock through it. The bright moon reflected in the fragments of glass on the ground and the door was partially open.

"This doesn't look good," Drake pointed out obviously.

I sighed. "Axel and Sasha are going to be devastated." Since we'd beaten them to the store, I guessed that they hadn't heard about the robbery yet.

Bobby came out the front door, saw me, and shook his head. "It's a mess in there."

"Was anything taken? Or was it an act of vandalism?"

Bobby looked back at the shop. "We'll have to wait and see what Axel and Sasha say after they walk through, but right now it looks like vandalism."

Fred and his wife, Molly, were standing by their antique store, watching the situation play out. "This is such a horrible shame," Molly said. "They're good kids trying to make it and they don't deserve to be treated this way."

I couldn't agree more. "Were you here during the robbery?" I asked them.

"Molly had run over to Sticks and Pie to grab us dinner. I was in the back working on a piece I recently got in," Fred said. "I heard glass crashing and thought someone was in the shop. When I got out to the front, I saw the glass on the ground and called the police."

"Did you see anyone?"

Fred shook his head. "They must have left before I got there, or maybe they went out the back way."

"Any cameras in the area?" I asked Bobby.

"Not that we know of."

A car came screeching to a halt in front of the store and Axel and Sasha jumped out. Sasha looked at the front door, the glass and their plans for the future littering the sidewalk, and immediately broke down in tears. Molly went over to comfort her. Axel's expression wavered between defeated and rage. I felt awful for them. They spent some time talking to Bobby and walking through the store while I waited and asked some questions of the other officers. When the officers gave me the okay, I took photos. Axel and Sasha finally came out of the store and I went over to them. "I'm so sorry."

"Maybe it was a mistake to come here," Sasha said.

I shook my head. "No. You need to be here. Your presence matters. Not only because you matter, but because being here is showing the people who live in Branson Falls and communities like it that just because you're different, it doesn't mean you're bad or scary. You're brave and I hope you continue to stand your ground."

Sasha sniffed at my words. "Thank you," she said, giving me a hug.

"Were you able to tell if anything was taken?"

"Four of our art pieces hanging on the walls," Axel said. "They were all pieces I'd painted."

My heart clenched at that. Having someone break into his space and take his personal property was one thing, but when that property included something he'd created from his heart using his talent, it must feel like a whole different level of violation.

"Do you have insurance?" Drake asked.

Axel nodded. "We'll be able to cover the damages and the missing pieces. But I don't know how long we'll be able to stay in town if something doesn't change."

"There was another note left on the front desk by our computer," Sasha said. "We gave it to the police"

My eyes widened. "What did it say?"

"We warned you. Get out, or you'll get worse next time." Sasha looked totally defeated as she relayed the message.

I pulled Sasha in for a hug and could feel the tears falling on my shoulder. I glanced at Drake and Axel across from me. Axel looked as discouraged as Sasha. "The police will put more patrols on your building. We're going to find out who did this and make sure it doesn't happen again. No one is going to run you out of town or stop you from pursuing your dreams."

Drake patted Axel on the shoulder. "I'll get you in contact with my convention friends and make sure you're in business for a long time."

"You're talented and excellent at what you do," I said, putting my hand on Sasha's arm. "The police will figure out who did this."

Axel looked off in the distance like he wasn't even really

there. I was sure he was absorbing everything that had happened and trying to process it all.

"Let me know if you need anything," I said.

They both nodded, and I walked over to talk to Bobby.

"Sasha and Axel said a note was left. Did they tell you they also had threatening notes left at Inked AF and mailed to them before it opened?"

Bobby nodded.

"Can I see the note?"

Bobby shrugged. "Sure, follow me."

I walked into the building with him where the note was still sitting by the computer and hadn't been picked up for evidence yet. It was a standard white paper, with the words printed in a large Times New Roman font. There was nothing about the letter that would help me track down the author of it. "Do you think you'll be able to get prints off the letter?" I asked.

"Don't know, but we'll try."

Branson Falls was a small police department which meant any analysis would have to be sent off to a lab and it would be awhile before we heard back. "Let me know if you hear anything."

Bobby nodded. "Will do."

Drake and I walked back to the car.

"I need to get these notes written up and start this story, but I can drop you back at the carnival," I said.

Drake nodded and leaned against the door as I drove. "That's the first time a business has been targeted by the thieves."

I'd had the same thought. "That's true."

"Doesn't that seem strange?"

I shrugged. "If they're looking for items they can sell, businesses are full of them, and those items are usually harder to trace."

"Yeah, but they didn't take anything that was generic and easy to sell. They took Axel's original art."

"It's odd," I agreed. "It feels different than the other robberies. Like this person had a vendetta against Axel, Sasha, or the shop."

"That wouldn't be shocking considering the amount of pushback they got when they moved into town," Drake said.

"Almost as much pushback as I got when I became the *Tribune's* newspaper editor."

"Well," Drake said with a grin as I pulled into the parking lot of the community center where the carnival was being held, "you *are* a Democrat."

I rolled my eyes. "See, this is exactly why a relationship between us would never work. We can add our difference in political ideologies to the top of the list—"

Suddenly Drake was right there, and closing his mouth over mine. His mouth was soft but with a touch of pressure as our lips parted. One of his hands tangled into the back of my hair, pulling me closer, while the other ran down my side, hesitating on my chest and continuing a trail down to my hip. I reached my arms around his neck, pulling him to me. He smelled like the woods after a rainstorm and I could kiss him like this forever. He pulled away, taking a piece of me with him. "I'm great at compromises, and I love a challenge. You give me both, Katie. And I can't get enough."

I couldn't either, and my eyes must have told him so.

He swore under his breath, a serious swear—which was

kind of a big deal for a Mormon—and opened the car door. "I'll see you. Soon."

It wasn't a statement. It was a promise. And every womanly part of me reacted to it.

Drake shut the door and I sat there for a full minute, stunned. Kissing Drake was always like kissing a fairy tale. He was the handsome prince fairy tales had taught me to yearn for as a child, and the same prince I'd rebelled hotly against as an adult. But holy ovaries, I was yearning. His lips were soft, his body hard, and he was everything I'd ever dreamed of, both physically, and as a person—I mean, aside from the whole Republican bit. Still, he was a good man, in every sense of the word, and I could easily see myself getting lost in him.

In that moment, I had a sudden realization that the getting lost part was one of the things that scared me. Drake was a force. So was I. I needed someone who would fan my flames, not try to contain them. I wasn't sure if Drake was capable of that. I worried that he'd try to overshadow me or mold me into something I wasn't—those things didn't make for a healthy relationship. I'd been trying to analyze my feelings about Drake and Hawke for months and was grateful for the realization. It was another thing to think about as I considered my future, and who I wanted it to be with.

I slid my Jeep into drive and went home.

Since my mom and dad had both been at the carnival tonight, Gandalf had stayed home alone. The goddesses only knew what he'd gotten into while I was gone. I'd probably walk into puppy rumspringa. I worried, but in all honestly, Gandalf was actually pretty good when I left him alone. He was a confident and independent little guy, and he had a whole trunk of toys and a doggy door and knew how to use them. I didn't like leaving him for long periods of time, like all day, but a few hours here and there was fine. I suspected that he mostly slept when I wasn't around, but I was seriously considering a doggy cam to check in.

I pulled into the driveway and shut the garage. I was on my way inside when I saw Phyllis coming up to my house. "Kate! Kate!" she said, waving her hands. I wondered if she had some pressing reality show information to share. "I'm so glad you're home. I almost called you. Gandalf was barking up a storm!"

"He was?" I asked, worried. He rarely barked unless he heard something unusual outside.

She nodded and we both rushed to the door to check on him.

I opened the lock and Gandalf came bounding up to me, his tail wagging and licks all over my hands before he did a series of spins and went running out to the backyard to zoom around it.

"He seems okay," I said. "Let me check the rest of the house."

I walked through, flipping lights on as I went, and nothing seemed out of the ordinary. I went back to meet Phyllis at the door. "Everything here looks okay. It must have been something outside." Gandalf came running back into the house and was doing his best to trip us all.

Phyllis put a hand to her chest and breathed out a grateful sigh. "I'm so relieved! You know how much I love your little guy." She bent down to give him a pet.

"Did you see anything out of the ordinary while he was barking?"

She shook her head. "I got up a few times to look out the window. There were some people walking up and down the street, but that's not unusual."

"Did you recognize them?"

"No," she said. "It was too dark to see faces, but they were some bigger guys."

"Like the ones we saw wandering on our street the other day?"

She put her finger to her lips and thought about it. "Maybe."

That didn't make me feel better. "I'm sure it's nothing," I said, trying to be reassuring. "Let me walk you home, and you make sure to lock your doors."

"Oh, Kate," she said with a laugh. "I always do." I wasn't confident in that fact since most Branson residents had lived there for a lifetime and couldn't fathom someone entering their homes uninvited. The recent robberies had changed some door locking opinions though.

I walked her home, Gandalf in tow, and then immediately went home, shut the door, and followed my own advice. I hated fear and paranoia. Gandalf was a good guard dog though, and made me feel better. I kept all my outside lights on, and some inside ones too, then wrote up my notes for the carnival story and the break-in at Inked AF. I fell asleep curled up next to Gandalf and thinking about who would have targeted a tattoo shop, and why they'd taken Axel's art.

Chapter Seventeen

"I heard you were fondling your own boobs in front of Drake at the carnival last night," Ella said as I dropped my bags on my desk the next morning. "And that Drake looked like he wanted to help."

She was standing in the corner like a specter and had startled me so much that I almost dropped my coffee mug. I took a deep breath with the hope that it would give me enough patience not to march immediately over to Amber Kane and Jackie Wall's houses and punch them both right in the boobs. I'd had self-defense training and that combined with my current rage left me feeling pretty confident I could break an implant or four with my bare hands.

"I wasn't fondling myself," I defended. "I dropped some chocolate candy down my shirt and had to get it out before it melted all over my bra like chocolate lava."

Ella's expression was dubious.

"Did you hear about this from The Ladies?" I asked, already knowing the answer.

"The Facebook page had all sorts of gossip from the event, but your post is the most popular one."

Of course it was. I hadn't heard any reports about Drake and I kissing in the car though, so hopefully that had gone unnoticed. "I'm surprised no one tried to talk to me or call me a hussy directly at the carnival." I had no tolerance for people who spoke unkindly about me behind my back but refused to say it to my face. They were cowards, plain and simple.

"People were busy with their kids," Ella said.

"But not too busy to watch my every move."

Spence's voice came from his office. "It was kinda hard to miss from what I understand."

"Not you too!"

He came out of the room, leaned against the door frame, and shrugged.

"Why weren't you there?" I asked Ella.

She tapped her phone. "I had active bids!"

I wondered if she realized that Not Just Junk was taking over her life. They probably used the same addiction tools as social media and casinos.

"Jackie was none too pleased about you being at the carnival with Drake, I'll have you know," Ella said.

"Well, I wasn't very pleased about having to deal with her either, so the feeling is mutual."

"Jackie said you made some horrific reference to flying monkeys?"

I rolled my eyes. "Horrific? Really? I simply inferred that Jackie would need to make sure her costume could accommodate her flock of flying monkeys."

Spence spit out his coffee and laughed. "Oh good grief, you're going to start a Lady war."

THE DEVIL HAS TATTOOS

I gave him a look. "I'm pretty sure they started that with me as soon as I moved back to Branson Falls. I'm not the one with an entire Facebook Group dedicated to gossiping about them."

Spence tilted his head in concession and changed the subject. "What did you find out about the robbery at Inked AF?"

I took a sip of my coffee. "The front door was shattered with a rock. Police weren't sure if it was vandalism or a robbery at first, but the thieves took four pieces of Axel's art."

"Do you think it was the same person who has been committing the other robberies?" Spence asked.

I shook my head. I'd been thinking about it all night. "I don't think so. It was a business instead of a house, and they stole something personal to Axel. It felt more like vandalism than a robbery. I think the person who did it was probably someone who isn't happy about having a tattoo and piercing shop in town and they were hoping to get Axel and Sasha to leave."

"Do you think they will?" Spence asked.

"I'm not sure. I hope not, but I know Axel and Sasha have been struggling."

"That's too bad. I hope they'll give it time to make it work."

"They might still. They have some good ideas for expanding into things that people in the area might be more receptive to."

My phone buzzed with a text.

Don't forget about the event tonight. Your outfit is in your living room.

I frowned at my phone and texted back.

> How did you get in my house?

He sent me a gif back indicating that was a silly question and he could basically do anything he wanted, including sneaking into a terrorist camp if he was so inclined—and he probably had.

I responded with a gif back rolling my eyes.

> I'll pick you up at six sharp.

Six meant I'd have to be home a lot earlier than that to see what outfit he'd chosen for me, and figure out how to style my hair and makeup to compliment it. I was hoping it was a real outfit and not a costume like I'd suspected. Then again, if it was a costume, I wouldn't need to worry about hair and makeup. I'd probably be wearing a full animal head.

I texted back.

> I'll be ready.

I worked on the carnival and Inked AF robbery stories and then got a call from my dad.

"Hi, Kate. I got the name of the other people missing Ron Storm sculptures."

"Great!" I said, grabbing a pen.

"Brady Gard, Carter Finn, and Laura Innot."

"Perfect! I'll find their numbers and give them a call."

"I also told Aaron Storm you were looking into the pieces and that you might contact him. I asked him to let you know if he had any other information."

That was really nice of him. "You're really hitting the whole dad thing out of the park today," I said.

He laughed. "I try."

I hung up the phone and looked up the numbers for Brady, Carter, and Laura. I called Brady first. He said his Ron Storm wood sculpture had gone missing during a move. They'd built a house and they suspected it was put in a mislabeled box, but after they were done unpacking, they never found it.

Carter told me his sculpture was an heirloom passed down from his dad. It had gone missing around the same time his dad had passed away and he assumed another family member had grabbed it. He didn't care as long as it was in the hands of someone who would take care of it and love it as much as his dad had.

The only person who was adamant that their sculpture had been stolen was Laura. "You're certain it wasn't misplaced somewhere?" I asked.

"Definitely. My husband and I came home from a trip to Salt Lake and the back door was unlocked. I never leave it unlocked. We have a cat and she's usually pretty mellow, but she seemed totally freaked out when we got home. She was meowing like crazy and didn't want to leave our sides. Nothing was disturbed but I had a feeling like someone had been in my space, you know?"

I did, unfortunately.

"I looked around the house and nothing seemed out of the ordinary or misplaced so I locked the doors and we went to bed. I didn't notice the sculpture missing until I dusted later that week. I reported it to the police, but by then there was really nothing they could do."

"Do you have any idea who might have wanted it?"

She paused like she was thinking. "No. There are a lot of collectors who buy Ron Storm's pieces. I imagine it was someone who wanted to sell the piece. The police said they'd let me know if it ever turned up, but I haven't seen it since."

"I'm sorry. I hope it will get back to you one day."

"Me too. Let me know if you need help with anything else."

"Thank you," I said, hanging up.

I sat back in my chair and wove my pen between my fingers as I thought about it. In addition to the Collins' Ron Storm sculpture, there were three other missing pieces, and only two of the four were stolen for sure. It made me wonder how many of his other sculptures were also missing or stolen that we didn't know about. My dad said Ron Storm had been sick for a while, but his family kept a list of the people who owned his sculptures. If someone had lost or stolen pieces, the Storm family would probably know more about it than the police. I needed to ask the Storms some questions.

I grabbed my bag and keys. "Where are you going?" Spence asked.

"To talk to Aaron Storm."

Aaron Storm's house was a palatial white brick affair in the French colonial style that sat smack in the middle of about five acres of land. I wasn't sure what Aaron Storm did for a living, but whatever it was, he did it well. I knocked on a giant crimson red door that had to be twelve feet tall and five feet wide. I hoped he didn't have toddlers. They'd never be able to get the door open. The house had a video doorbell and within seconds, I heard the microphone click on and a pleasant female voice say, "One moment, please."

I waited patiently, trying not to make any weird faces on the camera that could be used against me later.

The door swung open revealing a tall, lithe woman with stunning red hair and the prettiest emerald eyes I'd ever seen, holding a baby. She looked about thirty thanks to Botox, but was probably closer to forty, and her smile seemed familiar. I was sure I'd seen her around town. "Hi," I said. "I'm Kate Saxee, the editor of the *Branson Tribune*. I'm working on a story and was hoping I could talk to Aaron. Is he home?"

The woman's smile stretched, warming her entire face. "Of course! You're Damon Saxee's daughter. He said you might be stopping by. Come in!"

"I'm Cadence," the red head said as I followed her through their mansion, complete with sweeping staircases, iron stair rails, and an intricate glass chandelier that hung down from a twenty foot ceiling. It was beautiful, and it would be a royal pain to clean. Then again, they probably had a housekeeper to do that for them.

Aaron was in his study on the main floor. Cadence led me inside. "Babe?" Cadence said, opening the door. Aaron glanced up, his eyes clear and his expression kind. He was wearing a dress shirt and pants with a dark blue tie. He looked like he was in his mid-forties, some of his dark brown hair greying at his temples, but the grey was the only thing that gave his age away. He seemed fit, and I noticed several medals behind him on a shelf and pictures of him running in races. He must be some kind of marathoner. "This is Kate Saxee, Damon's daughter."

Aaron's smile widened. "I've heard a lot about you from

Damon and I read your articles in the *Tribune*. It's nice to finally meet you."

"Thanks," I said, smiling back. "My dad's been telling me about you too. I've been investigating the Ron Storm sculpture that was recently stolen from the Collins family. My dad said other sculptures have gone missing in the past year as well. I have a couple of questions for you about those if that's okay?"

The baby started to cry and Cadence excused herself, though her wide eyes made me think she was interested in the conversation and would have liked to stay around.

"Sure," Aaron said, motioning to one of the chairs in front of his desk. He came around and sat in the chair next to me. It was a nice gesture, and a way to be disarming and let me know we were on the same level, as opposed to him sitting across the desk from me in a position of authority. I appreciated that and it immediately made the interview feel less formal.

"I've been told that three sculptures have gone missing in the last year, four if you count the one that was stolen from the Collins family."

He nodded.

"How did you find out about the other pieces?"

"We keep record of all of the owners of my dad's work. When someone buys one of his pieces, they agree to keep us notified of where the piece is. If they choose to sell it, our family gets the first option to buy it back at current market value."

"Do people always comply with the request to notify your family and sell it to you first?"

He shifted in his seat, crossing one leg so his ankle rested on his other knee. "Generally they do. There's a hefty fine if they don't. Most people would rather do something as simple as send an email than have the threat of the fine hanging over their heads."

A fine? This was serious art ownership. "I imagine an agreement like that makes your dad's pieces even more valuable."

Aaron tilted his head to the side. "It definitely helps. They're one of a kind pieces and people like owning rare things."

Having that much control over Ron Storm's pieces could also help the Storm family inflate the prices.

"Who manages the inventory of pieces?" I asked.

"My brother and I."

"Do you both do it full time?"

Aaron shook his head. "No, I'm a financial planner and my brother works in marketing. My dad's work is something we oversee on the side so my mom doesn't have to worry about it. She's got her hands full taking care of my dad."

I nodded, feeling for them. I couldn't imagine watching a parent decline in health and wasn't looking forward to the day when I'd have to.

"What do you do in cases like the ones I mentioned above—where people simply don't know where the pieces are?"

He lifted a shoulder. "There's not much we can do in those cases. We try to watch private sellers, but there are many, and the underground art world is so massive that it's almost impossible. But it's heartbreaking. My dad's health has been in decline for some time. He's not able to work much at all anymore. The pieces that currently exist are likely the only pieces that ever will."

"I'm sorry to hear about your dad's health."

"Thank you."

A little girl with strawberry blonde curls came running into the room dressed like Wonder Woman complete with the bracelets and crown. I wasn't sure if that was her daily outfit, or special seasonal attire for Halloween, but I felt an immediate kinship with the little Amazon. "Daddy!" she yelled. She jumped into Aaron's arms and gave him a huge hug.

"Hi, pumpkin," he said. "Did you have fun playing outside?"

"Yes!" she said with enthusiasm. "I jumped in leaves and beat the bad guys!"

She was freaking adorable.

"Come jump with me!" she said, tugging at his hand.

He laughed. "Give me a few more minutes and I will."

"I've taken up more than enough of your time," I said, standing. "Thank you for your candor and for being willing to meet with me."

"Of course," Aaron said, rising.

"Have fun playing in the leaves," I said to them both.

He chuckled. "It took me two hours yesterday to rake them up. I imagine it will take another two hours tonight." He watched his daughter go running outside. "But it's worth it."

I smiled at him as I left and could see why my dad liked him so much. His wife and kids were the quintessential perfection many Utah families endeavored to become, and he seemed like a good guy. The background about his family and the sculptures was also helpful, though it didn't seem to point me in any direction to continue my search. I knew Hawke was on the lookout for any Ron Storm sculptures going up for sale. Hopefully he'd get a hit and we could go from there.

Chapter Eighteen

Since I wasn't sure where Hawke and I were going tonight, what we were doing, or what I'd be wearing, I thought I better grab a late lunch before heading back to the office to finish things up.

I stopped at Fry Guy and got a chicken sandwich, fries with the best fry sauce—a mixture of mayo and ketchup—in the state, and an Oreo milkshake. I probably shouldn't have gotten that, especially considering my lack of information about tonight's events, but fat and carb filled comfort food sounded the best. A bright neon sign on the counter announced that the fast food place would soon be offering tater tots and a taco salad option. My brows rose. That was not going to make Tres Tacos, the Mexican fast food place, happy in the least. Tater tots and taco salads were their staples. I wondered if they knew about it yet. Tres Tacos and Fry Guy co-existed in small town fast food harmony because of their vastly different food offerings. This menu change was an unabashed act of aggression by Fry Guy.

I was contemplating the fight that would break out between them when Bobby came in.

"Hey ya, Kate."

"Hi, Bobby. What are you doing here?" I wondered if Tres Tacos had already heard about the tater tot mutiny and Bobby was here preemptively.

"Gettin' some food. Long day."

I nodded in agreement. "Hey," I said, still thinking about my conversation with Aaron Storm. "Aside from the Collins' robbery, were there ever reports filed for other missing Ron Storm art pieces?"

Bobby thought about it for a minute. "I'd have to check. I remember one a while ago, but that's it."

"It was probably Laura Innot. She reported her piece stolen in the past year."

"That sounds right," he said, putting a finger to his lips. "How did you find out about that?"

"My dad mentioned more than one Ron Storm sculpture has gone missing or been stolen recently. I was looking into it to see if that was maybe a motive for the robberies."

Bobby lifted his hand and stroked his chin with his fingers as he thought. "Interestin'. Only one house had a Ron Storm though. Why were the others robbed?"

I shrugged. "That's what I'm trying to figure out."

My food order was called.

"Let me know if you hear anythin' or have other ideas," Bobby said.

"I will," I answered, taking a bite of my shake as I walked out the door. It was creamy with the perfect ratio of Oreo to ice cream and I was going to enjoy it for the rest of the afternoon while trying not to think of my outing with Hawke tonight.

It wasn't a costume, but it might as well have been.

I gave myself one last look in the mirror. When I'd taken the dress out of the box, I'd thought Hawke might have confused the word "dress" with "lingerie" and had perhaps lied to me about the *Eyes Wide Shut* party. I'd pulled it on thanks to prayer, and it had fallen in beautiful folds down my body. The whole dress was lace, bright red, with intricate lattice designs, and to say it was form fitting was an understatement. I was worried I'd break a seam or five from breathing. It had a plunging neckline that showed more of my boobs than anyone other than my past boyfriends had seen, short cap sleeves, and it fell to the floor, the back of it pooling slightly in a tiny train. A slit went up the right side that threatened to show everyone my lady bits if I moved the wrong way. We were either going to a very fancy party, or the slit was like the tear strip on bags from the grocery store—the ones that help get you started at tearing things, and we weren't really going anywhere. Truly, the dress was gorgeous, and fancier than anything I'd ever worn in my life. And it probably cost more than my Jeep...which was a sobering thought.

A knock sounded on the door. Normally Gandalf, chief notifier of the house, would have been on guard and barking like crazy. But since I wasn't sure about the night's events or when I would be home, he was having a sleepover at my mom and dad's.

I picked up my clutch containing essentials like lipstick, and opened the door to find Hawke wearing a black dress shirt, a red tie that matched my dress color perfectly, and a black tuxedo that draped over him exquisitely in the way only outrageously expensive clothes do. He was intimidating normally, but Hawke in a tux was a whole new level. He stood in the door frame, taking up all the space—polished, refined, and powerful. His cool countenance betrayed nothing. He could be planning to take me to bed, or he could be planning to murder someone. I really had no idea. And I'd never been more turned on.

His eyes trailed over me from head to toe. When they finally came to rest on my face, they were a deep green, and looked like they'd been heated from within. Every part of my body felt like it was tuned to a channel only Hawke was broadcasting and that channel was screaming at me to rip his clothes off. Based on the barely contained lust in his expression, I had a feeling his parts were screaming the same thing. We might not make it to the super-secret rendezvous.

"I'm not interested in the event anymore. Let's stay here," he said.

"I thought this was for work?"

"It is. And I don't care."

I pushed him out the door and locked it behind me. "One of us has to be responsible." Something flashed behind me, a blink of light, and I whipped my head around squinting into the darkness to see what it was. But I didn't notice anything out of the ordinary. It was probably just some car headlights on the street.

We walked out to the driveway where a sleek, silver Audi R8 sat. Seriously?! Hawke had an Audi R8? That was in addition to the sexy '67 Shelby Mustang and black as pitch Harley he usually drove during warmer months. He had a garage on his property almost as big as his house and I still hadn't been in it. I'd always wondered what other treasures it contained. Now I knew one of them, and wanted to see the rest.

He opened the car door for me and I slid inside while trying to arrange the slit so I didn't flash every traffic camera on the way to wherever it was we were going. Hawke got in the other side and the car immediately felt like there wasn't enough air. Hawke took up a lot of space, and his presence commanded even more of it than the average man.

He turned the engine over as his eyes slowly moved down my body and then back up in a way that felt like a stroke of his hand. "That color is beautiful on you."

"The color of blood?"

His eyes heated and I couldn't decide if I was turned on by the fact that blood did it for him, or terrified by it.

"That red lipstick isn't going to last, either," he warned.

"It better. Otherwise everyone is going to remember your date as the one who looked like the Joker with boobs."

His lips moved into a slow, sensual smile as he turned onto the street and we started our journey. "Or they'll remember you as the one who had six orgasms in the car."

I swallowed, trying to get enough moisture back in my throat to respond. "Six, huh?"

"We'll start low." He gave me a wink.

It was a really good thing the dress had a slit that ran all the way to China, and the lace gave it air movement because I was burning up. I reached over and attempted to fiddle with the air controls. I'd never been in a car that cost more than a house so I had no idea how to make any of the fancy things work.

"It's really hot in here," I explained. I started giving myself a little pep talk in my head that went: Don't think of how he looks good enough to lick in his tuxedo, or how much you actually want to rip it off him and start a taste test.

Hawke swore under his breath. "It could get a lot hotter."

I needed to change the subject, and fast.

"Do you realize the amount of restraint it has taken me to not ask more questions about tonight?"

His lips tipped up. "Oh, I know."

"I don't like secrets."

"I know that too."

"Are you going to give me any information about this evening?"

He went silent for about ten years just to exasperate me before finally answering, "It's a very private auction about an hour away. I have no idea what will be sold there. I'm not going for the items; I'm going for the networking and information."

An auction? I'd always wanted to go to one, but was worried I'd have to sneeze and accidentally end up buying a gold toilet.

"So are we buying things at this very private auction?"

"I will, because it's important to look like we're there for the items, not recon."

Ah ha. "So I'm here to help distract people while you observe them, network, and get the information you're looking for?"

"Exactly."

I breathed a little sigh of relief that I wouldn't be wearing a mask and getting naked in front of a room full of people.

He looked over at me. "Relieved?"

I gave him a look as he hit the gas to get around another car. The engine purred and the sound went straight to my core.

"I can't believe you have an Audi R8 and I didn't know about it." I let a hint of annoyance show in my tone. There were a lot of things I didn't know about when it came to Hawke.

"The Ferrari seemed a little too flashy for this evening, though it would have worked as well."

My eyes were the size of the Branson Falls rodeo champion's belt buckle. "Is that a joke? Because I really can't tell if you're joking?"

One corner of his lips ticked up. "It's not a joke."

My mouth fell open. "You own a Ferrari?!"

"Two."

My jaw dropped even more, and this time I was pretty sure it hit the floor. "What do you do for a living?!?" I tried not to shout. I did not succeed.

"Lots of things."

Murder. He murdered people. I knew it. I was sure he had good justifications for it, but seriously, he wasn't that much older than me...maybe early-thirties. There weren't many things you could do by that age that paid as well as Hawke seemed to be paid. He couldn't possibly own the things he did and not be killing people to afford them. As the car glided down the road like we were being carried on a cloud, I had the uncomfortable thought that despite the fact that he could very well be a mercenary and a murderer, his car collection might be able to make me forgive those things entirely. Selective ethics and all.

Regardless, if a relationship were to ever happen between us, I needed some answers from him. I needed him to open up and let me in. If he didn't, I wasn't sure how we could build a bond. Hawke glanced over at me. He must have sensed my frustration.

"Life wasn't always like this for me," he said, his expression tight.

I looked at him, surprised that he was opening up. I waited to see if he would go on.

"My childhood was difficult. I left as soon as I was able. I had a certain skillset that fit well with the military, so that's where I went. I moved up the ranks quickly, and did things that still haunt me to this day. Over the years, I've learned how to deal with them, but it doesn't mean I don't have regrets about some of my actions.

"Is there a particular regret you want to tell me about?"

The corner of his lips turned down in an expression that told me that question was not easy to answer.

When I'd first met Hawke, I'd done a background check on him and didn't find anything shocking. Then again, he could have had information redacted from his files, he'd told me in the past that he carefully managed his image and personal and professional information. I was curious about his history and what he'd been through, but didn't want to push him too far. I decided to give him a nudge and see where it went.

"I did a background check on you when we first started working together months ago on the Bradford case. I didn't see a criminal record or anything shocking."

A muscle worked at his jaw. "Because there isn't one."

I had so many questions, but I had a feeling Hawke opening up like this with anyone was new, and rare. If I pushed him, he wouldn't keep talking. I needed to be there for him. To let him know I wasn't afraid of his ghosts.

He kept going. "My point is I'm not the knight in shining armor you were taught to want. I know you're working through things. You're trying to figure out your feelings, what you want for a future, and who you want as a partner. I'm not saying I'm going to be that person, but if I'm anywhere close to being on your list, you deserve to know the real me—and the real me isn't always on the side that many people view as good. I'm not the white knight. I survived by embracing darkness and while I do my best to err on the side of good, that's a very subjective line."

Ah, so he was trying to protect me. He didn't want to push me away, but he also wanted to make sure I knew what I was getting into. I did. I already knew that Hawke's business wasn't entirely on the up-and-up. I knew he had a history, and some of it would be shocking. It worried me because I didn't know how his past would affect our potential relationship, but it wasn't going to push me away either. I knew he had a dark side—we all did. I wasn't afraid of his.

"Are you telling me this to try and scare me?" I asked.

"No. I'm telling you this because I want you to be aware of what you're getting into. I'm compassionate. I'm kind. And I've also killed people. Some people live in shades of grey. Things are very black and white for me. It's how I am."

"Black and white is a difficult barometer. Who gets to decide what's right or wrong?"

"Me."

213

"Okay," I said slowly. "Have you ever been wrong about someone?"

"Yes."

"Do you feel bad about that?"

He paused. "No. There are things I do feel bad about, but that's not one of them. I did what I had to do to protect myself and those I'm responsible for. I made the best choices based on what I knew at the time, and I own my actions."

The phrase that caught me in that explanation was protecting those he was responsible for. I wondered how much of his life had been composed of protecting others, himself included, and how much of that he was still doing. Feeling like the world is constantly on your shoulders is a lot to manage. I was sure I hadn't felt it to the extent Hawke had, but I knew it must be heavy.

I reached my hand out and rested it on his thigh. "I don't know what you went through growing up, Hawke, and I don't know what our future holds. But I want you to know, I'm always here for you. In whatever capacity that ends up being —friend...something more than a friend. You are not alone, and you don't have to carry the weight by yourself."

His eyes softened for a moment and he placed his hand over mine before his eyes flashed back to steel as we turned onto a private lane. We pulled up to a home that looked like a stone mansion, complete with turrets, and tucked back on the middle of a sprawling estate. It was incredible and I'd never seen anything like it.

Hawke looked over at me. "Try not to say too much and follow my lead. You're here as my date, but I'm counting on you to be my eyes and ears as well." The valet opened the R8's door and Hawke flashed him a solid gold ticket with black writing on it. We'd entered the world of Willy Wonka. I glanced around for the river of chocolate—not that I'd be able to drink it in this dress, but still. The valet nodded and Hawke handed him the keys before he got out and came around to open my door. Hawke helped me out of the car, and I managed to keep my slit in place for the maneuver. I took Hawke's elbow and followed him in to the mansion.

We met a woman with impeccable hair and makeup, wearing a dress almost as form fitting as mine, and followed her down the hall to a large room where about fifty chairs were arranged in five lines with an aisle down the middle. There was a stage at the front of the room with a stand and microphone in front of it. We were led to our seats and I glanced around. Everyone in sight was dressed as exquisitely as we were, and I was fairly certain there wasn't a person in the room worth less than a million dollars—except me. I recognized several of the attendees—politicians, celebrities, and prominent members of the predominant religion.

A voice came over the loud speaker. "Bidding will begin in five minutes. Please take your seats."

There was a lot of shuffling while people moved around, sat, and got settled. I'd never been to an auction before so my idea of what to expect came mostly from movies, and this seemed far more intense than anything Hollywood had come up with.

An auctioneer went to the front of the room. "We'll open the bidding tonight with a piece from a sixteenth century master artist. This piece is well known and while a copy hangs in a popular museum in Europe, this is the original, and documentation verifying that will come with the piece."

Bids started shooting up around the room. The total

climbed to over five million dollars before a man sitting on the row in front of us won. My mouth dropped and I quickly picked it back up so it would seem like I was actually supposed to be at this fancy auction and wasn't an interloper.

The auction continued in the same fashion for an hour.

Hawke bid on a piece of glass art by a master artisan who had worked in Murano, the glass island near Venice, Italy. The glass had a portrait of a face inside the piece and the level of detail was unreal. It looked like a special effect, but it wasn't. The artist developed the particular style of glasswork and his method died with him. Hawke paid a hundred thousand dollars for it. The house I rented wasn't even worth that much.

Another piece was brought out and displayed. "This is a sculpture by the well-known western artist, Ron Storm." My eyes widened and I sat up straighter to see it. I glanced at Hawke. He nodded in response. "This piece is called Ride of Thunder, and features Ron's trademark mountain landscape overshadowed by clouds. Ron Storm's pieces are all original, numbered, and have been highly sought after by collectors. We expect their value to skyrocket in the years to come. We'll start the bid at twenty thousand dollars."

Hands immediately shot up and the bids increased exponentially. By the time bidding was finished, the final price came to eighty-five thousand dollars. I had no idea Ron Storm sculptures sold for that asking price.

I needed to check and see if it was one of the pieces that had gone missing or been stolen. Maybe Aaron had arranged for the auction.

The auction ended and Hawke placed his hand on my lower back as he escorted me out of the room, stopping to speak with a few people, including the ones I'd recognized. Hawke knew everyone, and everyone seemed to know him.

We made our way out of the auction and into the hall,

"Did you know a Ron Storm sculpture would be sold tonight?"

"No. An item preview wasn't included with the invitation. I was as surprised as you were."

"It seems coincidental," I mused.

"I agree," he said.

We continued down the hall. A door opened, laughter floating out of the room, and I saw a flash of something that looked a lot like naked skin. "What's going on in there?" I asked, craning my neck to try and see through the slit in the door before it snicked shut.

"All kinds of things," Hawke said.

"*Eyes Wide Shut* things?" I asked.

He stopped and gave me all of his attention. He pushed me against the wall, caging me with his huge arms and body the size of a tank. One hand came up to my cheek and his eyes looked like they were on fire. He pressed his lips to mine, hot and full of want. My mouth opened for him and electricity shot through me, pooling low in my stomach. Suddenly his hand was between my thighs, inching up, and I vaguely remember hearing my dress rip right before he got to the good spot. He pulled back, his gaze searching mine as my breath came in uneven gasps. "Do you want to find out?"

Yes.

Absolutely.

With every one of my ovaries and some of my friends' ovaries too.

"No." I shook my head, trying to convince myself as much

as him. "No." As much as I wanted that, with every fiber of my body, I knew it wasn't the right call. I still had no idea what I wanted when it came to relationships, and Hawke's revelations about his past and the litany of questions his history predicated were all things I needed to deal with. If I gave into my hormones and had sex with him, especially *Eyes Wide Shut* sex with him, it would cloud my judgment one-thousand percent.

We waited for Hawke's R8 outside and when it pulled up, he opened the door for me before handing the valet a hundred dollar bill and getting in the driver's seat.

"Did you get what you needed tonight?" I asked, still uncertain about what exactly he'd been hoping to accomplish.

His eyes met mine, looking like they were on fire from within. "For work, yes." The implication that I had something he needed was obvious.

I would not have sex with Hawke. No. No. No. I needed to figure my shit out first.

"Are Ron Storm sculptures common in private auctions like this?" I asked.

Hawke settled into his seat, relaxing more the farther away from the mansion we got. "They're collector's items and the right buyers would see value in them."

"I didn't realize they commanded that high of a price."

"Neither did I."

I needed to take a harder look at the sculptures. I was now even more convinced that they were the reason for the string of robberies. There was some connection and I needed to figure out what it was.

"Oh, I traced the names of the users on the Not Just Junk site," Hawke said.

My ears perked up. "Were they connected?"

Hawke shook his head. "Not at all. One was based in Wisconsin and the other in Florida."

Dammit. I knew it was a long shot, but it had seemed like such a coincidence that the stuffed animals and VHS tapes had been stolen and then the same items had gone up for sale on Not Just Junk later that week. But even my mom still had those VHS tapes—I'd checked during one of Gandalf's pick-ups. And the stuffed animals were also common.

We drove in silence the rest of the way back to Branson Falls. So much had happened and I was still trying to process the information Hawke had told me earlier about his past.

Hawke glanced over at me as we cruised into town. Several people stopped and stared. If we'd been in the Ferrari, the story would have landed on the front page of the *Tribune* whether I approved it or not.

"I forgot to tell you, you can't use any information you gleaned tonight for articles," Hawke said.

I stared at him, slack jawed. "You're kidding me, right? Do you know who some of those people were?"

He gave me a dangerous look. "I know exactly who every person in that room was. And that's why you can't do anything with the information. I'm scary, but I'm not nearly as scary as half of those people. I'm not telling you this for their protection. I'm telling it to you for yours."

Well that wasn't the least bit comforting.

He pulled his super car into my driveway and walked me to the door. I stared at the R8 longingly. "That's a really pretty car."

His eyebrow arched. "Maybe I'll let you drive it sometime."

My eyes widened. "Seriously?"

He shrugged. "Sure."

"Oh my goddesses. Please let me drive it right past The Ladies. Multiple times."

He laughed. "I can make that happen."

I flashed him a huge smile before turning to unlock my front door. "Ryker Hawkins, making dreams come true."

I turned around and he was right there, our noses practically touching. He reached over and tucked a piece of hair behind my ear before pressing his lips lightly to mine. "I never really cared about dreams...until I met you."

He walked away, and I spent the rest of the night thinking about Hawke, his past, and what I could and couldn't live with. I didn't get any answers.

Chapter Nineteen

I stopped in to see Gandalf at my mom and dad's house on my way to work the next morning.

My mom met me at the door, eyes slitted. Even her shoulder towel looked perturbed. "I didn't get a chance to talk to you about this yet, but you made quite a scene with Drake at the carnival."

"Good morning to you too, Mom," I answered with a smile. Gandalf came running over and I fell to the ground giving him pets and loves that he returned with licks and spins. "Hi, little buddy! I missed you so much! Did you have tons of fun sleeping over with grandma and grandpa?"

He responded with multiple jumps and brought me a toy.

"What was happening with Drake?" my mom asked, undeterred by my efforts to deter her. I knew the look she was currently sporting. She was prepared to stand there until I answered, or the end of time, whichever came first. "Are you two dating?"

She asked me this at least once a week. She asked me the same question about Hawke nearly as often. She routinely got the same response about him that I was about to give her regarding Drake.

"We were there together. I was working. He was walking with me. I don't really think it fits the traditional definition of a date."

She folded her arms across her chest. "You were mauling your breasts in front of him and the whole state! And Drake looked more than willing to help!"

"He offered," I said, throwing Gandalf's ball.

My mom sputtered something nonsensical. She gathered her wits and tried again. "What was going on?"

"There was a Rice Krispie situation. Some chocolate escaped down my shirt, and then I tripped," I explained.

She shook her head. "I'm talking about the two of you looking like you wanted to rip each other's clothes off in the middle of a public event with small children present."

I gave her a dubious look. "If we looked like that, I'm sure it was an error in perception."

She smacked me with her shoulder towel. "I've been around a lot longer than you, Katherine Violet Saxee. I know exactly what that look meant."

"Have you come up with an emoji for it?"

She rolled her eyes. Hard.

"And don't even get me started about Hawke," she said. "I've seen those photos."

My uh-oh sensor immediately went off. "What photos?" I asked, concerned.

"The photos of you at your house last night." She looked like she might pop a vein in her forehead. "I thought I was going to see parts of you I haven't seen since I changed your diapers."

My mouth dropped open. "There are photos? Where?"

She gave me a look. "I was sent copies by no less than ten people asking me if I knew what my daughter was doing and if I'd seen her outfit."

"Dammit!" I hissed. I was so irate that I didn't even care that I'd sworn in front of her.

"You grew up here, Kate. You know how small towns work. Almost every move you make is the subject of gossip. You should know to be careful."

"I shouldn't have to be careful when all I'm doing is walking out my front door."

My mom gave me a look. "When you're walking out your front door in a dress that barely covers your who-ha, you should be prepared for the consequences."

Blood boiled in my veins and I seriously wanted to murder The Ladies. I'd seen the flash of light the night before when Hawke picked me up, and knew they'd probably had someone staking out my house like usual. I was sick of living under this microscope and trying to adjust my life to fit their expectations and dilute who I really was, and the person I was continuing to become. "No," I said with steel in my voice as I shook my head. "I refuse to be peer pressured into living someone else's life—a life they agree with. I'm going to continue to do my own thing and people, especially the asshat Ladies, can suck it."

My mom bristled at the swear and shook her head. "Oh, I'm sure they'll talk about that too." She paused. "Your dress was something."

I smiled at that. "Hawke thought so."

She raised a brow. "I'm sure he did."

"He picked it out."

Her other brow followed. "Where did you go?"

"I actually can't say because I was sworn to secrecy. But it wasn't a date. It was to help Hawke with something for his business."

She eyed me like she knew better. "I have a feeling that dress didn't last long."

My cheeks pinked. "It's still in perfect shape." Well, almost perfect. It probably needed a few things mended after the kiss against the wall at the auction.

"Sure it is. Bring it over when you get a chance and I'll fix anything that got torn...any more than it was already torn with that slit."

I was about a block from the *Tribune* when I got a call from Spence. "Another robbery on Oaktree. It's the Skinner house."

I wasn't far from there so it didn't take me long to arrive. Bobby was outside.

"Hey," I said. "Spence called me. Did the robbery happen last night or today?"

"Last night. The Skinners were out and didn't even know about it until this mornin'. It looks like it was a botched attempt though because the thief didn't get in the house."

I raised my brows. "How do you know?"

Bobby walked me over to a side door of the garage. "I always tell people not to put these dumb doors in when they build homes. Every door is an access point and another place you have to secure. The harder you make it for people to get in, the better." Good to know. I'd make sure my next house was located in a tree. He showed me the frame of the door, cracked, but not broken through. "Standard doors are usually pretty easy to break into, but the Skinners were smart and put longer screws into the faceplate and through the frame, which makes the door more secure. The robber tried to kick it open and couldn't. He must've given up after a while."

Larry Skinner came out of the house. "So you found the damage this morning?" I asked him.

Larry nodded. "I know it wasn't there when we left last night because I went out this door. Our neighbor has a great guard dog and they said he was barking around nine o'clock. They checked on him and said they saw someone in a dark outfit running through the backyard, past the trees and into the alley."

"Any idea what they might have been looking for?" I asked.

Bobby shook his head and Larry raised his arms in an "I don't know" gesture. I lifted my brow with interest as a thought occurred to me. "You don't happen to own a Ron Storm sculpture, do you?"

Larry gave me a funny look, but answered. "Actually, I do."

I looked at Bobby and his eyes went wide. "If that's what they were looking for, they'll probably try again," I said.

"They want my sculpture?" Larry asked, confusion in his tone.

"I'm not sure, but you're not the first house with a Ron Storm sculpture to be targeted."

"We'll put extra patrols on your house, Larry," Bobby reassured him.

I took some photos of the damage, then Bobby walked me to my Jeep. "He has a Ron Storm sculpture. I don't think that's a fluke."

He pressed his lips together. "I don't think so either. Do you have any leads?"

I might. "Let me check into some things."

I got to the office and after going through my inbox and taking care of a few items for the paper, I called Aaron Storm.

"Hi, Aaron. This is Kate Saxee again."

"Hi, Kate. What can I do for you?"

"I was wondering if you could tell me the names of your dad's sculptures that have gone missing or have been stolen. I know he names his pieces."

Aaron paused on the other end like he was trying to come up with an answer. Or maybe he was busy or caught off-guard by my question. That's what I hated about the phone—I couldn't read voice reactions as well as I could by watching expressions in person. "Sure. I'll have to look them up, but I can email you later today."

"Great!" I answered, and gave him my email address.

"Can I ask what this is about?" Aaron said, his tone wary.

"I'm trying to figure out what's happening with the robberies. I think there might be a connection to the recent robberies and your dad's pieces."

Aaron sounded stunned. "Really?"

"I'm not certain, so don't get your hopes up. I'm trying to do some more research and cover all my bases."

"Okay," Aaron said. "Let me know what you find out."

The first few robberies made no sense, and neither did the robbery at Inked AF. But Laura Innot's Ron Storm sculpture being taken in addition to the Collins sculpture was odd. And now this possible sculpture theft attempt was a common thread and my gut told me to follow it.

I proofed a couple of articles and dropped them into the design software for the next *Tribune* issue. I was finishing that up when Spence yelled, "Kate?"

I rolled my chair over so I could see him in his office. "What's up?"

"I got a call about someone in costume causing shenanigans."

I raised a brow. "Shenanigans?"

"That's what they said. The excitement is at the Mayfair house over in the Desert Ridge development. There was a police call on the scanner. It sounded frantic."

"I'll go check it out."

I'd seen some pretty crazy things as a reporter, even more so since moving back to Branson Falls and covering stories for the *Tribune*. But nothing could have prepared me for the scene I came upon today.

A septic tank truck was parked sideways on the street, half of it on the grass like stopping was an afterthought. Don Peabody, owner of Happy Poop Septic, and driver of the truck, was standing over a struggling goat, who looked way past the level of agitated. The goat was tied up with what looked to be a shimmering silver ribbon.

A police car was next to the septic tank and Officer Bob was talking to Don.

I had no idea what had happened here, but it seemed like something straight out of the apocalypse.

"Hey," I said, walking up to Don slowly. Who knew what other animals he'd pissed off.

"Hi, Kate," Don said with a smile. Sweat shimmered on his brow like he'd just finished a really hard workout.

"So…Spence got a call about an interesting situation." I still hadn't seen anyone in costume, but maybe the person who called it in mistook the goat for a Speedy Superhero. "Do you want to tell me what's going on?"

"There was a goat incident," Bobby offered.

The hogtied goat on the ground made that pretty clear. "I can see that. Can you start at the beginning and tell me what happened?"

It was at that moment a large purple dragon complete with sequins and gold filigree, came trotting around from the back of the house, tail swinging, with a young girl who couldn't have been more than fourteen. I put my head in my hands. Of course she was involved. Half of the *Branson Tribune* stories on any given week starred her.

"Kate!" she said, clapping her sparkly claws together and flashing a grin. "You're here for my first big criminal capture!"

I closed my eyes for a minute and took a breath. This story was going to be a doozy. "A goat, Mom? Your first capture is a wayward goat?"

"Yes!" she beamed. "I brought down Humperdinck!"

I stared at her. "Humperdinck? As in Prince Humperdinck?"

She nodded. "That's the angry little goat's name!"

Of course it was.

I gave my mom a once over, my usual check for bruises or broken bones. Though the costume was so padded I didn't think I had anything to worry about. The back of her dragon costume looked ripped. "What happened to your costume?" I asked, pointing to a Grand Canyon size tear.

"Oh," she said, waving her hand like it wasn't a big deal, "after the vacuum robbery, I learned that my costume needed a little practicality."

I arched a brow at that. "Because a dragon costume is practical in general?"

She glared and put her claws on her hips. "My costume is stunning, but it needed easier access points for quicker outfit changes. I added some Velcro to make the costume easier and faster to get on and off. It popped open while I was distracting the goat."

At least she had something on underneath it, or this story would have gotten even more unbelievable. And the headline would not have been flattering: Local Woman Wrestling Goat in Dragon Costume Moons Kids.

"Do you want to tell me why a goat is on the ground wrapped in silver ribbon made of tulle?"

She wrinkled her nose. "I'm not happy I had to sacrifice my bow to subdue that wily Humperdinck, but sacrifice is what superheroes do."

I wasn't sure a ribbon should be put in the realm of great sacrifices, but I wasn't going to argue semantics with her at this juncture.

"Trina here was babysittin' for the Mayfair family and their goat got itself worked up into a dither and attempted an attack," Bobby said.

"What happened?" I asked a pale Trina. She was obviously still struggling to cope with the goat assault.

"The kids wanted to go play outside. Literally minutes after we went into the backyard, the family's pet goat,

Humperdinck, broke free from its chain and came after us. I grabbed the youngest son and ran because the older son had already beaten us to the door." She paused like she had realized something. "You know, I think maybe this has happened before because Humperdinck was fast and knew exactly where to charge and the older son got inside lightning quick...like he'd had practice. We made it inside the house and I slammed the door before Humperdinck could get in. I thought we were safe, but then Humperdinck started ramming the door. The kids were freaking out and I was too, so I called the police for help. I warned them to be careful and not get hit by Humperdinck's horns. It's a *mean* goat!"

That would be part of the frantic call Spence must have heard.

"We were waiting and Humperdinck kept ramming the door. I thought for sure it was going to break through and kill us all, and then I saw this septic tank truck careen into the driveway and out popped a guy wearing a little poop hat and he had a dragon sidekick!"

I stared at my mom. I had questions. So. Many. Questions.

I took a deep breath. "How did you know about this goat situation and get here before the police?" I asked her.

"It's right around the corner!" she said, like I was ridiculous. In truth, it was almost a mile away. "And I heard Trina's call on the scanner, silly!"

"Where did you find the police scanner?" My dad had a scanner to keep track of my mom, but after her last crime fighting costume attempt, he'd told me he was going to keep it hidden where she couldn't access it. The potential for her to cause a disaster while trying to help someone was high.

"I couldn't find your dad's so I bought another one!" she

exclaimed. "How else was I supposed to help the superheroes fight crime in a timely manner?"

Right. What was I thinking? I had bigger questions, however. "How did you drive over here in that dragon contraption?" After a recent adventure where her truck somehow slipped into gear all by itself while she was shopping and took out an entire Branson Falls building, she'd decided to get something sportier. I didn't want to know what favors she'd promised the insurance agent to make that happen, because there was no way an insurance company should be willing to insure her at all, let alone for a sports car like the Corvette she'd managed to acquire.

She turned her nose up in offense. "It's not a contraption. My Cuddles dragon persona is a carefully designed crime fighting uniform."

I managed to hide my smile with my hand over my lips. Judging by her narrowed eyes, I didn't think it fooled her.

She continued, "Don Peabody, the septic tank cleaner, saw me trying to get my tail in the Corvette." She paused like she was considering something—it was an expression that usually sent my dad to the garage to work on his Mustang. "I might have made the tail too poufy. I'm going to have to alter it to be more sporty for the Corvette." I didn't tell her there was no need since the new car wouldn't last long.

"I'd finished up at the Howard house across the street when I saw her strugglin' and came over to help," Don confirmed.

My mom nodded in agreement. "Don tried to squish me all in, but it wasn't successful. So he drove me over in the back of his truck."

A vengeful dragon careening around corners in the back

of Don Peabody's Happy Poop Man septic truck was absolutely already being reported on the town Facebook page. I knew it.

"Next time I have to go somewhere in the costume, I'll take your dad's car," she said in a reassuring manner that wasn't very reassuring at all, and almost sounded like a threat.

"Bad idea," I said, shaking my head. "Last time you did that his Mustang ended up in a pond."

"Don't be ridiculous. Cuddles couldn't fit in the Mustang either. I'll take the truck."

"You started that one on fire."

She rolled her eyes like I was making a bigger deal out of things than I should have. "He got a new truck. I made him cookies. It was fine."

I had a feeling my dad would disagree.

"So you rushed to Trina and the kids' defense with your trusty sidekick, the Happy Poop Man?"

She nodded. Don backed up her nod.

I tilted my head to the side, considering. "Did it occur to you that Don's business logo is a poop, and he was wearing a poop shaped hat?" She pressed her lips together and didn't answer. "Did you also think that Don sold happy chocolate ice cream?"

She narrowed her eyes and looked at me like she was contemplating methods of murder so I thought I should probably get the rest of the story before I died.

"So Don, the very nice Happy Poop Man, dropped you off and decided to stay and help you with this dumpster fire?"

She gave me an odd look. "What are you talking about? There was no fire in a dumpster. There wasn't even a dumpster involved. It was just a fed-up goat." She looked at me like

I'd lost my mind, and considering I was talking to a woman dressed as a giant sparkly purple dragon who'd saved some kids from an angry goat with her poop sidekick, I thought the look was rather hypocritical. "Anyway, Don stayed because he knows some stuff about goats."

I blinked at that. "Knows some stuff about goats?" I looked to Don.

"I grew up on a farm," he answered. "I know how to handle an angry goat."

"The dragon didn't have it as bad as I did," Trina explained. "By the time the dragon and Happy Poop Man got there, I'd already tired Humperdinck out from his chasing us and ramming the door."

"How did you distract the goat from its original kid targets?" I asked Don and my mom.

"I got out of the truck and immediately walked up to that goat, looked it right in the eyes, and *dared* it to come at me," my mom said.

"You challenged an angry goat?" I asked, the disbelief evident in my tone. I was surprised she wasn't in the back of an ambulance right now. Again. "Was that wise?"

She stomped a claw covered foot. "Of course it was! Don't you know anything about goats?" She asked, a skeptical look on her face. "You're supposed to flap your arms at them."

"Flap your arms," I repeated, dumbfounded.

She nodded and then waved her arms up and down, her fluffy purple wings flapping in the breeze. The sequins and glitter made her flying apparatus seem less formidable than she probably intended.

I suspected that the person who had told her about the arm flapping goat defense was joking and truly believed she'd never be in a goat battle situation. That person evidently didn't know my mom. "Where did you hear that?"

"I read it somewhere. But they were right! As soon as I started flapping my wings, Humperdinck backed down for a minute! Then I tried the other suggestions of screaming and throwing rocks." She paused. "Those didn't work as well."

"I think maybe the goat backed down not because it was terrified of your arm flapping dragon, but because it knew it was up against Sophie Saxee and your reputation precedes you," I offered as an explanation.

She glowered at me. Most people would back down from that look—including angry goats—I, however, wasn't one of them.

"Humperdinck started chasing me around," my mom said. "I probably sprinted a good mile back and forth across their yard!" I was skeptical of that distance estimate, but the Mayfair yard *was* large. "I started to get tired and knew I didn't have much running left in me. Don was trying to catch Humperdinck unaware so I decided to distract the little bugger. I stood my ground, wiggled my bum and tail at the goat, looked over my shoulder, and stuck my tongue out. It did the trick! Don came at him from the side, grabbed his horns, and wrestled him to the ground while dodging the goat's kicking hooves. I grabbed my pretty silver bow from the top of my dragon head and we wrapped Humperdinck up so he couldn't hurt anyone else."

"You're making it seem like the goat was about to go on a killing spree," I observed.

"Humperdinck was practically holding the whole town hostage!" my mom exclaimed. "My dragon wings saved us all!"

I gave her a dubious look. "I think it was about ten percent dragon wings, and ninety percent your Happy Poop tackling sidekick."

She waved her hands in the direction of Don. "Well, of course," she conceded. "It was a team effort."

Don nodded. "I couldn't have snuck up on him without your mom's talent for distraction. It's like the sequins mesmerized the goat."

I'd thought the attention grabbing sequins would hinder her crime fighting abilities so she'd proven me wrong there. Still, it was quite an event. "I think we can safely file this under Catasophie."

She scrunched up her nose. "No way! This was a Sophie Saxee victory! The kids were saved, Humperdinck is going back in his shed tied up with a stronger chain, and all is well with the world."

I took some photos and some more notes and then got some quotes before I wrapped things up. "I have to get back to the *Tribune*," I said. "Will you be okay getting home?"

My mom nodded. "Bobby said he'd take me. I can't wait to ride in the police car!"

I didn't tell her that Bobby had once informed me that I should avoid the backseat of police cars at all costs because the back of every patrol car in history was tainted with all sorts of bodily fluids. Her dragon costume would need a hazmat team after the ride.

"Thanks for your help," I said to Don, the Happy Poop Man.

He nodded. "No problem, I was happy to do it."

"And thanks for taking her home," I said to Bobby.

"Yep."

I got back in the Jeep, already thinking of a headline: Horns of Terror.

"So what happened?" Spence asked, as I plopped down at my desk.

I closed my eyes and sank into my chair, wondering how I'd survived twenty-five years of my mom's Catasophies and how I'd survive seventy more. Someone had once called my dad a saint for his ability to deal with my mom's adventures. I had to agree.

"Trina was babysitting the Mayfair kids. They have a goat. The goat got loose and started chasing them, then tried to break down the house door. She called the police and my mom heard the call for help and got there first, Happy Poop septic tank man in tow."

I gave Spence the whole rundown of the situation and he was laughing so hard he had tears.

"The fact that no one has a video of this goat/dragon battle is one of the great losses of our time," he said.

"I know. Cuddles the dragon, goat attack hero. My mom is convinced she was the only one who could save the kids—by flapping her dragon wings."

We laughed and laughed. Spence ordered some food for us as we continued working to put out the upcoming paper.

About an hour later, a notification popped up on my phone. It was from Not Just Junk. A new piece of art had been listed in the art section. I pulled it up and gasped. I'd seen that piece of artwork before. In Axel and Sasha's shop. And it had been stolen.

I immediately called Hawke. "Can you track down another user from the Not Just Junk site for me?"

"Sure," he said. "Text me the name."

I texted him the seller of Axel's art. As soon as I heard back from Hawke, I'd contact Axel and Sasha and let them know I'd found Axel's pieces.

I sat back in my chair, tapping my pen against my leg. Whoever took the pieces had to be a complete idiot to turn around and sell them on Not Just Junk so quickly. And another thing bothered me. The pieces that had been taken were huge. I wondered how the thief had gotten them out of the building so quickly and without being seen.

Fred had been at his antique shop that night with Molly. Maybe there was something they'd missed and I could ask them some more questions.

"I'll be back," I said to Spence, and headed out the door.

Fred and Molly's antique store was like walking into another time. Old trunks, pottery, vases, furniture, and art were scattered around the eclectic shop and it smelled distinctly of history mixed with a little potpourri. A tiny bell chimed as I walked through the door and Fred came from the back wearing dark slacks and a red sweater. He had always reminded me of Mr. Rogers, and he was just as nice.

"Kate," Fred said with a smile. "What brings you here?"

"A couple of questions, if you have time?"

"Sure do!" He leaned his elbow against the counter and gave me all of his attention.

"You said you were here at the shop the night the tattoo shop got robbed?"

He nodded. "I was here all day and stayed late to continue working on a project."

"Did you see anything odd happening that day?" I asked. "Even before the robbery occurred?"

Fred knitted his brows in thought. "Not that I can remember. Is there a specific reason you're asking?"

I had to be careful here because I didn't want to lead him or alter his memories with my suggestions. "I was thinking about Axel's art pieces that were stolen. They're quite large and I think it would have taken some time for the thieves to move the pieces."

Fred nodded. "One of the pieces was actually split into three canvases. I helped Axel hang it, so I know. But Axel told me four pieces of art were taken in total. Whoever stole them would have needed a truck or an SUV to move them all."

Or a convenient store right next door with plenty of space to store them, I thought. I hated that I was even considering Fred as a suspect, but I couldn't ignore how easy the crime would have been for him, and no one would ever suspect our sweet local antique dealer. I was having a hard time even convincing myself to question him.

"And you didn't see anyone with a truck or SUV around?" I asked.

"Not that I remember," he said, thinking back. "I was working on a table restoration in the basement and barely went outside that day. Molly had left to get us dinner so she wasn't around either."

I understood getting wrapped up in a project, and restoration of any kind of antique was meticulous work. But I wasn't sure that was all Fred had been doing. I'd known him my whole life and didn't think he was the type to steal, but you never really know everything about a person and I felt like I was still missing some information. As an antique dealer, Fred had a decent working knowledge of the art world.

"There's a lot of art being stolen lately," I led.

Fred nodded.

"Do you know much about Ron Storm sculptures?" I asked.

Fred stood up straighter, almost like he had something to prove. "Quite a bit, actually. I've known Ron for years."

"You know one of his sculptures was stolen from the Collins' house during the recent robberies, right?"

Fred's expression turned somber. "Yes. It's a shame."

I agreed. And I wanted to find out who was taking them, and if Fred had any awareness of the theft ring. "I've been looking into it and the price of Ron Storm sculptures has gone up a lot recently."

Fred's brows shot up at my information. "Sure has. By about forty percent in the past year."

"Forty percent?" I said, eyes wide. I knew the auction price had been high, but I had no idea the value had increased by that much so quickly. "Is that because of his ailing health?"

"Could be part of it," Fred said, rubbing his chin with his thumb and forefinger, "but that doesn't totally explain such a drastic jump."

"What would explain it?"

Fred shrugged. "A lot of interest all at once. Someone fluffing the market."

"Fluffing?" I said, questioning his verb choice. "As in a porn fluffer?"

"The same idea works here as well," Fred explained. "Someone keeping the market hot and people interested."

I tried to reconcile my vision of grandpa Fred the antique store owner and Fred who knew what a porn fluffer was, and couldn't. "What would—" I tried to think of a word other than fluffing "—stroking the market do?" Stroking wasn't a much better word choice.

"It creates demand and increases the price for pieces by a specific artist."

Several things clicked together at once in my head. "So someone who controlled the inventory would be able to accomplish that fairly easily then," I said, making it more of a statement than a question.

Fred sliced his head down once. "Yes."

"That helps a lot, Fred. Thanks!"

"No problem," he said with a wave. "Let me know if you need anything else."

I'd come into the store with a hunch about Fred having something to do with the theft of Axel's pieces, and maybe even the Ron Storm sculptures. I still wasn't sure that Fred was uninvolved, but I had a pretty good idea of someone else who might be. I knew exactly who controlled the Ron Storm sculptures inventory. Now, I needed to prove Aaron Storm was somehow involved in robbing people of his dad's artwork —and I needed to figure out why he was doing it.

Chapter Twenty

I'd tossed and turned all night trying to figure out Aaron Storm's motives for stealing his dad's art, and how it was being done. He'd seemed so proud of his dad's talent, and committed to keeping the Ron Storm legacy pristine. He didn't seem like he was hurting for money. I remembered he said he managed the pieces and inventory with his brother. Maybe his brother had something to do with the price inflation and robberies? Or maybe they were both working together. The only other reason I could come up with was that Aaron was trying to inflate the prices to make his dad's pieces, and legacy, seem more valuable. I needed to chat with Aaron and ask some more questions.

As the sun started to rise, I got out of bed and took Gandalf on a brisk early morning walk. The cool air and blood movement helped wake me up, and my morning coffee with milk and lots of creamer didn't hurt either.

I dropped Gandalf off at my mom and dad's and then spent the morning working.

Aaron Storm hadn't emailed me the list of names of his

dad's missing art pieces and I needed to talk to him anyway so I decided I'd drop by his house later today.

I lost track of time editing, but my stomach didn't. By lunch, I was starving. "I'm going to grab some food at Fry Guy. Do you want anything?" I asked Spence.

"Yeah, a salad would be great."

I stopped in my tracks. "A salad?" Spence and I had pretty specific food orders that rarely wavered. A salad had never been on his Fry Guy list.

He lifted his shoulders, the movement slight. "I'm trying to be healthier."

I gave him a knowing look and smiled. "This wouldn't have anything to do with a certain love interest, would it?"

His cheeks pinked slightly and I chuckled on my way out the door.

I placed my order at Fry Guy and was waiting patiently when I heard the door open, the bell jingling like Thor's hammer had hit it. Johnny Fern, owner of Tres Tacos, came storming through it like a hurricane. He walked straight to the front counter, pulled the announcement about tater tots and taco salads off, and started ripping it to tiny pieces.

Colby Zimmer, the actual Fry Guy and restaurant owner, rushed out from the food prep area. "What in tarnation are you doin' to my signs, Johnny?" Colby demanded.

Johnny looked up at him, pure rage in his eyes. I'd never seen someone so mad over modified potatoes and lettuce. "I'm fixin' them, that's what!"

Colby came over and tried to take the next sign away from Johnny and it wasn't long before they were both on the ground and a full-fledged brawl was taking place. A few patrons tried to stop them, others called the police, and I mostly tried to stay out of the way. Since I happened to be at the location of a breaking news story, I took some photos. Police sirens wailed and pretty soon, Officer Bob and his partner were there, breaking things up.

After they got things settled, Bobby came over and asked me what had happened, which was new since I was usually the one getting an event summary. I told him and he wrote it down for his report, shaking his head while he muttered about stupid people, emotions, and dummies who made him do paperwork.

The commotion meant my lunch was delayed since most of the food that had been cooking was now burned. I texted Spence to let him know what was happening. When I looked up, Nut Man was standing in front of me. I jumped back, startled. "Hey," I said, always a little thrown to see him at a police scene and six inches from my face. "Did you come to try and help with the fight?"

He nodded, then said, "I saw you though and wanted to follow up on something you asked me about before."

"Okay," I said, listening.

"You were asking about the person who paid our Speedy Superheroes application fee."

"Yeah," I answered. "But you said they haven't been around for a while."

Nut Man nodded. "They haven't, but yesterday they started signing up for watches again. We haven't heard from Speckles for a while and it seemed sudden and kind of strange. I wanted to let you know."

My eyes got bigger. "The person's superhero alter ego is named Speckles?"

"Yeah. Their costume is all black, almost like a leotard, and it masks Speckles from head to toe. It's covered in various shades of paint splatters all over it. That's why Speckles is named Speckles."

Drake had told me the Popes' son had an imaginary friend named Speckles. Was it possible they were the same? The person couldn't be dumb enough to use the same name for the Speedy Superheroes and robbing people, could they?

"That helps me out a lot," I said. "Thanks for letting me know."

"No problem. We're here to help."

I tried to hide my opinion and not let it leak out onto my expression—which unfortunately, happened often. I felt like the majority of the Vendetta League members were probably there to help, but maybe not all of them, and Speckles was now on the top of my nefarious deeds list.

If the robber was using the Speedy Superheroes as a cover, the thief should have been on watch with the Vendetta League during the times the robberies happened. But maybe they just knew where watches would be taking place, so they were able to plan the robberies around those areas. I needed to ask Drake some more questions about Speckles. I jotted some notes down on my pad and made a reminder to call Drake after lunch.

I filled Spence in on everything that had happened and was about to call Drake when he walked through the front door.

"Well, this is handy timing," I said, finishing the last bite of my lunch. "I was about to call you."

Drake waved to Spence in his office before coming over to

my desk and resting his hip against the side of it. "Couldn't wait to see me again?" The corners of his lips turned up in a flirty grin.

I rolled my eyes. "You already have a big enough ego; I don't need to add to it."

"What were you going to call me for then?"

I ran my tongue over my lips while I grabbed my notebook. Drake's eyes snagged on my mouth and his gaze did funny things to my stomach. I immediately directed my attention to my notes instead. "You mentioned that the Popes' son had an imaginary friend, Speckles. He said Speckles looked like he was covered in paint. Did he ever give more details about Speckles's appearance?"

Drake thought about it for a beat. "Not really, only that Speckles glowed like stars."

I tilted my head. If any of the paint on the costume was glow in the dark, it would probably look like stars.

"Why," Drake asked.

I shrugged. "Following a lead. It's probably nothing." I moved some flowers on my desk that I'd picked from my garden. Drake noticed them and his expression hardened for a moment before he got control of it. I tried to hide my smile. I was certain he thought Hawke had given them to me but I didn't need someone else to get me flowers; I was perfectly capable of acquiring my own—though I didn't mind when they were gifted either. "What are you doing here?" I asked. He'd gone out of his way to find me at the *Tribune* so I assumed he needed something.

He leaned more heavily on my desk, his eyes sparkling in a way that was both alluring and slightly worrisome. "There's a community Halloween party next week," he said, watching my reaction. I wasn't sure where he was going with this so my reaction was pretty neutral as he continued, "Costumes are encouraged. I'm hoping you'll accompany me."

And there went my neutrality. It seemed Drake was determined to ask me to every possible Branson Falls town event— as if The Ladies didn't have enough to talk about already. Drake wasn't the first to invite me to the Halloween party, however. "Annie already invited me, so I'll be there."

He bit the corner of his lip. I could practically see how hard he was straining to not press me into going with him as his date instead of going as an independent party with friends. "I'm glad I'll get to see you there then."

"Me too," I said, and meant it. Just because I wasn't going as his date didn't mean that I wasn't interested in seeing him —or the costume he decided on. "Hopefully it will be less eventful than our Halloween carnival adventures."

"I don't think they're serving Rice Krispies on a stick, so you should be fine," Drake said with a grin.

I rolled my eyes. "I have no regrets."

"Neither do I," he said, his gaze heating. We sat there staring at each other with scandalous promises playing across our irises for approximately one year, before Drake changed the subject, "I was able to get Axel and Sasha hooked up with the comic convention. I think it will help their business a lot."

I snapped out of Drake's dark magic eye trance. "I think so too. That was really nice of you. They still don't know who vandalized Inked AF. And I saw one of Axel's stolen pieces listed on an auction site."

Drake's eyes went wide at that. "Did you look up the seller?"

"I have someone on it." Drake didn't need to know that

someone was Hawke, but judging by his clenched jaw, I was pretty sure he suspected it.

"I still think there's something off about the whole thing," Drake said, his brows narrowing in thought. "It doesn't feel like the other robberies."

I leaned back in my chair, mostly to get some more distance between us because I didn't trust my own two hands. "I agree. I had some questions about Axel's art pieces and stopped to ask Fred about them. They were huge pieces and wouldn't have been easy to transport. I feel like someone would have seen the thief moving them."

Drake's expression turned skeptical. "Or the person who stole the art was someone close by who had access to an entire store with a basement that they could have easily moved the pieces into."

I stared at him, surprised his thought process had gone the same direction as mine. Talking to Fred hadn't convinced me of his involvement one way or another, so I wanted more detail about why Drake thought Fred might be the culprit. "You think Fred stole Axel's art and vandalized the store?"

Drake shrugged. "I'm not sure, but it's a possibility."

Despite my own suspicions, my mind was still having a hard time wrapping itself around the idea of Fred being a thief, but there were a lot of things pointing in that direction. He knew art, and knew the value of various pieces—whether they be art canvases by a tattoo shop owner or renowned sculptures. He would also know where to find a market for them and get a solid return. And he'd have a good idea of where to find Ron Storm pieces around Branson Falls to steal as well. As much as I wanted to rule him out as a suspect, I couldn't. But since Drake had come up with the same suspect, I wanted to know his take. "Why would Fred steal Axel's art?"

Drake shifted against my desk, crossing one leg over the other at the ankle. "Any number of reasons. Maybe Fred and Molly really aren't that happy to have a tattoo shop next to their store, despite what they say. Maybe he saw value in Axel's work and thought he could sell it. Maybe it's another reason entirely. I'm saying it's a bad idea to rule suspects out unless you're one-hundred percent certain they didn't do anything wrong."

Okay, I'd give Drake that, but I still wasn't sure. If Fred was involved, I didn't think he was working alone, and it didn't explain why Axel's art was being sold on an auction site. Fred was smarter than to sell a stolen item in a public setting so soon after the crime.

Drake stood. "I have to go get some things done before tonight."

I gave him an interested look. "What's going on tonight?"

"I have an event to go to," he said.

"Work stuff?" I asked, internally wondering why I was suddenly so curious about his evening plans, and kicking myself because it probably came off like I was fishing for information.

He moved his head back and forth in a non-committal way. "Kind of."

I narrowed my eyes, wondering if he was going on a date. And then realized I had no claim on the man, and it really wasn't my business even if he was. But I was bothered by the thought, and the fact that I was bothered, bothered me even more. "I bet it won't come with Rice Krispies on a stick," I said, trying to push aside my impending jealousy, "so my work is more fun than yours."

He lifted a brow. "It certainly won't come with you doing a search and rescue mission for chocolate in your cleavage, and that's a damn shame."

I rolled my eyes, secretly happy that he was thinking about my boobs. "Well, have fun at *work* tonight," I said, putting the emphasis on work since it didn't sound like that's really what he'd be doing.

"I'll be thinking of you the whole time," Drake teased as he walked out the door.

I sat there for a minute stewing in my thoughts until I heard Spence make a tsk, tsk, tsk noise from the other room. "You're in trouble with that one," he said.

"I'm in trouble with a lot of ones," I answered, thinking of Drake, Hawke and the epidemic of feelings I seemed to have caught.

"No kidding," Spence said with a laugh. "You need to figure out your boyfriend situation."

"They're not my boyfriends." I tried to say it convincingly. I failed.

My phone rang, the seductive melody of "Play Me" dancing through my speakers. I picked it up. "Hey," I said, wondering if he could hear the smile in my voice.

"There's my favorite person," Hawke answered.

I smiled even wider. "That's quite a compliment."

"I mean it." He paused momentarily. "I found the person

who was selling Axel's art. His name is Jordan Sider. He lives here in town."

Holy crap! "Did you talk to him?"

"I did. And I'm confident he didn't take the pieces or rob Inked AF."

I slitted my eyes. Jordan lived in Branson and was selling Axel's pieces on an auction site that a lot of Branson Falls residents were using. It felt like there was a good chance he was our guy. "How confident?"

"One thousand percent."

Wow. "Why?"

"Because he's fourteen and has had a broken leg for a month."

I shook my head. Evidently, Not Just Junk didn't enforce an age limit on sellers. "Then how did he get Axel's art pieces?"

"He said he and some friends were going to a party. They had to park a couple of blocks away on a side street and they passed a dumpster. Axel's pieces were resting on top of the trash."

My heart twisted. "Someone went to the trouble of vandalizing Inked AF, stealing cumbersome pieces of Axel's prized artwork, and then threw them in the trash?"

"Seems like it," Hawke said.

"That makes no sense."

"I've found that most things people do make little sense."

Fair point.

"Okay. Thanks for letting me know," I told Hawke.

"No problem. You can pay me later."

I raised a brow. "I didn't realize we were on a payment system."

I could hear the smile in his voice as he answered, "I'm keeping a tab."

My brain wasn't sure it wanted to be there when he decided to collect. My body was on board in every way.

"Are you going to the Halloween party at the town hall next week?" Hawke asked.

Geez, this Halloween party must be a serious event if everyone was asking me about it. "I am," I said. "Annie invited me."

I could almost feel him grinning through the phone. "Then I might start helping you pay down your tab there. I'll see you soon, Kitty Kate."

Oh boy. I was committed to going to an event where both of my not-boyfriends who were more than capable of doing bodily damage to each other would be present. It would be an eventful evening, I was sure.

I stopped by Aaron Storm's house on my way back from dinner.

He opened the door, the lines of his face pulled back and strained. He seemed upset. "Hi, Aaron," I said tentatively. I wasn't sure what was going on, but it felt like I'd intruded on something.

"Oh. Hi, Kate," he said. "Come in. I totally forgot to email that list to you but I can get it now."

He pulled up the list on his computer and jotted down the names on a piece of paper. "I hope this will help."

"I'm sure it will." I took the paper and started to glance at the list when Aaron's phone rang and he frowned at the number.

"I have to take this. I'll be right back."

As he walked out the door, I heard him say hello and mention something about evidence. My ears perked up at that, but once he was out of his office and the door was shut, I couldn't hear anything else.

I looked at the list he'd given me and Ride of Thunder, the piece that had been sold at the auction I'd attended with Hawke, was at the top. I pressed my lips together, my reporter instincts running wild. Aaron had to be up to his eyeballs in this robbery mess and sculpture price manipulation, I just didn't know his motive and reasons.

I shifted so I could see him better as I tried to figure it out, and noticed Aaron gesturing wildly, a frustrated expression on his face. I had about a hundred other questions for him, but as he came back into the room I realized I wasn't going to get to ask them right now. He scribbled something on a notepad on the desk: Forty-three west Stardust Street. It was obviously an address.

"I'm sorry, Kate," he said, ripping the paper off the notepad and putting it in his pocket. "I'd like to talk to you more, but I have a pressing matter I need to attend to. I hope you'll excuse me."

"Sure," I said. "I hope everything is okay."

He pressed his lips together. "Me too."

I left the house, pulled around the corner in my Jeep, and waited for Aaron to leave. Wherever he was going, I was going there as well.

Chapter Twenty-One

I followed Aaron, hanging back so he wouldn't notice my Jeep. It was a common SUV in a non-descript color, no hot pink cars for me, so it shouldn't stand out—especially not to a financial planner who wasn't used to being tailed, but I was still careful. A couple of hours and another state later, we'd crossed the border into Wyoming. It was a good thing I'd had a full tank of gas when I started this unexpected journey. We pulled up to a beautiful home with large white columns, surrounded by towering evergreen and maple trees. It looked like it doubled as some sort of event center. Aaron got out of his car and grabbed his suit jacket, putting it on as he walked in the front doors. I examined the building, certain that I'd be seen if I went through the front. There had to be another entrance, especially if it was used for events.

I got out of my Jeep and went around the side of the massive structure. I found a staircase with a door at the bottom, tried the handle, and it was unlocked. I thanked every deity I could think of for that small favor.

The door opened into a hallway. I started down it, trying

to look like I belonged there when a woman dressed in a deep purple cocktail dress with shiny dark hair and perfectly applied makeup walked by, gave me a once over, and rolled her eyes. "I told them to have the girls go in through the back, not the side. Come on, you need to get dressed."

I had no idea what was happening, but I'd learned a long time ago that you get more information by playing along than by trying to explain, so I followed her to a room full of six other girls, all in various states of undress, as they got their hair and makeup done.

"I'm Pam," she said, the authority clear in her tone. "I run the back end of things, and we need to get you a costume."

She walked to a rack in the middle of the room and pulled two costumes off, flipping them around so I could see them both. I fought not to roll my eyes. "This is pretty stereotypical for Halloween."

Her lips slid into a knowing grin. "But the players love it, and your tips will be through the roof."

Players? Tips? What in the world was happening here?

I looked at the costumes, trying to decide between them. I grabbed the black one.

"Good choice," Pam said. She pointed to a chair and I settled in for whatever came next.

The makeup artist had done my makeup and hair. Heavy black liner highlighted the fake eyelashes that framed my eyes. She'd contoured my face so my cheekbones looked like Angelina Jolie's, something I was not sad about and needed to learn to do on my own. And she'd topped it off with a dark red lipstick that sparkled like blood red roses dripping with rubies. My hair was teased, curly, and approximately the size of the state of Montana.

The black lace corset I was squeezed into was studded with red crystals. A black leather skirt that definitely would not have met Utah's three inches above the knee length requirement, swished around the tops of my thighs, and barely covered my butt. The heels were about six inches tall but they felt like they were around seventy. And the whole ridiculous outfit was topped off with a headband of red and black sequined devil horns.

Between the makeup and the costume, I wasn't sure if I was trying to draw attention to my face or my body, but thought I'd probably manage both. If someone tried to touch me when I hadn't asked them to, they'd get a swift kick to the ass with some very sharp heels that could easily double as weapons.

"What exactly are we doing here?" I discreetly asked one of the girls I was walking next to down the hall.

"We're basically décor and entertainment," she said, rolling her eyes. "But it pays well."

The idea of being described as décor and entertainment got my hackles right up.

"I'm Sandra, by the way," the girl said.

"Kate," I said, managing a smile. "Décor and entertainment for what?" I asked.

"The game."

I must have looked at her like she'd started growing carrots out of her ears because she gave me a strange look back. "Gambling," she said slowly, like she needed to lengthen her speaking patterns for me to comprehend.

"Gambling?"

The girl shook her head and sighed. "Sometimes the entertainment agencies are lax when it comes to giving girls information about events. Yes. It's a series of poker games and we're here to wander around the tables, flirt with the players, look pretty, and keep them distracted and entertained."

The feminist in me rose up, incredibly unhappy with my costume and role for the evening. The reporter in me calmed her down by saying cool your tits, Kate Saxee, we're undercover.

We walked into a room dripping with chandeliers and four poker tables set up throughout the space. A bar with an attendant stood in the corner, and the room was full of men dressed in everything from expensive suits to hoodies and jeans. They were the who's who of Utah. I recognized several of them, and a few had also attended the super-secret auction I'd been to with Hawke. Based on the overlapping attendees, I had a feeling the auction and game were connected.

I watched as men came in, got their chips, and settled at their tables. I'd played a little in college—strip poker, mostly—but I certainly couldn't compete in the games these guys were about to start, and I definitely didn't have the bank account for it.

"Just be flirty and smile a lot," Sandra whispered. "And don't be surprised if your ass gets slapped."

If my ass got slapped, there would be a very quick end to this undercover situation and probably a broken nose.

I looked around the room and while I didn't see Aaron Storm wandering around, my eyes quickly caught on another set of shoulders I'd recognize anywhere.

Hawke.

His eyes met mine from across the room, surprise flitting across his face. I got the impression Hawke was rarely caught off guard, so his expression was entertaining. He made his way over to me, taking my arm and leading me slightly away from the group. "Nice costume," he whispered.

I made a face. "I was only given two choices."

He raised a brow. "I'm certainly glad you chose this one."

"Well, you could have corrupted the angel if I'd chosen option two."

He thought about that for a minute. "Good point. Wear the angel next time."

I gave him a sweet smile and tried not to roll my eyes.

"What are you doing here?" he asked.

"Following a lead. Have you seen Aaron Storm around?"

"Ron Storm's son?" Hawke asked, confusion playing across his face. "I thought I saw him at one of the tables by the door." He looked around and nodded toward a table with about six men sitting at it, chatting. Aaron kept glancing around the room like he was waiting for someone. "What are you looking for?" Hawke asked.

"I think Aaron's been controlling the market for his dad's sculptures. I was over at his house to ask him some questions when he got a call. He looked upset and started talking about evidence, then he hung up the phone, told me he had something urgent to attend to and needed to leave. I followed him here."

Hawke's expression turned wolfish. "Interesting. We should have a chat with him."

I gestured up and down my body. Hawke's eyes followed, and held. "That's why I'm here, in this ridiculous get-up." I paused, looking him over in his exquisite suit, perfectly coiffed hair, and his no BS expression. "What are you doing here?" I asked. He was definitely in work mode. I wanted to know why. "Just a little October weekend gambling? Did you bring the Ferrari this time?"

He took my arm gently, moving me over to a more private area so it appeared that we were doing something illicit and should be left alone. Given that he looked like someone had put a ten thousand dollar suit on a statue of a Greek God, I kind of hoped we would be. He put an arm against the wall, leaning into me, managing to shelter and claim me all in one movement. "I'm in the middle of an investigation I've been working on for weeks."

I gave him a suspicious look. "Does this have anything to do with the auction we went to?"

"Yes."

"Were you using the auction to get an invitation to this gambling game?" I asked him.

"Yes."

"Well, apparently you didn't need to spend a hundred grand on some trinkets. You simply needed to waltz in the side door looking lost and in need of a costume."

His eyes ran over me, taking in every inch of my body and leaving a trail of fire in his wake. "I lack the attributes that would have gotten me as easily admitted as you were."

I let my gaze fall from his wide shoulders to muscular thighs, and everything in between. I begged to differ with him on that count.

His eyes heated at my perusal. "Careful, or you won't be wearing that costume long, and neither one of us will get the answers we need."

He pressed me against the wall in a heated kiss, his lips

dancing with mine in a promise of things to come. I forgot about the robberies, work, and pretty much every other thing on the planet until his lips were no longer grazing my skin. My chest heaved with deep breaths and Hawke's lungs didn't have it any easier.

"I want to drag you down the hall to an empty room." His voice was husky and carnal and my hormones were screaming.

I took a deep breath, attempting to calm myself. "That won't help either of us figure this mystery out."

He closed his eyes, his expression that of a man who was at the end of his rope. "When this is over, you're mine."

"Or you'll be mine," I said. "We'll see." I gave him a wink.

He flashed a wicked smile and moved away from the wall.

To be honest, I still wasn't sure who I actually wanted to be mine, but Hawke was hot, looked carved from marble, and standing right there—and that was mighty tempting.

Hawke moved away from me and I made my way around the room, complimenting men, twirling my hair, swishing my hips, and being as charming as possible. I loathed it. I wanted a game where women were the power players and the men were the ones being trotted around like walking candy.

The games had been going on for almost an hour and I was still trying to simultaneously watch, and not be seen by, Aaron Storm. He seemed—uncomfortable wasn't the word...maybe unsettled. I wondered why. Most of the men were caught up in their play and the money they were winning or losing.

I was flirting with a well-known Utah businessman, playing my part, when a new player walked in, all dark hair, huge arms, and thighs the circumference of watermelons.

Drake.

Of course. Because my life needed an extra level of complicated right now.

I glanced at Hawke, who narrowed his eyes in Drake's direction.

I followed Hawke's gaze back to Drake, and saw Drake's attention resting on me, his deep blue irises heated from within. He walked over to me immediately.

"I was wrong," he said, taking my hand and guiding me away from the table and a crap ton of tips. "My work *is* going to be interesting tonight."

I gave him a sideways glance. "It doesn't really look like you're working."

"It doesn't look like you are either," he said, his eyes dropping the length of me and slowly lifting back up.

I scoffed and whisper-hissed, "Do you think I'd wear something like this in public by choice?"

He licked his lips slowly, one corner of his mouth hitching up. "I've seen you wear skimpier things."

I blushed, recalling the night I'd been heavily under the influence of a controlled substance and invited him over to my house.

"I bet we can still make the chocolate in your cleavage work," he suggested, referencing our previous conversation at the *Tribune*, his eyes warm with desire. "I just need to grab some candy."

I ignored the cleavage and chocolate comments. "This is work for you? Because it looks like an illegal poker game to me."

"If it were in Utah, it would be illegal. Wyoming is a bit of a grey area—which, I imagine, is why the games are held here."

Utah's gambling laws were the strictest in the nation. No monetary wagers were allowed at all, even among friends, and if you wanted a lottery ticket, you had to be prepared for a road trip because you couldn't get one in the state. If the poker game had been held in Utah, it wouldn't have lasted long. "So this is an ongoing game? Who plans it?"

"A game runner organizes it, from what I understand."

"Who's the game runner?"

Drake lifted his shoulders. "No idea. I've never met them; I only know the runner is the one in charge."

I scanned the room, taking in all the Utah power players at the tables. "How are people invited?" I knew Hawke had to work to get an invitation.

"I was recommended for the game by another Utah House of Representatives member, so that's how I got in. A lot of business and political negotiations take place off site. This is one of the locations."

I was accosted with irritation. "I find that rather hypocritical considering the predominant opinions on gambling by the Utah religious majority." In Utah, politics was frequently controlled by religion, and gambling was considered a sin by the Mormon Church. I was shocked a game like this was allowed for any sort of networking.

He shrugged as we sat down on a comfortable couch, far away from the game tables and noise. "Some people are orthodox when it comes to religion. Some aren't."

I rolled my eyes. "It's not a buffet, Drake. You don't get to pick and choose what rules you follow in a religion. You're not deciding between chicken and roast."

"Actually, you do get to choose," he said, leaning closer to me. "Everyone has different viewpoints on right and wrong, and all churches give members leeway to have opinions and make their own choices. The way I see it, religion is really about being an upstanding person who helps others, and deciding what beliefs work for you personally to help you achieve your good human goals."

I knew all about that. Drake was not one of the strict Mormons, but he pretended to be to fit in and win elections. The problem was I didn't know exactly what his beliefs were, or which of the rules had more meaning to him than others. It kind of seemed like religion should be an all-in sort of thing. I didn't like the obfuscation that came with justifications like Drake's, but I saw his reasons for it. "I'd like to know where you fall in that category."

He eyed me, rolling his tongue over the inside of his cheek like he was trying to decide what to say next. "I saw a photo of you the other night in a red dress," Drake said, a muscle working at his jaw. "There wasn't much dress."

I swore. A big one. And not quietly. He'd seen the photo The Ladies posted of me leaving with Hawke, those covert Lady asshats! Jackie had probably sent it to him personally. "The Ladies need to mind their own business." The problem was that they had no business to mind, and their lives were so unsatisfying that they resorted to gossip and talking about other people because they had nothing interesting happening in their own lives to discuss instead. The gossip smacked of jealousy and unfulfilled dreams. If I were nicer, I'd feel bad for them for their lack of life achievements, but considering I was constantly the subject of their ire, I wasn't feeling in a particularly compassionate mood.

"You weren't with me in that dress," Drake said, and I

couldn't tell if his tone betrayed anger or hurt—or both. It was also pretty clear that he hadn't seen Hawke yet and didn't know my red dress date was right across the room. "And if you had been," he continued, "you wouldn't have been in that dress for long."

Hawke had given me the same speech when he'd picked me up in his fancy Audi, and we almost hadn't left my house.

I took a deep breath. "Again, I was working that night."

Drake blinked. "So when you're working with me, I get you wearing Rice Krispie treat confetti. When you're working with Hawke, you look like you're about to rip your clothes off and go straight to bed."

"Two totally different situations," I said without apology. "Both predicated on something that related to my job."

Drake's eyes went up and down my current costume, complete with the corset, skirt so short it showed my frilly black and red panties when I moved too fast, and devil horns. "And this is work as well?"

"Yes," I hissed. "If you don't screw it up for me. Be quiet, go flirt with some angels, and pretend I'm not even here."

He breathed out a long sigh. "Number one, pretending you're not here will never happen. You haunt my waking and sleeping hours."

I scowled. "I don't really think that's a compliment."

"Two," his eyes darkened and his whole body shifted, radiating sensual energy, "I'm much more interested in flirting with the devil tonight."

If that wasn't a double entendre, I didn't know what was.

I leaned in closer to him, my breasts pressing against his hard chest, and whispered, "There are plenty of devils here to choose from." I got up slowly, and walked away from him. And it took a serious amount of willpower to do it.

I wandered the room, trying to figure out the connection between Aaron Storm and this game. I'd been watching him all night. He'd moved around, talking to people like they were all old friends—and they probably were. He was a financial planner. Maybe he was inviting wealthy clients to play and taking a cut of the game percentage? But what did he mean when he'd mentioned evidence on the phone? And what did his dad's stolen art have to do with it all? I was lost in thought, when I suddenly found myself between my two potential love interests by the bar.

"Hi," I said, looking from Drake to Hawke and trying to act like this was all totally normal. It totally wasn't.

"Did he bring you here?" Drake asked conversationally, tilting his head toward Hawke. Drake's tone was so even and contained that I knew he was anything but calm.

"I brought myself here." I smiled and ordered a Utah staple, a Sprite-spiked fruit punch. I wanted something much harder, but I needed all my synapses firing at full power for this evening.

Drake shook his head. "I don't believe it. There's no way you'd wear that outfit in a place like this without peer pressure."

I took offense to that. "I'm excellent at my job and I do what I need to in order to get information. Not unlike you," I said pointedly, reminding him he was currently networking at a place that was definitely not sanctioned by his religion.

"I think she looks great," Hawke offered, purposely provoking Drake.

"Of course you do," Drake said, a muscle working at his

jaw. "You'd have her in something like this all the time if you had your way."

"Nah," Hawke said, tipping back his glass and swallowing what looked to be a sip of whiskey. "I'd have her wearing much less."

I could actually see Drake's blood pressure rising in the vein at his temple. His face was frozen into a falsely composed mask that was trying very hard not to break. "You're dangerous and you put those around you in danger. She's not the one for you, Hawke."

I held up my hand between both of them, annoyed as hell. "First of all, I'm the only one who gets to decide who the one for me is, so back off, Drake. Second, the men in my life don't pick my clothes, I do, and I'm usually wearing jeans and a t-shirt, so deal with it. Third, I'd really like to know what the bad blood between you two is. Care to enlighten me?"

Both Hawke and Drake immediately clamped their mouths shut.

"That's what I thought," I said, pressing my lips into a line so nothing would come out that I might regret later. "I have a job to do, and I'm going to get back to it." I turned and looked them each dead in the eye. "Stay out of my way. Both of you."

I walked off and spent the rest of the night trying to gather information and figure out more about the game. I'd learned that the stakes were high and people had lost and made thousands and tens of thousands of dollars tonight. Most of the people in attendance had been to the games before. There was someone behind the whole thing—a game runner who organized each event. I wasn't sure who that was, but looking around the room, Aaron Storm seemed like a pretty good bet for that position.

An hour later, Pam came in and announced the end of the evening's play. She then informed the attendees that the game runner wanted to say a few words. My eyes went directly to Aaron Storm, and I waited for him to stand up and start speaking.

A hush fell over the crowd and everyone's attention swung to a doorway on the other side of the room. An exquisite woman wearing an emerald green gown that hugged each of her stunning curves and looked like it was made of pure silk, walked into the room. She was a study in refinement, grace, and she practically dripped money. The dress complimented her skin tone perfectly. Her cheekbones were high, her frame slender, and she had brilliant red hair and gorgeous green eyes that had been just as pretty the first time I'd met her. At Aaron Storm's house.

The game runner was Cadence Storm, Aaron Storm's wife.

Chapter Twenty-Two

It took a few seconds for the shock to wear off. I glanced at Aaron Storm. His face lacked all expression, but a muscle was moving at his jaw like he was highly irritated.

"I'd like to thank everyone for coming tonight," Cadence said, a kind smile flashing across her lips and warming her eyes. "You can settle up your accounts with Pam, and in a few weeks, invites will go out for our next event. Keep in mind that patrons who show their appreciation are significantly more likely to be invited back. Thank you for coming, and we'll see you next time."

Cadence was the game runner? Was she working with Aaron on the games? She had to be! I didn't have long to stay stunned because Cadence walked off to the side of the room before exiting. The game players went back to their conversations and some got up to wait in line to settle their accounts with Pam.

I immediately followed Cadence out the door and down the hall to another room where she was talking with a woman. A burly man wearing a suit, ear piece, and gun holstered at his waist, stood behind her. He was unmistakably some form of security.

"Cadence," I said, a question in my tone.

She glanced up, startled. It took her a minute, but she eventually recognized me. "Kate Saxee? From the *Tribune?*"

I nodded.

Her eyes widened. She turned to the woman and security guard. "Can you give me the room?"

The woman and Cadence's security guard walked out the door.

"I almost didn't recognize you," she said, the surprise evident on her face. "Are you working with one of the entertainment agencies we hired?"

I laughed. "No, I was following a story lead and it led me straight here."

A streak of anxiety crossed her face. "A lead about what?" Her tone was full of caution.

"The robberies in Branson Falls."

"Oh dear," she said, her face falling as she sat on a chaise lounge in the corner of the room. "I didn't mean for this to happen, but things got out of hand."

I sat across from her, trying not to seem too eager for answers to the story I'd been chasing. "What exactly happened?" I asked. "Why don't you start from the beginning?"

She took a deep breath, her hands worrying over each other in her lap. "I've been working with Betty Turner."

My jaw dropped. "Betty Turner? The same Betty Turner who was robbed a couple of weeks ago? The same Betty Turner who had an anonymous potato casserole dropped off at her house?"

Cadence nodded. "Betty and I met during a painting event at the craft store in town."

I knew I'd seen Cadence somewhere before! She'd been the woman walking out of Get Crafty with Betty Turner the day I'd followed the Speedy Superheroes! She'd been wearing a beanie cap at the time or I probably would have remembered her striking red hair.

"My family lives in another state, and with the kids, I wasn't getting out much. I needed to make friends and have a social life outside of being a mother and wife. I decided to attend a painting event at the craft store one night and that's where I met Betty. She was widowed and her family didn't live close either, so we started talking and bonded. Craft night became a weekly thing."

"How did craft night turn into a gambling ring?" I asked, confused.

Cadence closed her eyes and took a deep breath like she'd been holding in the truth for too long. "Betty used to run a gambling game in California when she was younger. It was lucrative and she was very successful. She confided in me that she wanted to do it again, but she wasn't as young as she used to be and she needed some help."

You could have blown me over with a feather. Betty Turner, sweet widow and anonymously dropped casserole food critic, had run a gambling game in one state, and started another successful game targeting players who lived in one of the strictest moral states in the union? I would have had an easier time believing that Keanu was an actual unicorn.

Cadence continued, "I was desperate for something to do. Anything. I'm a mom, and I love being a mom, but it's not all I want to be." I could hear the guilt in her tone and my heart went out to her for feeling like she was stuck in a specific role and couldn't embrace any others. "I'm more than just my kids. I double majored in college. I had dreams and goals before I met Aaron. But then I fell in love and everything changed. And not in the direction I wanted, but what Aaron wanted."

"So you changed your goals and life path for him?"

She sighed and picked at a piece of string on the couch. "He's very traditional. He wanted a wife who would stay home, raise the kids, and take care of the household while he worked. I thought his perspective stemmed from the fact that he was young and that kind of attitude was simply what he'd been taught. I thought that as we got older he'd eventually change his mind, but he never did. I've been stuck at home, helping him live his dreams instead of pursuing my own. It was suffocating me, and I knew it. I have interests and passions and I haven't been able to pursue them for years because I'm expected to stay at home and support him instead. Betty's proposition was perfect for me. She does the game organizing, finds the locations, vets the invite lists, and chooses the people who will be invited to gamble. I simply have to be there to manage the night, keep things calm, deal with tempers, and be the face of the game."

I knew what feeling unfulfilled could do to a person. I was glad Cadence had taken her happiness and future into her own hands, but based on what she'd said about Aaron, I wasn't sure he was going to see it the same way. "This is a big game, and it's been a large part of your life for a while now. How did you hide it from Aaron?" He seemed like a pretty savvy guy, and considering he was a financial planner and they had one of the biggest homes in town, I guessed he'd be difficult to keep a large influx of money from.

"He knew I went to craft class once a week. Betty and I would discuss business afterward for an hour or so. I told him I was spending time with her because she was lonely."

"What about when you have to be gone on poker game nights?"

"We only host the game once every two months," she explained. "I tell Aaron I'm going for a spa weekend with my girlfriends. It's not a total lie. After the game, I always spend a day at the spa. The games are full of entitled, brash, and frequently unkind men. I need time to decompress before going home to my family."

That made sense. If I were her, I'd take longer than a day. "If you don't like the players and the game is stressful for you, why did you keep doing it?"

She thought about the question for a minute before answering, "It's not all the players, just some of them. And I'm the game runner so if any player makes me uncomfortable, I note it, and they don't get invited back. I have control here, in a way I don't have control in other areas of my life. Running the game gives me a purpose, and makes me feel alive in a way I've never felt before."

I could understand that. She was doing something she knew her husband didn't approve of, and rebelling in a way. There was probably also an adrenaline factor to it since she was doing something illicit...and possibly in a grey area of the law. "How are these games not illegal?" I asked.

She nodded like she was expecting the question. "For two reasons. One, we hold the game in Wyoming, and social gambling among friends isn't outlawed here like it is in Utah. Two, because we work off of tips instead of raking the pot and taking a cut of the winnings as a commission," she explained. "That's why Betty needed me as host—to help get tips because that's how we get paid."

Understanding dawned. "So that's why you asked for tips at the end of the evening tonight."

"Yes. If people don't tip, and tip well, they don't get invited back to the next game. And they know it. My games are safe, exclusive, and full of wealthy individuals spanning everything from politicians to the CEOs of Silicon Slopes. An invitation to one of my games is in high demand, and isn't easy to get."

If the game was connected to the auction like Hawke thought it was, then that's why he'd gone there before attempting to get an invitation here. He was showing them he had money, interest, and could play with the big boy crowd. I still wasn't certain how the two were linked though.

"Isn't forcing a tip for an invitation a little like blackmail?" I asked.

She shook her head. "No. I view it more like a ticket fee. People who pay for the ticket get to come, people who don't, don't get invited again."

I couldn't argue with that. A lawyer probably could, but I couldn't.

"So you split the tip money with Betty," I confirmed.

Cadence nodded. "We also pay the girls from the entertainment company ten percent of the tip pot and it's split evenly among them. They keep any additional tips they were personally given."

That's what Sandra was talking about when she told me how to act to get better tips.

"How much tip money are we talking about here?" I asked.

She shrugged. "It depends on the game, what players are there, and how generous they're feeling, but usually we make at least fifty thousand a game, sometimes a little less, sometimes more."

My mouth fell open. I was obviously in the wrong business.

"Aaron never found out about the money?" If not, this didn't bode well for his financial planning skills.

"I set up an anonymous LLC for the business in Delaware so it couldn't be tracked to me through a social security number. All of the money is deposited into a Delaware business bank, and my accountant takes care of everything. I consulted accountants and lawyers and made sure the game and everything about it was legal and above board before I got involved. The game has to be held in Wyoming, and has to be considered strictly social among friends. As long as we're not taking a cut from the pot, we're only earning money on tips, and we make sure to pay our taxes on those tips, we're fine."

Interesting. I knew about anonymous LLC states, but had no idea those gambling loopholes existed. That still didn't explain the robberies, or how the auction Hawke and I had gone to was involved with the game. "So how did the robberies and Ron Storm sculptures get involved?"

Cadence took deep breath and let it out, disappointment showing in the lines of her face. "The mob started threatening us."

I lifted my hand, palm up, to stop her for a moment. "Wait a minute," I said, trying to compose myself. "The mob? Like the actual mob? We have one of those in Utah?" I truly had no idea, and I was an investigative reporter who covered things like that. I should have known about something as monumental as organized crime infiltrating the state.

Her shoulders slumped like she was carrying a heavy

weight. "Betty previously had dealings with them when she was running the California games. Once she moved to Utah and stopped her game, they left her alone. But word moves quickly in dark markets, and it didn't take long for the mob to find out she was involved in running a game again."

"What does the mob have to do with poker?" I asked, still baffled.

"The mob wanted to be our enforcement to make sure debts were paid, to head our game security, and for intimidation. They force their services on people. Betty and I didn't want their help and they wouldn't take no for an answer. Betty was adamant that we not cave, but the mob approached me separately from Betty and threatened her if I didn't cooperate. I knew my family was probably next on the list of people who would be put in jeopardy. I couldn't stand the thought of Betty being hurt, and they told me I'd have to pay them to stop that from happening. Betty would know if I was taking the money from our joint business account, and I couldn't take it from my family account because Aaron watches our investments daily and would notice it immediately." She breathed out a deep sigh. "So I came up with another option."

Understanding dawned. "Your father-in-law's sculptures."

She nodded, her face visibly relieved that she was able to talk openly about what she'd done. "They're valuable now, but they're going to keep going up in value over time. I thought if I gave the mob one or two sculptures, they'd leave the game, Betty, and my family alone. I couldn't give them one of our pieces because Aaron would know it was missing and start an investigation. But Aaron has a master list of where all the other sculptures are so it was easy to find them. I picked a family that was moving and took the first sculpture from them."

I was stunned at the idea and its effectiveness. She was able to stop the mob, keep the game going, and keep her secrets all with a simple robbery, one that she executed seamlessly.

"The first time was easy. I simply offered to assist the family with their move," she explained. "I helped them pack, and loaded several boxes—including the one containing the sculpture I'd helped pack—in my car. Then I took the sculpture out and handed it over to the mob as my payment."

I marveled at the simplicity of her plan.

"That lasted a couple of months before the mob got restless. I've let them have more control than I probably should have—even inviting players they suggested to the games."

Which was how Hawke had gotten his invitation. The mob ran the auction and suggested new players who should receive invitations.

"I realized they weren't only going to settle for one or two sculptures, and I needed a way to get more. I'd heard about the Speedy Superheroes in a news story one night and realized if we had a chapter in Branson Falls, I could use it as my cover. Betty and I had a mutual friend who occasionally helped us in the game. He had more moral dexterity than Betty and I, and was willing to do things we weren't—like breaking and entering. I spoke to him privately about the mob situation, paid him, and he opened the Speedy Superheroes chapter in Branson Falls. Then he started stealing things."

My mouth dropped. My gut had told me the Speedy Superheroes were involved, but I hadn't figured out how. I never would have guessed a superhero was stealing sculptures to help pay off the mob so a poker game could continue with no one being harmed.

"But there were robberies at multiple homes," I said. "With various odds and ends taken, and some of the homes didn't even own Ron Storm sculptures."

She nodded. "That was done on purpose. If we would have gone around only stealing Ron Storm sculptures, it would have been obvious the sculptures were the target. We needed to be more covert than that. The pattern needed to be odd and random. So odd items at random locations interspersed with the actual thefts is what my associate focused on. I honestly think no one would have suspected anything if my associate has spaced the thefts out more."

I had to hand it to her; she was committed to this business and didn't seem to feel too bad about felony robbery.

"So the robberies had nothing to do with Inked AF opening in town?"

She shook her head and her face fell. "No. The additional pressure from the mob started happening at the same time, and I had to get more sculptures so the robberies became more common. I felt awful when I found out the tattoo shop was being blamed for the thefts."

Relief washed over me. It meant Axel and Sasha weren't involved and once the story broke, I hoped people in town would rally around them and make them feel more welcome in Branson.

A noise from behind Cadence startled us both and we jumped up.

"Did you hear that?" she asked.

I nodded, wishing I'd figured out a way to conceal my stun gun or pepper spray in my skintight costume. At least the outfit gave me a lot of flexibility because my heart was racing and I thought there was a good chance I might need to use my Hawke-taught self-defense skills on whoever was in the room with us...and I really hoped it wasn't a mob member.

We heard a click, each of us bracing for whatever was about to appear, when Aaron Storm stepped through the door that led to another room, his face a combination of fury and pain. "I heard everything," he said, his voice shaky with hurt and anger. "How could you do this to me? To my family? To my dad?"

Cadence's surprise turned to sadness as tears welled up in her eyes. "I'm sorry, Aaron. I'm so sorry. I didn't mean to hurt you."

Aaron paced the room, strongly resembling a rhino getting ready to charge, and I wasn't sure he was any safer to be around than the mob at the moment. I stayed back, watching him closely, and ready to protect Cadence and I both if it came down to it.

"How did you find me?" Cadence asked.

I'd been wondering that myself. I'd followed him here, but someone had to have told Aaron about the game and his wife.

Aaron looked up at Cadence. "You seemed preoccupied and were spending a lot of time at your craft nights. Then you kept leaving to go out of town on spa weekends. During your trip two months ago, I ran into Dorinda Fromm. I knew she was supposed to be with you that weekend and asked her why she'd decided not to go. She had no clue what I was talking about. I asked you questions and tried to get you to open up to me, but you wouldn't. So I hired a private detective. They called me earlier today and said they had evidence you were involved in something dangerous and illegal, and told me you'd be at this address at seven o'clock."

Ah, that was the call I'd heard Aaron take.

"It's not illegal," Cadence insisted. "We're outside of Utah, and we don't take a commission from the gamblers."

Aaron looked at her like she'd lost her mind. "You're facilitating a game that allows players to exchange money they've won and lost. I'm not an attorney, but I'm sure that makes you complicit somehow."

Her lips pursed with resentment. "I'm not stupid," she said, her words pouring out with years of regrets and pent up frustrations. "I consulted my own attorneys and accountants before I got into this. They say I'm fine." She stood her ground against him and I was proud of her for it.

Aaron's expression was full of anger. "The area is grey at best."

Cadence looked down. "I needed to be something more than a mother, Aaron. I told you that from the beginning of our relationship. And I told you that again repeatedly throughout it. You never listened."

He leveled her with a hard stare. "And I told you I wanted a housewife."

Cadence breathed out a ragged sigh, her eyes liquid. "I guess we were both hoping each other would change. We shouldn't have moved forward and gotten married with those presumptions."

The conversation felt like it had taken a very personal turn and I shouldn't be there. I quietly exited the room and told Cadence's security officer to keep the door ajar and go in if he heard anything that sounded like Cadence was in danger.

Hawke and Drake were both waiting outside the door,

directly across from the security guy. From the tension in the air, it seemed they'd all had words.

"Are you okay?" Hawke asked, his voice clipped.

"I'm fine," I said, pulling off my ridiculous devil horns headband. The adrenaline spike I'd had was going to wear off shortly, and Cadence had downloaded a crap ton of information on me that I needed to get written down immediately so I could consult my notes for the complicated article I'd need to write.

"What happened?" Drake asked.

"A lot," I said. "And right now, all I want is to get back into a comfortable pair of jeans, go home, and cuddle my dog."

Drake and Hawke both looked like they had murder in their eyes. I couldn't handle it at the moment. "I promise I'll give you more details, but I need to go home. Alone."

I was shocked when they both let me pass by them without more discussion. I went back to the changing room, switched into my regular reporter clothes, and made my way back to my Jeep, happy to no longer be a devil pin-up girl, and even happier I hadn't been murdered by the mob tonight.

Chapter Twenty-Three

I sat in my Jeep for at least thirty minutes taking notes, then recorded more voice notes as I drove home. I thought of the game, Cadence, and how Betty and Cadence had come together. Betty, alone and wanting some connection and something to do; Cadence feeling lonely and unfulfilled in her own life. No wonder the two of them had bonded. On the surface it didn't seem like they shared much in common, but they were both in the same emotional place and needed each other.

I hoped that Cadence and Aaron would be able to work things out. Cadence had betrayed him in a horrible way and that wouldn't be easy for them both to come to terms with. And Aaron had asked her to be someone she wasn't—a person she had never wanted to be; that wouldn't be easy to resolve either. I couldn't imagine how difficult it would be to explain the thefts of her father-in-law's sculptures to the Storm family. Those pieces had been sold by the mob, who had purposely inflated the prices to get more money and create a higher demand in the market. Cadence couldn't get the pieces back. Her gambling game might straddle a legal grey line, but robbery didn't, and even though she hadn't committed the crimes herself, I was sure there would be consequences.

It had been a long drive home and as I took the freeway exit for Branson Falls, I sighed. I'd be home, makeup free, showered, cuddling with Gandalf, and eating ice cream soon. Not thinking about work or anything else for the rest of the night, and definitely not worrying about being robbed because I certainly didn't own a Ron Storm sculpture.

The thought of the robberies snagged in my brain. I was missing something, I knew it. I paused, trying to put my finger on it. Betty had been one of the robbery victims, but that didn't make sense since Cadence and her associate were the ones organizing the thefts. They wouldn't have robbed her business partner, and Betty said she'd been targeted by two men instead of one.

There had been a game tonight, and Cadence usually paid the mob's game fee in Ron Storm pieces. But the last robbery targeting a Ron Storm sculpture had been botched. The sculpture wasn't taken, and no Ron Storm sculpture had been stolen since.

My heart started beating a little faster. That meant that the mob payment hadn't been made. If the mob hadn't gotten their fee, they might follow through with their threats to hurt Betty Turner, and Cadence probably hadn't even considered that because she was currently in the middle of a discussion trying to salvage her marriage. Betty was at risk. I had to warn her. I pressed on the gas and took the turn to Betty's house faster than I probably should have, judging by the squeal of my tires.

I pulled up to the house, grabbed my stun gun and pepper

spray from the glove compartment, flung open my Jeep door, and ran up Betty's front porch stairs. Her door was already cracked open and a horrible feeling settled in my stomach.

"Betty," I said her name softly, hoping that maybe she was hanging out inside her living room with the door slightly ajar on purpose, and no mob members had come to hurt her.

No answer.

Dammit!

I grabbed my phone and dialed the police, then spoke as quietly as could, "This is Kate Saxee. I'm on the scene of a break-in. I need the police at Betty Turner's house."

I hung up the phone, and quietly stepped inside the living room.

The room looked fine. Lights were emitting a warm glow like she'd been home recently, and might even be there still.

I took my stun gun out of my pocket and held it in one hand, and pepper spray in the other. Hawke had told me repeatedly to get an actual gun, but I didn't trust myself with it. I'd probably end up shooting a house plant or animal instead of a bad guy.

I made my way down the hall as softly as possible, and that's when I heard a deep male voice. "I know she's here! We saw her!"

I heard a sigh and another deep voice. "We've looked through the whole house. I don't see her anywhere, Carl."

"Maybe she has a panic room? We saw her through the window. She's, like, eighty-something. She can't have gotten far."

I heard some grumbling and swearing. "Okay, let's look again."

If they didn't know where Betty was, that was a good

thing. Hopefully she'd stay hidden until the Branson cops could arrive.

Rustling noises started and got louder as they came toward the hall. I quickly jumped into a room to hide, and closed the door behind me. The room was lined wall-to-wall with shelves and cabinets full of bolts of material, ribbons, and a couple of sewing machines. It looked like a craft room.

The noises continued down the hall, getting closer. "Hey," the voice who was definitely not Carl said, "did we check this room? The door is closed."

I swore in my head. Repeatedly. Like, the only words coming out were swears. I should have been more careful and left the door open like it had been before I arrived.

"I thought we checked it," Carl said, his voice intrigued. "Check again."

I nestled behind the door, next to a wall of cheery printed fabric. Carl and the other guy came in and looked around. "Hit the lights," Carl said.

His buddy did, and that meant if they moved the door, I would be one hundred percent on display. Carl moved around the room. "I don't see anything," he said. He started to pull on the door. I had my stun gun and pepper spray in attack mode when I heard a scream that sounded a hell of a lot like a warrior princess coming from the area of the craft closet. And then I heard a gunshot. Carl went down, yelling in pain.

"Take that, you dirty mob ninnies!" Betty, warrior princess yelled, marching into the center of the room, gun in hand. She planted her feet and lifted her arms in a shooting stance. "Think you can beat me up to scare me? Well I'd like to intro-duce you to Bambi, bitches!"

Betty fired another shot, and took out mob muscle number two.

"Holy…" I trailed off, not wanting to swear in front of someone who was older than my grandma but could clearly kick even my ass and seemed to have no problem with swears herself.

Betty beamed and put the safety back on her gun before turning to me with a wide smile. "Bambi never disappoints," she said, lifting the gun and petting the barrel.

Carl and his friend were on the ground. She'd shot one of them in the leg, and the other in the arm. She grabbed some orange fabric ribbon off one of her shelves. "Here, help me tie them up."

Luckily, I'd recently witnessed a goat subdued by ribbon and had a good idea how this worked. Too bad my mom wasn't around to help since she'd shown some serious skills.

"Damn mob asshats," Betty said, shaking her head as we tied them up with various bits of fabric and tulle. "This is the second time they've tried to threaten me into submission."

I glanced over at her while she tied an impressive knot. "So the robbery that happened to you earlier was the mob as well?" I'd already figured as much but it was good to get confirmation.

She nodded in response. "Same guys. They think they can intimidate me! Well they have another think coming!"

I sat back on my legs and looked at her. "I know about the game."

She lifted her brows slightly in surprise.

"Did you know Cadence was paying the mob off?" I asked.

She pressed her lips together. "I had my suspicions."

Interesting. I wondered why she hadn't talked to Cadence

about it. "How long have you been running games like this?"

The two guys were on the ground, whimpering in pain, but they hadn't passed out, so that was a good sign that their blood loss wasn't critical—yet. We finished tying them up and Betty checked her knots as she answered, "Years. Started when I was in my twenties. My husband was an alcoholic and couldn't hold a job. We had kids and I had to find a way to make money. I'd grown up watching my dad run poker games and decided to try running one myself. It did well. So well that the mob got wind of it and wanted a piece of the pie. Sometimes I'd have to float players who overextended and couldn't pay what they owed. The mob wanted to go after the game players who were in debt to me, and take a chunk of the money. I said no. They weren't happy with my resistance and threatened my family. I'd made plenty of money at that point so I shut my game down. But years went by and I realized I missed the excitement of the game." Her eyes got bright with the memory. "I'm too old to run it by myself. I needed someone young and smart and beautiful. Cadence was perfect for the job, and she not only wanted it, but she needed it too. We've made a great team."

"What happens now?" I asked. Wondering if the game would continue. I wasn't sure how it could considering Cadence was going to be in a lot of trouble for her part in the robberies.

Betty shrugged. "Who knows?"

We heard Bobby's voice yell from outside, "Drop your weapons!"

"It's fine, Bobby," I yelled back. "We're fine. But you might want to bring handcuffs. I don't know how long this ribbon will hold. And you're going to want to call an ambulance."

Chapter Twenty-Four

"Well!" Phyllis said, "that was dramatic!"

"Honestly," I answered back, scooping up a huge amount of her amazing cheese dip. "I didn't think they could make two strangers marrying each other any more awkward, but they managed to do it."

"Trust my words," Phyllis said, "it won't end well."

"Reality shows rarely do." Gandalf climbed onto my lap and curled into a little ball. He was basically a tiny heater, which sucked in the summer, but was awesome for fall and would be even better come winter—and snow would be falling soon.

"Tell me more about this gambling game," Phyllis said, switching off the TV.

I'd written the article about the game and the connection to the robberies for the *Tribune* last week and it had been the talk of the town ever since. Gambling was a no-no, and the fact that a prominent mother and grandmother from Branson Falls had been the masterminds behind the game was basically a small town gossip orgasm. "It's been going on for about two years. The mob found out about it a year ago, so Cadence started paying them off with stolen Ron Storm sculptures. The mob took the sculptures and auctioned them off to the filthy rich, inflating the worth of the pieces, and the prices."

I'd done some research on the game, and other games like it, for the article. In the process, I found out that organized crime is no joke and they have their hands in pretty much everything. All around the world. It's scary.

"Why didn't Cadence explain things to Aaron and Betty?" Phyllis asked, grabbing a few more pieces of the caramel popcorn I made.

I took a drink of my hot chocolate—real hot chocolate. Phyllis had a recipe so scrumptious that I liked it as much as coffee. "Betty refused to pay the mob. Cadence felt like she had no choice. Betty was probably right and could have held out, but they saw a weak link in Cadence. Cadence has a lot of people she cares for and would do anything to keep them safe. As for Aaron, he wouldn't have been supportive of her having a job, and given their religious beliefs, he definitely wouldn't have been okay with Cadence managing a gambling game. He also never would have sanctioned his dad's sculptures being used to help fund the mob payoff so the game could continue. Cadence wanted to keep the game, her family, and make sure everyone was safe. She had to find a way to take care of it all on her own."

Phyllis shook her head, her lips turned down in sadness. "It's too bad she didn't feel like she could go to her husband for help."

I shrugged. "Relationships are all so different and expectations can cause a lot of problems. Cadence and Aaron both had different goals and expectations for the future, and that affected everything else."

"Will Cadence go to jail?"

I refilled my popcorn bowl and started snacking on it, one by one. "She has a long legal road ahead of her, but I talked to some attorney friends today and they told me that Cadence will likely make a deal in exchange for giving the FBI information about the mob and the contacts she was working with. She'll probably have to do some volunteer work, but with the information she's offering, I don't think she'll have to go to jail. She and Aaron are going to start counseling and try to work things out. You don't throw away that many years of marriage. I hope they'll be able to reconcile."

Phyllis nodded like she was pleased to hear it. She took a couple of bites of popcorn. "What about the Speedy Superheroes? Do you know who was helping Cadence and robbing people?"

Speckles' identity was something that still bothered me, and I hoped I'd figure it out eventually. "Cadence refused to give Speckles' real name and took all the responsibility for Speckles' crimes. But I'd be surprised if it doesn't come out at some point. Nut Man said Speckles had started taking superhero shifts again, but after the mob attacked Betty and things came out about Cadence and the game, the Speckles persona vanished."

"Do you think Speckles is gone for good?" Phyllis asked.

I shrugged. "You never know. The Vendetta League is still active in Branson, and Nut Man says it's growing, so I don't think we'll stop seeing the Speedy Superheroes any time soon. Maybe Speckles will be back."

Phyllis clapped her hands together like she was excited.

"Well, that's good because I haven't seen the superheroes at all yet!"

Gandalf stirred and Phyllis petted him back to sleep. "Oh!" she said with excitement, "I almost forgot! What ever happened with the casserole caper? I'm still pretty upset I didn't get a meal!"

I laughed. Of course she'd be concerned about that. "Bobby called me about that mystery. He said it was some kids having fun. They decided it would be hilarious to anonymously drop casseroles on doorsteps so they picked people they thought might need help with a meal or five. About a week after Betty was attacked, they realized the casserole might get tied back to them and came forward with the truth."

Phyllis nodded like it made perfect sense, but when Bobby had told me, my first thought had been: only in Branson Falls.

"Have you heard from Sasha and Axel about Inked AF?" she asked.

I had, and this update broke my heart, but I still hoped it would have a happy ending. "The vandalism that happened was organized by Axel," I said. "He took out a big insurance policy on the shop and his pieces to help cover the debt they were under. He wrote the anonymous note that was left at the crime scene, and arranged for the pieces to be stolen. It's not good, but he hadn't taken payment for the fraud yet, so that should help his case. Drake is representing Axel and I think he'll be okay, though he might step back from the business for a while and let Sasha run things."

It turned out that Fred didn't have anything to do with the vandalism, which made me pretty happy because it meant my childhood vision of him as a sweet and kind antique shop owner who'd let me wander his store making up stories about items, could stay firmly intact.

"Drake hooked Sasha up with one of the comic conventions in Salt Lake, and she's been working with some of the film studios in Utah too, so I think she's had a lot of doors opened for her. She's expanding the business to include things that people in Branson are interested in, like temporary tattoos and cosplay. It's a smart move for her, and I think she'll be able to pull the business out of the debt it's in and do well."

"Good," Phyllis said, nodding. "Because I've been eyein' a tattoo and I want them to do it!"

My eyes widened in surprise. "I've never thought of you as the tattoo type."

She gave me a conspiratorial grin and a wink. "I like to keep people on their toes. Speakin' of that, did they ever find out who egged Drake's house? I'd kind of like to give them a high-five for the giggle."

"No," I said, taking a piece of candy out of the bowl on her coffee table. "They avoided the cameras, but I'm pretty sure it was an angry constituent, and Drake thought so too. Nothing has happened since—that I know of—but it surely won't be the last time."

All of the mysteries had been solved for the moment— well, at least most of them. I still had no clue who I wanted to date, or what to have for dinner, but I could figure both of those things out with time. One mystery did remain, though. "The only thing that still bothers me is that I can't figure out who those big guys were that we saw walking by our houses," I said. "And then you saw them again a few days later and said Gandalf was barking. It makes me uneasy." At first I thought the guys had something to do with the robberies, but I now knew that wasn't the case. I'd pondered whether they might be part of the mob, but I'd seen them walking down the street and they weren't the same guys who had been arrested at Betty's house. Maybe they were other mob members though.

"Oh!" Phyllis said, clapping her hands together. "I solved that mystery!"

My eyes widened. "Who was it?"

"Salespeople," she said with a grin. "They were tryin' to get people to buy solar panels. They'd been up and down the street for weeks. Their plan is to get one neighbor on board and then go back to the other neighbors and tell them their friends are doin' it and they should too. That's why they didn't talk to us that first day. They didn't have any sales yet. But they did later."

I nodded in realization. "It's a solid tactic for sure. They're trying to use peer pressure to their advantage."

"Yep," she said, pressing her lips together. "They stopped by the house and talked to me a couple of days ago. I told them I'll probably croak before the solar panel loan is paid off, so no thanks. I also told them you're a renter and aren't interested so they should leave you alone too."

"Thanks," I said, and meant it. I was rarely home and when I was, I didn't like to be bothered by salespeople. I had a no soliciting sign that said, "No soliciting unless you have Thin Mints. The dog will bark, shit will get real. Don't make it awkward." The sign didn't seem to work. I also had two very large not-boyfriends, but they didn't seem to be much of a deterrent either.

I frowned. "It's weird they weren't wearing company shirts, or badges, or something." Most home owners don't allow people in the door without identification anymore. Not that it mattered though since identification was easy to fake.

"I think they were a newer company and not the most professional."

"Well," I said, gathering my things. "Thanks for letting me know, and for always watching out for me. And for being my reality show watching buddy."

She smiled. "I love our date nights."

"Me too," I said, giving her a hug. "I better get home and put Gandalf to bed."

"He's been sleeping all night," she said, "but I'm sure he could sleep some more."

I smiled and petted his little head.

"I'll watch to make sure you get home safe."

She did, and she blinked her outside lights at me once I'd gotten the door open. I blinked mine back at her, our little message that all was well, and got ready for bed. It had been a long few weeks and I was exhausted.

Considering the last costume situation I'd participated in had ended with the mob and gunshots, I hadn't been too interested in repeating that scenario. I'd been hesitant about coming to the Halloween party—held the weekend before Halloween so parents could attend—but I needed to get out more, and Annie had invited me. Relaxing and not thinking about work for a night sounded lovely. Plus, the other two invitations I'd received had been too tempting to pass up.

"Nice costume," Annie said, looking me over as I walked inside the party and found her standing by the food and drinks. I'd opted for a Wonder Woman theme. My mom had made it, and Gandalf got a Steve Trevor pilot outfit, though he was staying home with my mom and dad tonight. We would dress up for Halloween together though. I expected lots of kids to stop by, and they'd love Gandalf's costume.

I laughed. "Thanks. I like your costume too." She was dressed as a Viking shield maiden, her blue/black hair arranged in an intricate braid. She looked amazing and like someone you definitely didn't want to mess with.

"Shield maidens kick ass," she said, ignoring the glare she got from a couple of other people at the table for her use of a swear.

I grinned as I finished filling my glass with Sprite-spiked fruit punch. "I couldn't agree more."

"You've had a busy few weeks," Annie mused as we both walked over to an empty table. "Robberies, vandalism, theft, superheroes, gambling games, the mob, The Ladies—"

"—The Ladies could give the mob a run for their money," I said, lifting my glass.

Annie laughed, clinked her plastic cup to mine, and took a drink of her Sprite-spiked fruit punch. "Did you ever find out what Hawke was investigating at the game?"

I shook my head. I hadn't seen Hawke or Drake since the game. They'd both contacted me after the incident at Betty's and I had no doubt they were keeping tabs on me in multiple ways, but other than texts, I hadn't spoken with them in person. But they'd both texted to tell me they'd see me tonight. So far, I hadn't run into them—that I knew of. A lot of townspeople were in full costume and totally unrecognizable.

"Not entirely," I answered. "But I know it had something to

do with mob. The mob was running the auction, and they were threatening Betty and Cadence's game. I think Hawke's still working on the case and that's why he hasn't told me more." At least, that's what I was hoping.

"And what about things between you, Hawke, and Drake."

I scrunched up my nose. "It's not a threesome."

She threw her head back and laughed. "If it was, you could probably sell tickets to it and make a fortune."

My cheeks went bright red and she laughed harder.

"I've been spending time with them both, trying to get to know them better and figure out how I feel."

She nodded. "Have you come to any conclusions?"

"Not really."

Her eyes twinkled. "Maybe tonight will help."

I gave her a look. "They're both supposed to be here, but I have no clue where they are. I haven't seen either one of them yet."

Her lips lifted in a half smile. "I'm sure you'll run into one of them soon."

Annie's husband, Rich, came over, dressed as a Viking to her shield maiden, and whisked her onto the dance floor. They were adorable together.

I made my way around the black and orange decorated hall, bats, ghosts, and witches adorning the ceiling and walls. Several areas were sectioned off, decorated with different themes so attendees could get the perfect Halloween photo for social media. People were dancing, playing games, and others were chatting. I saw The Ladies huddled in a corner, undoubtedly planning nefarious things. I avoided them like most people try to avoid vampires.

I was standing in the area decorated with a spider theme.

It was darker than the rest of the room, and a giant Shelob looking spider jutted out from the wall, webs threatening to ensnare anyone who entered. I hated spiders in real life, but was unafraid of the fake Shelob décor. I was leaning against a cocktail table in the space, drinking my Sprite-spiked fruit punch—because they didn't have anything stronger there—when a tall, broad shouldered man came up to me. He was wearing a dark black cape with a hood, and his face was completely covered like he was some sort of grim reaper. Based on his body alone, I couldn't tell who exactly he was, but I'd only seen shoulders like that on two men in Branson Falls, and I was waiting for both of them to show up here tonight.

"Hey," I said, taking a sip of my drink.

"Hi," he said back, lifting his hand to move some of the hair out of my face. His voice was muffled by whatever mask he had on.

"How's the party?"

"Better now," he said, his voice deep, but still unrecognizable. "I've been waiting for you all night. That costume is even better than the one you were wearing at the game."

I raised my brows. "So you prefer Amazon princesses over tempting devils?"

"With you, I get them both."

I smiled at him, needing this reprieve. This break from my hectic life.

He must have noticed the difference in my expression because he threaded his fingers through mine and pulled me around the corner, deep into Shelob's lair. He lifted his hand and started stroking my neck, before slowly moving his fingers, sliding over my shoulders and down my arms. I leaned into him, enjoying the feel of a big, male body close to me, holding some of the weight I carried. He pressed me against the wall, then he slowly lifted his mask, just enough to reveal his lips, and closed his mouth over mine. Suddenly, nothing else mattered. Warmth flowed through me, accompanied by an electric jolt of lust. Desire consumed my body as I wrapped my arms around his neck. He pulled me even closer and deepened the kiss, all of my senses lost to his touch. It was magic, full stop, and I could have stood there kissing him for eternity.

He broke the kiss and stepped back, searching my eyes. Whatever he saw there was enough. He took my hand and led me outside under a blanket of stars. "What if I don't know who you are?" I asked. Even though the kiss had made it pretty obvious.

"Then this should be interesting," he answered, and I could hear the smile in his voice.

He took my hand and I followed him. I had a feeling that tonight, I might follow him anywhere.

THE END

Check out Kate's next adventure in The Devil Shops on Sunday

Acknowledgments

Out of all my books, my best friend and editor, Ashley, loved my Kate Saxee Mystery series the most. After she passed away, I wasn't sure if I'd be able to write the series again. The Devil Wears Tank Tops was the last book she worked on before she died, and I tied her death to this series in my mind. Trying to continue the story without her to read it was painful in a way I can't describe. Humor eluded me, and I wasn't in the right head space to write the witty prose you've come to expect from these books. It took years, and a lot of mental and emotional work to get to this place, but I'm so happy to be back in this world, where I can be true to the characters and their stories again. I think Ashe would have loved this book, laughed a lot, and been as proud of it as I am. This is for you, Ashe—thank you for the lights.

Huge thanks to my talented cover designer, Kat Tallon, of Ink and Circuit Designs. And another thank you to all of my editors and beta readers who always catch the mistakes I miss.

Another giant thank you to Elana Johnson, incredible author, marketing guru, and friend. I'm so grateful for our lunches, chats, and your expertise! And to Jean Booknerd, thank you for your friendship, for always being there, and for telling everyone about my books.

My mom, who is the absolute best puppy grandma on the planet, and gives me so many ideas that my Kate Saxee idea file is almost as long as a full length novel. And to my dad and siblings, who keep me informed of all my mom's adventures—and occasionally participate themselves. Tash—I'm looking at you.

Dan, my soul mate. Thank you for always cheering me on, making me laugh constantly, adventuring with me, being my biggest support, calling me on my BS, and for the limitless pep talks. You are the best partner and friend I could have ever hoped for. I love you with my whole heart and soul!

The friends who have stood by me, pushed me with love, and believed in me and this series for years, specifically Karen DeVault, Britta Sorensen, Jennifer Miller, Brandy Korzep, and Athena Wikstrom.

And to you, my readers, for being patient, sticking with me, and continuing to read and tell people about my books. You are essential to my job, and I think of you all as friends. I hope you love *The Devil Has Tattoos* as much as I do. There's more Kate on the way!

Books by
Angela Corbett/Destiny Ford

<u>Kate Saxee Mystery Series</u>

The Devil Drinks Coffee

Devilishly Short #1

The Devil Wears Tank Tops

The Devil Has Tattoos

Devilishly Short #2 (Coming Soon)

<u>Tempting Series</u>

Tempting Sydney

Chasing Brynn

Convincing Courtney (Coming Soon)

<u>A Dude Reads Romance Series</u>

A Dude Reads Romance-Tempting Sydney

A Dude Reads Romance-Chasing Brynn

<u>Hollywood Crush Series</u>

A-List

<u>Fractured Fairy Tale Series</u>

Withering Woods

Scattered Cinders

<u>Emblem of Eternity Trilogy</u>

Eternal Starling

Eternal Echoes

For special sneak peeks, giveaways, and super secret news, join
Angela's newsletter!

http://eepurl.com/KhLAn

If you enjoyed reading *The Devil Has Tattoos*, please help others enjoy this book too by recommending it, and reviewing it on Amazon, Barnes and Noble, Google Play, iBooks, or Goodreads. If you do write a review, please send me a message through my website so I can thank you personally! www.angelacorbett.com

xoxo,

Ang

About the Author

Angela Corbett is a *USA Today* bestselling author, and a graduate of Westminster College where she double majored in communication and sociology and minored in business. She has worked as a journalist, freelance writer, and director of communications and marketing. She lives in Utah with her extremely supportive husband, and their sweet Pug-Zu, S'more. She loves classic cars, traveling, puppies, and can be bribed with handbags, and mochas from The People's Coffee. She's the author of Young Adult, New Adult, and Adult fiction —with lots of kissing. She writes under two names: Angela Corbett, and Destiny Ford.

http://www.angelacorbett.com/

Join my newsletter to get a free book!
http://eepurl.com/KhLAn

facebook.com/AuthorAngelaCorbett

twitter.com/angcorbett

instagram.com/byangcorbett